AF120983

"A unique writer voice, a refreshing storyline, and a future that we may all see before too long! Tension, pace, and real-life issues make this a novel to read. Wow, what a story!" - Jonas Saul, author of the Sarah Roberts Series

"Absolutely brilliant! Claudiu Murgan knocks another one out of the park with *Crystal Cloud*, his futuristic and daringly provocative sequel to *Water Entanglement*. Discerning readers will be impressed with the multiple layers of meaning embedded not only in Claudiu's word choice and intriguing story details, but certainly, throughout his penetrating vision of humanity's future. Claudiu easily succeeds where so many authors before him have failed—to envision a future worthy of humanity's attention—a future where the evolution of technology merges beneficially with the evolution of human consciousness. *Crystal Cloud* is a must read for anyone interested in water and its participation in the transformation of human consciousness. Highly recommend!!" - Rainey Highley, author of *The Water Code: Unlocking the Truth Within*

"Claudiu Murgan establishes his latest book *Crystal Cloud* with his prior brilliant novel, *Water Entanglement*. The significance of *water* is the manner through which it changes molecular structures to spur the health of the Earth and the humans who abuse it. *Crystal Cloud* provides a thrilling continuity. It shows an increased consciousness through crystal implants in the human brain so that the degradation of humanity on Earth is overcome and a new paradigm takes over the planet. The intricate tale provides an excellent read. The author brings in a possible retrofit for our future. Bravo." - Ian Prattis, author of Shattered Earth.

"Well done! *Crystal Cloud* shows a sweet passion for the environment and a genuine connection to a higher spirituality that transcends dogma. Claudiu's talent as a fiction author brings these two worlds together in this environmental sci-fi series. *Crystal Cloud* is an admirable sequel to *Water Entanglement*, continuing the story of the living properties of water and the importance of understanding nature's connection to it to preserve the Earth." – Nanette O'Neal, author of Beyond the Door Series.

"If *Water Entanglement* gave the critics a pleasant surprise at its release last year, the sequel *Crystal Cloud*, encores with continuous excellency into its literary genre.

In a mix of Tesla, Orwell, and Emoto, Claudiu Murgan's clear vision helps us see our planet Earth and ourselves differently. Consciousness and Science join together, resulting in an intense and indisputable quantum leap in how we view our world, and how we can redeem our planet's health as well as our future, realizing that water is the chief source for remodeling human consciousness.

Crystal Cloud is a wonderfully written story that offers permanent suspense and captivating action, making it a page turner, and a pure joy to read." — C.S. Douglas, Author; and founder of *AUTHOR-PÆDIA®—The World's Only Encyclopedia Dedicated to Authors.*

"Nature has something to say and we would do well to listen. *Crystal Cloud* is a story that hits chillingly too close to home! Author Claudiu Murgan has devised a way to expose the amazingly mechanical attributes of crystals and water working in tandem. Who could have known that water and crystals can provide a hyper-effective ways of communication and has the ability to store vital information within. *Crystal Cloud* is a must read...especially if we don't want to repeat current cataclysmic events that we are stuffing now in the future. This is an excellent piece of literature!" - Yvette Kendall, author of The God Maps Series.

"*Crystal Cloud*, Claudiu Murgan's newest book, is a one-stop literary environment which stacks a future not too far beyond us to inhabit now, a cast of players who wander through the story almost as if they were reading the book with us, and a strong broth of new science and ancient knowledge stirred together as one expanding perception of the inevitable interwoven fabric of Aboriginal Newtonian Darwinian Quantum Psychology, with water and crystals as conscious protagonists in this adventure, silently filling the spaces between biology and consciousness to unlock territories of awareness and enhanced physicality unfolding an inner regeneration of mind and body. Is it a novel, or a text book? Read it and see!" - Fredric Lehrman, author of The Sacred Landscape

Crystal Cloud

Claudiu Murgan

AUTHOR ACADEMY elite

Copyright 2020 Claudiu Murgan

Cover illustration and cover design: JetLaunch

Printed in the United States of America

Published by Author Academy Elite P.O. Box 43, Powell, OH 43035

www.AuthorAcademyElite.com

All rights reserved. No part of this publication may be reproduced, stored in a retrieval system, or transmitted in any form or by any means—for example, electronic, photocopy, recording—without the prior written permission of the publisher. The only exception is brief quotations in printed reviews.

This book is a work of fiction. Names, characters, places and incidents either are the product of author's imagination or are used fictitiously, and any resemblance to actual person living or dead, events or locales is entirely coincidental.

Paperback ISBN-13: 978-1-64746-415-8

Hardcover ISBN: 978-1-64746-416-5

Ebook: 978-1-64746-417-2

Library of Congress Control Number: 2020914481

CHAPTER 1

In Cherry Mortinger's nightmares, water and wind faced off as howling tornadoes, hurricanes, and torrential rainstorms in battle. Shards of ice mercilessly pierced metal rooftops, brick buildings, and flesh, mincing everything senseless in its path. Wind unleashed a ruthless interrogation of water as it demanded proof of humanity's innocence for misdeeds that happened not so long ago. Water screamed and twisted but refused to break her silence; she would rather endure blow after blow, suffering intimidation and abuse for mankind's mistakes. Neither side would relent, forcing Cherry to wake in a cold sweat, knowing her beloved Earth was left the innocent victim every time.

Cherry gasped at the vividness of the memory of these nightmares, even at noon day, and the clarity of her responsibilities as an activist became more evident. She knew water's humanistic secret: its crystallographic patterns remembered every evolutionary cycle on Earth, every birth of a child, every thought of doubt or happiness. Water had witnessed timid and supple seedlings of oak, beech, sycamore, silver maple, European ash, Douglas fir, and more grow into old forests, at liberty to expand unencumbered. No one had challenged the forest for its obsession of conquering new lands and claiming its own. Far into the past, water did not cry. Only much later, water witnessed the decimation of the wise overstory and learned about pain, suffering, and senseless death. Her memory was changed forever, now storing the history of the planet and its civilizations. Water's innocence melted in a fuzzy molecular structure that science, only recently, classified as unhappiness.

From the safety of her bungalow's windowless office room in Toronto, Cherry shook the nightmare from her mind and stood firmly. She glanced over at Hayyin's mask for the first time since the United Nations resolution related to the awakening of water and its repercussions on Earth had passed. "I'm a limnologist and water activist," she said aloud as if to remind herself of her credentials in this unstable world. "I'm registered with Water for All, and I should be able to handle this." She shook her head. Who was she kidding? She could barely keep track of the environmental changes threating to collapse delicate eco-systems all over the world.

She perused through the reports on her iPad screen. Reports from Brazil, Peru, Southern U.S. states, China, and India issued by environmental agencies or not-for-profit entities were beyond frantic, all pointing to the enormous ecological stress from continuous deforestation, wildfires, increased dead zones in the oceans, or uninterrupted rains followed by devastating tornadoes. Unable to ignore the hysteria or deny her research, she brushed the moisture from her upper lip and turned away. *It's quantum entanglement.*

The structural changes on a molecular level in the Ganges River that had replicated within hours to those of the Jordan River left no doubt in Cherry's mind that the quantum entanglement concept applied to almost anything else in nature. Quantum characteristics such as storing information, self-information, and self-organizing proved the behavioral nature of an organism. Only certain scientists understood this, Cherry included. Now the media seemed to be catching on, even labeled the phenomenon *the awakening of water.*

She envisioned the U.N. resolution signed by all member countries would be a welcome respite from a GDP-focused mentality that had driven the economies and the consumerism to dizzying heights. The awakening of water had given everyone the necessary slap in the face. For the last six months of 2057, the occurrences in Asia and South America of water changing its molecular structure had ceased, thus reinforcing the compliance of all U.N. signatories.

She picked up the mask and held it reverently in her hands. Now, using her hidden identity as Hayyin, Cherry aimed to deliver a friendly yet firm message to her followers while the world's biggest companies were still busy negotiating compensation for the loss of profits. It was a stratagem that, as long as the politicians continued to turn a blind eye, would be inserted in major trade agreements between powerful countries.

Cherry compared this approach to a polite dinner guest who suddenly turns nasty, claims ownership of her house, and demands a hefty payment before leaving. At any moment, any of the other guests might make a similar claim, leaving Cherry miffed and broke, both emotionally and financially.

Cherry pulled out an external microphone and plugged it into her tablet. Her hacker friends in the Anonymous Group would make the message available, posting it in a location that couldn't be traced back to her.

Seeing renowned companies haggling over a dry bone, a human DNA feature too hard to remove was still a sour sight for the eight-point-five-billion people who had no choice but to endure the consequences of the world's major industries coming to a halt.

She clenched her fists several times. Using Hayyin's identity to provide hope through a period of hardship and to let everyone know that she's still watching the international players subdued by the 'awakening of water' crises still made her uncomfortable.

Certain economies had to be saved, not bailed out. Cherry had read how this had happened many times in the past. Financial giants—those backing products with money that seemed to be pulled from thin air—owned the politicians.

Tired of being told what to do by companies controlling their purse strings, governments had agreed to accept nationalization. It was a concept hated by those who had embraced crony capitalism to justify their outrageous and unethically-generated profits. She clutched the mask to her breast and breathed in the familiar smell of the wood.

The important, egocentric CEOs would either take early retirement or become full-time government employees. Playing by the rules and reporting to bureaucrats would push most of them into settling for the former.

Cherry took a deep breath and slipped Hayyin's mask on her face. It felt natural, empowering, and right. After checking the strap at the back of her head, she stood upright with confidence. With the mask, there was no risk of being identified by any government-run face recognition software, and she smiled knowingly behind the façade. She gently caressed the aged wood with metal insertions on its outer edges like new skin. Hayyin's identity had become hers, replacing her teardrop-shaped face, blue eyes, and pixie-blonde haircut with a certain power and dignity only the mask could command.

By being Hayyin, she could expose shady deals between corrupt governments and corporations willing to buy their way in for water and oil rights with little or no respect for the will of the people. Switching between the identities was a conscientious move. It ensured against memory blackouts. The liability of her actions was hers and hers alone.

She motioned to her iPad to begin the recording.

"Hello, my friends," she said, her voice confident and dark. "We all should be proud of the latest achievement of a consensus on how badly we have treated the environment. Science couldn't explain the radical molecular transformations water went through in 2055. Sadly, people died, and we had to trigger significant changes in our global community. Halting oil and gas exploration in environmentally sensitive areas, reevaluating the intensive water usage for mono-cropping agriculture, and limiting air traffic have impacted all of us. The readjustment made us believe we suddenly switched from a period of abundance to one of scarcity. We knew a wakeup call was imminent, but as usual, our stubbornness threw another pinch of pixie dust at us, warping our minds against the lie that we kept telling ourselves—that everything is fine, and we couldn't possibly experience calamity in our lifetimes. Seemed that even the prolonged water restrictions in the highly populated cities on every continent sent a message few took seriously.

"Prevention has never been humanity's forte; damage control is. We would rather spend our money, time, and resources after the fact than be creative prior to the disaster."

For the first time, Cherry didn't feel the urge to scratch any itch or wipe perspiration from her hidden face. Her words evoked a tranquil awareness, trailing from her lips with a firm cadence even if the mask's narrow mouth slit made them sound slightly muffled. She dreaded the extensive water restrictions in Toronto, a temporary measure until additional industrial filters were added to the treatment plants serving the city. Lately, the trade winds from Africa that reached the eastern part of Canada and covered it with desert sand pushed even farther inland. With the help of the Maritime's own gap winds and capricious weather, the onslaught exposed Toronto to increased health challenges.

"I know some of you will smirk at my calling it a consensus. I admit—and it's no secret—the accord has been imposed on select companies for the greater good with disregard to the optics that in capitalism, only the fittest survive. And because these entities couldn't understand that not even the well-prepared and competent had a chance against the fluid fury behind the consequence of our actions, they had to be forcefully told. You know what I stand for, and still, I agreed with this approach."

For an extended moment, it appeared as if the wooden mask reflected on the glistening iPad screen shifted up and down, as if nodding in agreement. The fading red tears that had been painted on the wood also seemed to follow the pull of gravity, dripping off the edge, though she felt no wetness in her hand when she tilted it slightly forward. A low vibration in the mask tingled against her skin, releasing the scent of the wood. She inhaled the sweet smell, and her lungs heaved with relief.

"Coherence, as a concept, has been taught in school for the last twenty years.

We, as individuals, communities, social groups, and countries, have to be in coherence with one another to ensure sustained survival on Earth. The older generations still don't understand that we are all one, and the resulting grief, pain, and misfortune affects everyone in subtle ways."

Cherry shifted a bit in the chair and ran her sweaty palms on her pants.

"A lack of coherence is what has brought us to the tipping point of our existence. We live as a broken organism whose parts are pulling in different directions, the equivalent of the medieval punishment of horse dismemberment."

She chuckled at the comparison. It had flown from her lips without much thought, but she took advantage of it as she continued.

"I refer to a cycle in humanity's history. We repeat these cycles over and over because we forget what we learned the first time. Some of you might say this is nonsense. I say it is nonsense for the stubborn among us to endorse the idea that lack of awareness creates permanence for life's lessons. It was the twenty-first-century philosophers who pleaded with the world's leaders that enhancing our lives with spirituality would bring benefits to the individual and the whole of society. This is what they thought will keep us coherent."

The buzz of her cell on the floor distracted her momentarily, and she almost looked down.

"We've all heard renowned scientists debate how creating the specific language for water could bridge the evolutionary gap between humanity and water. It's like trying to communicate with an alien species that just arrived on Earth. But in this case, the alien has been living within and around us for millennia."

She chuckled again and stretched her legs for a better balance.

"What will be the medium that will properly transmit our intentions so they are not misinterpreted? Will water believe us?" She leaned in toward the iPad, feeling her heartbeat swell. "And how much more radical will the climate repercussions become before our communications and transportation infrastructure will be obliterated?"

The mask stared into the screen not sure if it should tackle any of her questions. Cherry sat back and folded her hands conclusively.

"Be vigilant. As always, there will be nefarious companies who think they can outsmart everyone while doing business as usual. Until next time, stay safe."

She saved the file with the encryption key provided by the Anonymous Group, then sent it to them. Cherry wished she could have a longer respite between Hayyin's appearances, but imminent crises always hurled nasty consequences. The Earth had reached a point where the saying, *you can't get blood from a stone* made perfect sense.

CHAPTER 2

Ilanda faced the spotlights hanging from the ceiling in CityTV's morning news studio, waiting for her interview on Toronto television to begin. She drummed her fingers and fidgeted too much for her liking on the tightly upholstered couch.

She would rather be in the lab working, but the mounting pressure from various opinion leaders on why she would not divulge openly the secret sauce of the crystal technology needed to be addressed publically. The anchorman, Wrightly, a man in his forties with a sharp nose and an angular chin, sat at the other end of the couch. His gaze was focused on the news as it scrolled on the AugReality app enabled on his oversized cell. His skin stretched on his face and the layer of makeup he used to cover the age spots that peppered his cheeks only slightly grossed out Ilanda. She had accepted only a minimal retouching of her face from the staff on hand before entering the studio for the impromptu interview.

Inside the studio, three drone-like cameras hovered several feet above the ground, trying to find an optimal angle for the broadcast. A commercial ran on the large screen in her right periphery.

She turned her gaze toward the wall of smoky glass facing bustling Dundas Square. The beginnings of a sunny, glorious, late

August day seemed gloomy through the tinted windows. Outside, passersby walked briskly, stealing furtive looks at the drones floating on the street corner directing traffic and scanning for illegal water and weapons possession.

The aroma of donuts and freshly brewed coffee permeated the studio. Ilanda knew the smell to be fake, chemically induced to stir memories still yearning for the lost privilege of drinking unlimited cups of java daily. The surrogate for water was unable to mimic the original taste, but the smell remained.

"Commercials will end in thirty seconds," a soft feminine voice announced.

The anchor raised his head and forced a smile at Ilanda, apparently worried about the news he'd just read.

"Dr. Mazandir, please remember that we only have ten minutes, so keep your answers short, but not so short as to lose their essence," Wrightly said. "It's a subject that won't go away anytime soon, and our viewers are hungry for reliable news." He tightened the knot of his tie—the purple and violet pattern contrasted with his light blue shirt and dark suit.

Ilanda nodded attentively, straightened her shoulders, and checked that her black-and-white dress didn't expose too much of her legs.

The same female voice said, "Three . . . two . . ." then mouthed *we are live* and pointed to Wrightly.

"We welcome you back to our live broadcast. As announced before the break, my guest this morning is a reputable neurosurgeon, Dr. Ilanda Mazandir. Thank you for accepting our invitation."

"No, thank *you* for the opportunity to talk about a subject so dear to me," Ilanda replied. Her eyes fixed on the floating camera behind the anchor.

"It's been almost twelve months since you successfully brought Kahuna Lapa'au, Hawaii's spiritual leader, back from an induced coma against all odds. We all remember the vivid images of the glass shards protruding from his skull after the explosion at the Water for All conference here in Toronto, and the extensive damage caused to his brain as a result. The procedure you used healed him and brought his mental and locomotor functions to normal conditions. Please, tell us more."

Ilanda didn't hasten to reply. She was determined to make them listen, thus easing the pressure on her through carefully chosen words.

"For a while," she began, "I've been fascinated by the interaction between structured water and crystals. Studied individually, they revealed fascinating patterns, but when combined, we started to observe hidden codes that we didn't know how to interpret—"

"Sorry to interrupt, but for our viewers that don't know what structured water is, could you explain in simple terms?" Wrightly said, his chin protruding forward aggressively.

She glanced furtively at the glass of water that had been left for her on the faux-wooden table in front of her. There was only a mouthful of liquid in it at best. She considered taking a sip but decided to continue instead. "Structured water is a type of water whose molecular structure has a hexagonal shape and is similar to water that hasn't been polluted or contaminated by human processes." She looked at the camera and then switched her gaze to the newsman. "Water that has not been touched by human processes is rare, so we had to employ unconventional methods to change it to structured water."

"What type of unconventional methods?" He leaned in.

At previous public engagements, she'd always site Dr. Masaru Emoto's famous research, exposing water to music and positive language. Ilanda didn't dare mention the praying of the monks on water or of the healers from Hawaii that helped with Kahuna's recovery. Play it safe, she thought. Only talk about the same believable story of the Japanese scientist. Wrightly nodded contently, and Ilanda smiled back while still feeding the audience the information they'd come to expect.

She kept to herself how the team sliced the crystal horizontally and loaded it with code routines that would use the crystal's vibrations to encode information, which could be accessed later using the right thought-commands. "The proprietary code we developed, along with the vibration generated by the structured water poured on the crystal, unlocks specific unused areas in the brain," she said.

"That's fascinating," Wrightly said. "This is a revolutionary scientific discovery that's worth sharing with the medical community, wouldn't you agree?"

It was the sensitive question she'd been able to dodge at every scientific conference she'd attended lately. In the end, she gave up accepting invitations to appear as her justifications seemed to ring hollow with her peers.

On the big screen to her right, she noticed the latest photo of Kahuna Lapa'au after his implant intervention. His head and face tattoos were gone, replaced with new, artificially grown skin that matched the dark nuances of the skin on his thick neck. The thin layer of amber-like crystal transformed his eyes into piercing flames, which simultaneously absorbed and reflected the natural light. His imposing stature—wide shoulders and a sheer force that affected everyone he met—had become secondary to his piercing gaze. The ghoulish look was in contrast with the warm, empathic eyes to which those around Kahuna were accustomed.

His gaze brought no comfort. Rather, the reality that this dear father figure had suffered a permanent psychological alteration evoked a visceral fear.

"I do agree with your statement, and up to a point, I did share the results of the unique surgical intervention we did on Kahuna Lapa'au—"

"But just the results. Not the process, per se," Wrightly interjected.

"I'm a doctor. I swore an oath to protect and save human lives, and for that reason, I choose to withhold the details of such a procedure until I've evaluated the consequence of embedding crystals in the population at large without discrimination."

Ilanda's shoulders slumped from exacerbation. Her mouth was dry, and she knew she could only hold her smile for so long. She wondered if the audience believed her forced smirk to be real. She grabbed the glass, barely tilted her head back before swallowing the lukewarm water inside.

The anchorman patiently waited for her to finish. Ilanda sensed he couldn't move on as of yet since she hadn't answered the question to his satisfaction. His chin pointed forward showing determination to extract whatever information the producer or his puppeteers told him to.

"What reassurance do you need before you release this proprietary procedure?"

Though it was live television, she desperately wanted to scream —her team's research and proven results couldn't fall in the hands of opportunistic corporations that were bound to find more malefic uses for it. She managed to restrain the liberating thought, responding, instead, with a coy smile.

"I'm no different than any other responsible scientist wanting to see his or her achievements improve—not destroy—lives. In the not so distant past, how many of us have been tricked by well-spoken politicians or military men into giving up scientific knowledge only to see it immediately shrouded with a top-secret halo and wholly misused to the detriment of society?"

Ilanda shifted on the couch, moving a bit closer to the edge. She sat there like a bird perched on a fence ready to take flight.

"Integrating such complex structures into our bodies has the ability to reverse damage spawned by today's faulty medicine, a concoction of chemicals so foreign to the natural processes running inside us on cruise control. And when I say that, I refer to things like autism, muscular dystrophy, and many more mutations resulting from the alteration of our DNA—"

"Do you mean intentional DNA alterations? You're a doctor, so we trust a statement like this when it comes from you. Isn't this a little bit extreme?" the anchor asked.

Ilanda saw him quickly glance into the blackness of the room as if uneasy to follow the producer's latest directive. She almost burst into raucous laughter at the silly question. Was he trying to corner her on a subject so familiar to her?

"Yes, I refer to the intentional ones. I only mention what I know as a matter of fact. The miracle Kahuna Lapa'au witnessed gives me a high level of certainty that combining crystals and structured water can reverse the DNA alterations caused not by a natural evolutionary process but by human interference. Food infestation with certain chemicals and vaccines premeditatedly loaded with pathogens stretched our immune system thin, allowing such DNA mutations to happen. As if someone wanted to see how much the human body can sustain and what's the trend of adaptation. In their pure form, crystals and structured water can reset the DNA. At least this is what I believe. More research is required though."

Ilanda cursed herself for not bringing some of her daily water rations with her. The glass in front of her was empty, and her mouth was parched from the focused lights and the emotion of having blown the lid fully off of a confession long overdue, showing her distaste with a certain sector of the medical field with no regard for rules and ethics.

The anchorman looked suddenly distraught. His mouth opened slightly. Ilanda sensed that even the producer had been fazed by her outburst, forcing the man in front of her to quickly improvise.

"I have to admit it's hard for me to understand your frustration. Regardless if this outstanding technology is made public or not, don't you think that even if it were used on a small number of patients, it would speed the theory popularized by author Dan Brown in his novel, *Origin*?"

Ilanda saw a haggard look reflected on her face in the monitor. "Sorry, but I'm not familiar with whatever theory you are referring to."

With an uneven voice, the man explained. "One of his characters, a brilliant scientist, an atheist, did everything in his power to answer two questions with which we, as a human race, have always struggled: where did we come from, and where are we going?"

For a moment, Ilanda wasn't sure if he were taunting her or if he were serious. She listened but showed no visible reaction.

"For the sake of this discussion, only the latter is important. After much iteration, the scientist, run by a sophisticated AI, concludes that we are moving toward a technologically-embedded society, edging out our humanity. So, I reiterate my question: by enhancing our bodies with crystals, even for purely medical purposes, aren't we sliding down a rampant curve, making it impossible to climb back up?"

Was he serious? Presented that way, he implied her scientific research had ghoulish connotations. Her left palm cupped the opposite elbow as she tried to settle on an answer that seemed like common sense. All she wanted to do was save lives, not turn anyone into a mindless robot. She searched desperately for a way out.

"You're asking me an ethical question," she said at last. "There's no doubt in my mind that the efficiency of our process will save lives. Could humanity evolve faster in the direction you mentioned if the technology were available to anyone for purposes other than medical? Of course, it's obvious."

"What if Crazy Velvet receives the implants and she's getting totally out of control? What example are we going to set-up for our children?" Wrightly said, his gaze fixed on her.

Ilanda arched her eyebrows and kept quiet as not to say something that might boomerang her.

"Oh, I assume you also haven't heard of the popular YouTube content creator Crazy Velvet." He smirked when he said *content creator*.

Ilanda pressed her palms together and leaned in with determination. "I am not interested in defending my actions against any potential lunatic that would misuse such technology. This is the reason I want to limit its reach. The pressure I'm under after Kahuna Lapa'au's recovery is unbearable." She dropped her gaze. Did she really let out that confession? She pinched her brow as her gaze focused on the floor.

"Dr. Mazandir, I'm told by my producer that we're going to invite you back next week for a one-hour slot we've entitled 'Latest Developed Technologies: Friend or Foe.' It will give us more time to expand on this captivating subject."

Ilanda lifted her head and nodded. "Thank you," she muttered weakly as she forced back the well of tears ready to erupt.

"We'll be back after a short commercial break."

The interview finished without her having the strength to publicly denounce the threats she'd been receiving since she'd made it clear that her ethical conviction forbade the release of the technology that had saved Kahuna. The distorted voice on the other end of the phone calling her at random hours had evolved from a polite request for the procedure's technical details to a nasty sting of threats on her entire genealogical tree. She couldn't block a restricted number—it was untraceable. The nastiness of the increased threats wrapped around her mind like a bandage hardened by dried blood, impairing her ability to think clearly. The invisible stalker could be anyone waiting in the fold to grab a chunk of a market worth billions in any currency.

Ready to leave, a thought snaked mischievously into her head. *Wrightly could very well be the caller.* Maybe he or the producer had gotten her cell number from the university.

She'd set out on a tortuous path that necessitating keeping her team out of it. They'd done a great job finalizing the correlation between crystals, sounds, and humans, and Ilanda didn't want to distract them from the delicious success they were experiencing.

"Thank you for coming. See you next week," the anchor said, briefly looking at her.

"Did you get all your answers?" she asked, stepping toward him as if it was her turn to challenge him. The crazy hypothesis of Wrightly turning into a villain in front of her eyes hung at the fringes of her mind like a pesky spider web brushing against her face.

Wrightly sustained her gaze, the smirk on his face like the one of a predator that has identified an easy prey. Was it really him, or was it her mind's carrousel stopping at nothing to drive her nuts?

Off the camera, his voice hissed as if trying to put a spell on her. "Your concern about the technology getting in the wrongs hands is partially justifiable," he said. "Simply weigh the benefits carefully. An opportunity like this could make a lot of people wealthy and provide jobs at the same time. Who wouldn't love you for this?"

Before she could answer, he winked at her and went back to the news desk while his assistant led her shaking out of the studio.

CHAPTER 3

"Kahuna Lapa'au was the real target of that carefully crafted explosion, and potentially his daughter, Marinka, if she would have been there," the Anonymous's email revealed several months after Water for All-2055 ended in flames and eighty-six people died. "The companies responsible for poisoning the Hawaiian Islands through their pesticide-promoting genetically engineered crops went after him. He opposed them too loudly, and his comments had gathered enough traction with activists on the mainland."

Cherry didn't believe initially the information. After the shock of the news had sunk in, she emailed back: "Are you one hundred percent sure?"

The Anonymous Group's intel was always reliable, though not easily verifiable.

In 2056, after all countries had signed the agreement under stringent United Nations supervision, things got quiet. Only the updates on negotiating the financial compensations for loss of profit made waves now and again.

"How can we protect him?" she had asked Anonymous, thinking about how she might avoid human collateral damage if another attempt on the spiritual leader's life was made by the same corporations. "He's still in an induced coma."

"We can't do much," they had answered. "We'll just monitor communication channels in case such planning goes online. If somehow he recovers well, keep him on the island."

It was wise advice from someone that made an art of concealing his own identity but, at the same time, a sacrilege containing Hawaii's recognized spiritual leader and preventing him from traveling the world to spread the message about Mother Earth's dire situation. He'd be filled with so much guilt if she ever mentioned the tragedy he'd indirectly caused. She intuitively knew that if she kept this detail hidden, he wouldn't take additional security measures, and she didn't want Kahuna Lapa'au to become a martyr just yet. He had so much to offer while still alive.

Choosing between ethics and practicality always proved a struggle for Cherry, and there were rare times when ethical practically fit the template of a clean consciousness. All this overthinking, added a cold sheen to her otherwise warm approach to people. Helping others was second nature to her, and shifting the burden of untold truths to her shoulders justified her actions or the lack thereof.

Ilanda's medical restrictions imposed on Kahuna and Marinka due to the crystal implants they received in Toronto limited their travels for a while, and Cherry knew that another attempt at the leader's life could only take place outside the island. Hence her decision to postpone informing Kahuna.

During one of their AugReality calls, Marinka invited her to Hawaii and saw the opportunity to finally share with both of them the terrifying information she'd been holding back. The trip also took her away from attending the two-year remembrance festivities of the Water for All explosion in Toronto, a commemoration that only accentuated the pain of those she knew, now gone.

Now, Cherry landed in Hawaii after a flight less tiring than anticipated, during which she had chosen a sound sleep over the entertainment.

"Aloha. I'm so glad you came," Marinka said after giving her a healthy hug. "We haven't had real face-to-face girl talk since I left Toronto with Father last year in March. It's time to catch up." She pushed an invisible lock of hair behind her left ear.

Cherry's face opened up and inhaled the scent of the fresh Plumeria garland Marinka had around her neck, and she forced herself to shed the bitterness behind the main reason for her visit.

"I'll get your carry-on," Marinka offered, and they walked out of the main building toward the parking lot.

The heat almost overwhelmed Cherry, but she kept pace with her friend. She felt the several degrees difference between Toronto and the island melting her skin, invading her body as if trying to know her better, checking if she was there for the first time, if she could be trusted. She instantly remembered the stories that Marinka and the Hawaiian elders that visited Kahuna in the hospital had told her about the spirits of the islands, embedded in every blow of the wind, in any whisper of the flowers and trees blooming with beauty. Now, looking around her at the nature's artistry, she built the confidence to believe them.

"Thank you for accepting our invitation instead of attending the memorial ceremony in Toronto. We're aware you could've been more useful in your own city representing Water for All."

"More vivid memories, more pain. I needed a faraway break, and your call came at the right time. On top of everything else, I had to use my vacation flight allowance. Toronto's security will be tighter than the eye of a needle. I'll still be there in spirit," Cherry replied. She put on a pair of shades and looked up at the svelte palm tree silhouettes edging the road.

Around the parking lot, white curb stones kept in check inch-high decaying grass as if afraid that the rusty contamination could become airborne and drift to green patches further ahead.

Cherry glanced at Marinka lovingly. The Hawaiian woman's crystal implants covering her eye cornea had a blueish hue that became the main features of her round face. 'Enhanced contact lenses' Cherry had labelled them, but much more potent, based on the type of crystal they were cut from. They connected to the pineal gland through nanobots. Marinka's long black locks were gone.

She'd cut her hair military-style, a sign of solidarity with Kahuna, who had lost his bushy ponytail before the surgery. The boyish appearance balanced well with her light cinnamon skin that had regained its elasticity in the steamy Polynesian weather.

"I know I've changed since the implants," Marinka said, "but my father needed my support in and out of the community. Re-acceptance is still work in progress for both of us. The other tribe leaders understood that using the implants to bringing father back was a gamble and the only viable option at that time." She drove the convertible Jeep Cherokee with a firm hand on the smooth road. She'd also put on a pair of shades, hiding the uniqueness of her sight.

Cherry remembered her pleading with Ilanda to test the crystal and structured water research on Kahuna right after the explosion in Toronto. And the doctor's acceptance became the spark in getting the funding, the building, the team around Ilanda, and finally, the daring intervention that rewired his brain, thus reinstating most of his body functionality.

"You know Ilanda kept her promise and didn't make public any information about your own crystal implant intervention."

Marinka nodded and glanced quickly at her friend.

"She calls on Father and me every month for a check-up. She takes our vitals, downloads the biometrics from the crystals into the app on her tablet, makes a joke or two, and that's it until next time. How is she? She never talks about herself and the loss of her husband."

Cherry nodded, acknowledging her in a way that said she understood what she was going through. Ilanda's internal mourning after Maahes's death in Egypt, wasn't healthy, but her offering of support remained unanswered. It seemed that the husband and wife needed closure for words that were said under the influence of anger, or for gestures that only remained in the form of a thought.

"I don't know any more than you do. Maahes's sudden death and the fact that she couldn't repatriate his body damaged her morale and changed her focus. After your surgery, no one else had the implants, as far as I'm aware. She took a break to mourn and heal, letting the team run with the preparations for the patients on the waiting list. My interaction with her was more constant during the funding and renovation of the lab and sporadically afterward."

"She might need a rescue team," Marinka said, her gaze focusing on the road ahead.

"I'll do my best to re-connect upon my return to Toronto," Cherry said. A muscle on her lower back throbbed with pain as a reminder of her inability to fracture Ilanda's shell of self-imposed misery and shine light and purpose to her path as a neurosurgeon.

"How's the legal battle going?" she asked after taking in the beauty of the relentless waves to her right as they broke into pulverized foam on the sturdy rocks. Flocks of seagulls scattered in the sky, moving up and down as if playing with the ocean as it threw its watery arms at them in a game of catch-and-miss. The high-pitched squawking melded with the caws of birds dotting the ground, but it wasn't enough to overpower the ocean's rumble. It was a mighty being, aware of its grace and strength.

"Recently, the positive tide's been in our favor. Some judges have been replaced, and new evidence has been accepted, so we're succeeding in pushing out the chemical companies, one legal battle at a time. This is justice we can touch, feel, and celebrate."

Cherry raised her hands, letting the rushing wind find the openings of her T-shirt and brush against her alabaster skin. She felt elated and wanted to release a happy scream, discharging the pressure valve of her psyche.

"Do it, Cherry," Marinka said, sensing the tension. "I did it, too, on this very road the moment we were back from Toronto. Let's do it together."

Cherry flashed a giddy smile. They howled in unison, Marinka speeding dangerously. They did it once, twice, until their vocal cords could no longer muster another pitched note. The wavy, low-grade hills on either side of the road amplified their voices, carrying them from treetop to treetop, echoing the frustration, disappointment, and grief that had accumulated since the tragedy in Toronto.

"Feels really good, doesn't it?" Marinka asked, her face radiating from the sun.

Cherry's chest heaved and swelled from the effort. Her previous dispirited look was now prickled with gratitude for the friend who had encouraged her in this much-needed exercise of relief.

Marinka swerved off the highway onto a patch of dirt big enough to host one care and fenced with waist-high bushes. "Where are we going?" Cherry asked.

"We're meeting my father at one of his favorite locations on the island. Wait and see—I don't want to spoil the surprise."

They got out of the car and started on the narrow path parting the bushes on the side road. It led to a valley with low, smooth, curved hills on either side. The grass had a sick, yellowish color, with no sign anyone having stepped on the hidden passage.

"The rains are scarce," Marinka said, and nodded towards the ground, justifying the anemic look of the grass.

Pockets of pink Plumeria and hibiscus shared the shoulders of the hills, bobbing their heads in the amiable wind, sending their fragrance afloat in the heated air, somehow proud of their insensitivity to the capricious weather.

The women climbed gently through the groove of the ground toward the plateau at the top. Meters away, Kahuna sat there with his back to them, straight and immobile as if his body had been sculpted from the lava stone beneath him.

He tilted his head slightly in their direction upon hearing their feet ruffle through the grass. When Cherry got closer to him, she noticed the multitude of healed scars marking his skull. The women walked around to face him. Without standing, Kahuna opened his thick, tattooed arms to welcome Cherry, who hugged him back with deep love, grateful that he was still alive.

"Both of you—sit beside me and take in this glorious sight that God has created for us. It looks so perfect from up here."

His old, imposing voice had gone, replaced by a synthesizer that had been implanted in his neck after the crystals had healed him. Having been uploaded with the latest AI application, the artificial voice was fairly close to Kahuna's real one, but a bit metallic.

Marinka and Cherry squatted on the grass, flanking him.

"Who would believe the waves smashing our shores are devoid

of life. No more fish, crabs, or stingrays—they're all gone, but that is not obvious from up here. One has to dive in for the proof. We were told about layers of water without oxygen that caused the damage."

Cherry smelled the salt. A layer of water vapors raised by the changing wind covered her face. She gazed involuntarily at Kahuna's eyes. The oval amber disk covering the cornea had a glow that stuttered in the angled light, giving the impression that he could see in all directions at once.

"The scientists called them blobs," Cherry said. "The lack of oxygen is pushing the marine life deeper and deeper and is changing their migration patterns. The more chemicals seep into the oceans, the bigger these blobs become. Some blobs merge with each other forming large dead zones."

"It wasn't until recently," Kahuna said, "that we could show the world the environmental and human devastation the Hawaiian people have suffered as guinea pigs at the hands of the chemical multi-nationals running their poisonous trials on our once pristine farm lands. Any GMO seed these companies develop is tested here first. And all the run-offs spill in the ocean expanding the damage. We've been blocked in every possible way to either stop the pollution or taking our lands back. But now, under the new U.N. agreement, they had to stop, and Pelé, the spirit of the volcano, is happy again, and he will start accepting our offerings."

He turned to Cherry and officially welcomed her. "Be blessed, you that helped us so much."

With cheeks throbbing from the heat of the sun, Cherry hastened a reverent nod. "The emotional healing process for your people would be extensive as your sacred places were desecrated and your customs disrespected. Now, we have the opportunity of making peace with water and apologize for what these foreigners did to her. Do you think it's possible?"

The air surrounding Cherry felt suddenly denser, charged by the invisible entities that had gathered to hear the wise statement, and she had no doubt the ancestors about which she had heard so much were listening.

Around her Hawaiian friends, she had the tendency to forget

her scientist persona and delved more into the spiritual side of the conversation. She would have said that with the diminished pollution along the shore, the ocean water will change its structure under the influence of the electromagnetic ley lines, vortexes, and nodal points, becoming healthy again and propitious for the marine life to return.

Kahuna said nothing, but he pierced her with his gaze for several minutes as if to temper her expectations.

Cherry cupped her knees with both palms and squeezed hard. The wailing of the waves reaching them on the top of the hill and the shrill call of the seagulls and Layson albatrosses hovering in the air currents lent a theatrical background to the somber news she could no longer keep bottled up inside. "You were the target of the explosion in Toronto, not the WFA's leadership. The chemical corporations you despise and fight against here in Hawaii are the ones behind it."

Cherry dropped her palms to the ground. The prickly touch of the grass felt comforting, and she pressed down harder, yearning to sync her body vibration to that of the Earth.

"When did you find out?" the Kahuna asked.

"While you were still in Toronto, just before the surgery."

"Why tell me now?"

Cherry had had the presence of mind to anticipate the question, and she'd rehearsed a crafty answer. She replied firmly, leaving no doubt as to how convinced she was of the righteousness of her decision. "Your consciousness would have succumbed under the heaviness of the indirect guilt. You might deny it, but please, use your introspective capacity to ask yourself if the limits of enduring culpability have been pushed beyond repair."

Talking freely to Kahuna Lapa'au made her body shiver with emotion and sweat. She licked the dry corners of her mouth. "Throughout history, human symbols have been protected. Those who didn't fear death became martyrs in the end. You are a symbol, at least for the people of Hawaii, and I'll do anything I can to convince you not to turn into an early martyr."

Kahuna's large chest shook with a high, rasping breath,

replacing what used to be a healthy laugh. If it weren't for the warm smile, she wouldn't have guessed his real reaction. The eyes, the mirrors of the soul, displayed no feelings.

"You've got one thing right: I don't want to become a martyr yet."

He patted her gently on the shoulder like an understanding father, ready to forgive a child's prank.

Encouraged by his attitude, Cherry got bolder. "Would you accept some kind of protection? Those thugs might try another attempt, especially now, when the legal battle is going your way—"

"Why is this information not public yet?" Marinka intervened. "It could help with our legal case . . . considerably." She had taken off her shades. The thin blue layer of her crystal implants sparkled when the sun caught their reflection. She changed her position on the grass to face both of them.

"Why hold back?" Marinka said, fiddling for a moment with the invisible hair—a habit that her brain no doubt had yet to overwrite. She caught herself and rested her hands on her tights.

"It's the wise thing to do," Kahuna said. "There is hope for extended peace between nations, between corporations and citizens, between the Divine Mother and us. This agreement might make it possible."

"Yes, but this happened in the past. Before the agreement was signed. We aren't talking about a commercial contract where the grandfather clause applies. This is intimidation and corporate terrorism," Marinka blurted, still struggling to understand the subtleties of what her father was trying to communicate.

In the air above, restless seagulls, propelled by strong gusts of wind, dared neither land nor get closer to the three human intruders.

"Mentioning the names of these corporations and their crimes against us will only divert attention from the negotiations and fuel more hatred. We'll forgive, but we won't forget, and moving forward, we'll be more vigilant."

Cherry nodded respectfully at Kahuna, confirming once more, how truly special the spiritual leader was. "Marinka, if it's of any consolation, the information came from one of the fiercest opponents of the corporate world. The message was similar to what your father just explained to you."

Without a word, the Hawaiian woman took her place beside her father. Cherry could cut the silence with a knife. Three immobile bodies gazing at the ocean's entropy, and she suspected each of them were building their stories of how they might bring life back to it.

Cherry's thoughts lingered on the enticement that she could join the group of scientists on the islands that would observe the healing of the ocean and of the fresh water resources. She needed healing too. Nature's trauma at the hands of irresponsible people was her trauma as well. The devastation of the Amazonian forest, the rising water levels affecting every coast line, and the plastic and chemical pollutants in the ocean unraveled in her mind as a black and white movie on an endless loop. More back muscle spams shook her body, pounding her flesh as if yelling a directive she couldn't translate into words.

Water is truth, water can't lie, and it cannot be tricked, she had read in a book whose title escaped her. But water was also sick and Cherry had to help disseminate the message that the humanity dying under the anesthesia of technology had to reconnect with the biological world that it came from. She still believed in the opportunity of developing a language based on frequency and vibration that structured water would understand. A language that would go beyond the display of single words that Dr. Masaru Emoto and others had achieved. She wanted to talk to water in a more fluid way. So far, her research using Ilanda's lab resources was as successful as the thirsty patch of dirt in her backyard growing anything green.

"LET'S WALK ON THE BEACH," Marinka said.

Cherry and Marinka had had an early breakfast on the porch of Marinka's house, a three-bedroom bungalow built on the same plot of land as her father's. No more than twenty steps separated the two structures, which were similar in design and exterior paint color. They both faced east and were perched atop a hill edging a narrow, stony beach in front of the ocean.

A precarious dirt path meandered down in tight swoops, and they climbed down, careful not to slip.

The sun was rolling over the line of the horizon, and an exciting day was ahead of them. Floating buoys carrying sensors set to alert changes in the water's structure bobbed at various distances from the shore. The closest one had turned green and was ten meters out.

"The beach of my childhood is gone. Thirty meters of sand heaven," Marinka explained when they reached down. "What's left are these black stones of lava, polished and sanded by the waves over billions of years."

"They're beautiful," Cherry said. She picked up a freshly washed triangular one and rubbed it against her left palm. "So smooth."

The light reflected on Marinka's implants, blinding Cherry for a moment. She giggled and almost dropped the rock in the water.

"It's getting hot," Cherry said, pulling off her T-shirt and tucking it into the back pocket of her shorts. Her bathing suit top was the same shade of blue as the ocean.

"Why don't we hear about any of the Hawaiians' ongoing legal battle on the net?" she asked.

Marinka grabbed her own stone to play with. "Because it's a subject that doesn't serve the powerful few. Our local protests—before and after the explosion in Toronto—have already made the tourists concerned about the quality of the food they eat and of the air they breathe while vacationing in this paradise. Word-of-mouth did the rest. Also, the internet provider claimed multiple outages over a very short interval, preventing us from uploading files or broadcasting live. As an island, we're looking for a way into crystal cloud hosting that Anonymous Group so tightly controls."

"So, you're saying that the corporations are fighting from the shadows?"

They walked slowly, measuring their steps. Marinka pulled out the garbage bag from her back pocket to collect some of the plastic litter lining the shore. "That's pretty much what they do. They have well-paid proxies," she said, her mouth twisting in a resentful grin.

"What's going to happen with the land they own if future chemical trials are forbidden?"

"Hawaii's political leaders representing us at the U.N. negotiations have put forward a buy-back proposal. This is our land, and we want it back."

"That's smart!"

"They'll get a fair price," Marinka said, "even if the land's contaminated, and there's no official evidence as to the amount of chemicals applied during the trials."

"The companies won't release any of the records?"

"No. They claim it is proprietary information. We expect the legal action to cease as soon as the agreement is accepted in principle."

Marinka added two more plastic bottles to her collection in the bag, and Cherry contributed the ragged remnants of a small lifejacket.

"So, this is the reason you think there won't be any other assassination attempts on your father?"

The Hawaiian woman nodded. "What else is happening in the world? What industries have shut down."

"It started with the main culprits: oil and gas have slowed down and were given additional six months to completely shut down. The water bottling companies have strict limitations in terms of the quantities they could extract and the locations. The initial draft of the U.N. agreement, along with a big push from the respective governments, forced all of them to reveal every single asset they had on and off the books," Cherry said.

"All of them?"

"Yep. An average of twenty-two percent of the assets was owned by shell corporations—not easy to dig up."

"And they just gave it up?" Marinka asked, probably sensing there were more details coming.

"The U.N. pleaded publicly for help from any hacker group, going as far as proposing a reward. On the other hand, the U.N. threatened the corporations that if any undeclared assets are found and tied to them, their CEOs would get life in prison."

"Nice," Marinka said, and kicked a deflated ball, its leathery skin had peeled off and it was marked by dried salt.

"It wasn't about the company being held responsible anymore, but them, individually, as CEOs and decision-makers. The legal bullshit of 'the company doesn't accept or deny any wrongdoing' used every time they broke the law, was disregarded. Considering that none of these guys or their predecessors had gone to prison in the past for the criminal acts they committed, it was a major win."

They approached a narrow bend in the shore and jumped quickly to the other side between the cycle of the waves.

"These bastards have always greased the legal system and get away with it," Marinka said with no contention in her voice, even a little amused, Cherry thought.

"The oil sands operations in Alberta have also closed down," Cherry continued her report. "The equipment is in the process of being moved out, and the workers have started a paid training program in renewable energies and solar, wind, and car batteries. They're helping to rehabilitate thousands of square kilometers of lunar landscape left behind by their explorations. The environmentalists estimate anywhere between fifteen to twenty years before the fauna is back at a decent level."

"What about underground infiltration of heavy metals into freshwater resources? It might be similar to what is happening on our islands," Marinka said. She picked an entanglement of mesh and plastic wrap and dropped it in the garbage bag.

"That type of pollution will last much longer, and it's harder to assess because the natural filtration system is gone," Cherry said.

A speedboat cruising close to the shore broke the cadence of the waves. The happy, noisy people onboard waved at them. There was no one else on the beach to share in their good mood, so the women waved back.

"What else?" Marinka asked.

"The deep-sea drilling has shut down, too. The platforms are being dismantled and carried off the shore, replaced by wind turbines and shallow water turbines."

"That explains the rare piece of news we got about the boost of the electric car manufacturers. It's time we ban the old and welcome the latest technologies that have been kept from the masses up until now."

"It finally happened. Another evil plucked down from its throne of indifference."

"And the flight restrictions helped, too, I assume?" Marinka asked.

Cherry didn't reply right away. A couple of meters away a sharp rock was protruding out of the water. It wasn't shiny—its sides were rough as if it had been recently dumped there. She thought of wading in to get a closer look. She pushed her hand into an incoming wave and the coldness of the water made her changed her mind.

Cherry took a moment to think how she might answer Marinka. The flight restrictions had decimated the airlines industry. Initially. Bright minds, thinking inclusively, suggested the establishment of an aerial flotilla owned by all countries, flying under one brand. Against all odds, the proposal was accepted as a clause by eighty-seven percent of the signatory under the same U.N. agreement addressing the climate change. It was a monopoly by any means but with its prices capped. Each citizen had the right to four flights per year for pleasure, business, or personal emergencies. Any additional trips were encumbered with a steep price that only a few could afford—it was so expensive, in fact, it was like paying for a trip to the moon.

The era of private jets was over. Shared ownership boomed, but it was still exposed to stringent restrictions.

"The awakening of water had done that to us."

"Sorry," Cherry said. "We did this to ourselves."

"Every single step in the right direction helps. Don't forget that we are not doing all of this out of good nature and maturity. Water forced us to do it. We didn't know when to stop."

The garbage bag became too heavy, so Marinka tied its mouth and leaned it against two oversized rocks. "We'll pick it up on our way back. I should have brought more than one. The plastic tide is still significant."

Cherry let the sunlight engulf her half-naked body, and she inhaled a whiff of salt. She put on her sunglasses so she could wander at the stirrings of the ocean and its rhythmic breath of waves. "Have you gotten used to the implants yet?"

"Not completely." Marinka blinked few times. "Some people look at me with awe, some with a sneer. At least, they don't dare take pictures and upload them to the net."

"It takes time for society to accept such a drastic shift. Ilanda assured me this sight will be commonplace thirty years from now."

"Yes—the usual tangle of rhetoric. They ask the silliest questions and debate them legally, morally, and religiously until the real meaning is lost like so many other issues."

"But aside from the odd looks, how do you feel? How's Kahuna feeling?"

Marinka bent down and let her palms be caressed by the water, rocks, and the healing touch of salt. "Physically, we're in top shape. Mentally it's like we're both on steroids. We see energies bouncing around us in a flow of colors invisible to the regular eye, the hum emanating from each stone, tree, and bird. We live in a thrilling space that continues to amaze us each day."

"Is that something Ilanda expected to happen?"

"She expected there would be all kinds of enhancements. She'd have declared victory over any concrete reaction on our part as long as she can record it as scientific data. As a scientist and neurosurgeon, she took a high-risk gamble, and she came up with a winning hand. Lucky for my father and me."

Marinka peeled off her T-shirt as well, revealing a floral tattoo arrangement of turmeric, bird of paradise, and kava-kava. Cherry couldn't identify the other buds. They were the plants her father and all the men and women in their lineage used in the healing ceremonies.

"Did she connect yours to the pineal gland as well?"

"Yes. She followed the same procedure as with my father. There was no time for tweaks or further research, but knowing Ilanda, she'll try different brain mapping for future implants."

"But only for medical purposes, I've heard. You were a special case due to your association with Kahuna Lapa'au."

"If you ask me, the genie's already out of the bottle, and there's nothing she can do about it." Marinka paused to jump over a large boulder, then turned around and asked, "Will you do it?"

Cherry looked back at the piercing blueish hue of Marinka's crystal implants, searching for the right words. "Maybe. Possibly. For the right reasons. Lately, my meditation sessions lack the motivation and the focus to expand my consciousness. Maybe it's the stress or some other worry I'm not aware of. Getting the implants might help open jammed or stuck doors in my head. I'd consider that a worthwhile incentive to do it." But she was only braving out in front of her friend with no clear understanding if her current emotional state would provide the energy for such decision. But she will definitely look for serendipitous signs that could trigger a justified reversal.

Marinka grinned happily and hugged Cherry in a quick gesture —alabaster skin against chocolate-milk, fragility and fitness contrasting with formed muscles and visible force. A picture of complementing identities, struggling between reality and the astral plane, between the tangible and the ethereal.

The shoreline turned into a narrow but extended bay. Seaweed, plastic bags, water bottles, energy drink cans, and thousands of other items sloshed onto the shore, making a sour sight. There were no more stones on the beach but a thick, uneven carpet of garbage pushed inland by the relentless frothy waves.

"They stopped producing those cans twenty years ago, and they still wash up so often," Marinka pointed at a pile of twisted red Coke cans. "Their trip through these waters is long and exhausting.

Do you really think the oceans will ever be clean in our lifetime?" she asked.

Oceans were not Cherry's specialty but the same effects in the ability of the metabolism of the organisms in the inland water systems to adapt growth responses to imposed changes applied to them as well. Excessive inputs seemed to exceed the capacity of the ecosystem to be balanced when high concentration of pollutants reached the oceans in various forms such as oil spills, chemical left-overs, and sewage dumps.

"It's hard to say," Cherry said. "We have to stop polluting them before we can reverse the tide. Lip service alone doesn't help."

They left the garbage inlet behind. Small crabs hurried away on fast legs to hide under the rocks. A handful of Layson albatrosses clustered above them, brought over by a sudden gust of wind.

"Water will remind us again, and brutally so if we don't keep up our end of the deal. No half measures." Cherry continued the previous thought. "She would sense any crooked intentions, and if necessary, twist the screw again."

"Like God, she's everywhere," Marinka remarked.

They both let out bubbly laughs.

"Yes, you can say that. Those who think they can hide from the Creator are so mistaken."

"Let's go back," the Hawaiian woman suggested.

Sweat shined on their skin. Cherry's shoulders were tinged with a nuance of pink.

"You should take one of these stones with you to Canada."

Cherry looked inquisitively at her friend.

"Its spirit will help you stay balanced. I'll ask which one is willing to start such a journey north. There are benefits, but only if there's an agreement. I know of stories you won't believe."

They reached the narrow inlet. A group of about fifteen to twenty teenagers supervised by three adults had arrived for a cleanup mission. Those wearing high rubber boots were in the water, racking out the slosh while the others remained on the shore, collecting piles of plastic, metal, and miscellaneous stuff.

They greeted each other, and Marinka congratulated and

thanked them for their efforts. She asked if any of the boys would pick up the garbage bag she'd left a short distance away. One of them offered, and together, they left at a quick pace. The bag was still there, smoldering in the heat and surrounded by a family of seagulls ready to poke their beaks into it. The boy slanted his body to the left to compensate for the weight of the bag and went back.

"All of that garbage will be back in less than a week," Marinka said. "There's something my father and I recently experienced as a result of the implants."

She grabbed Cherry's arm gently and stared her in the eyes. "And it has to stay between us until we decide to share it publicly. Or others will come forward after they get the implants."

Cherry blinked in unconditional acceptance.

"Those jammed doors you mentioned earlier have opened wide for us," Marinka continued. "Connecting with the spirits surrounding us is one thing, as we already knew that was possible, but reading each other's thoughts is a totally different level."

Cherry wasn't puzzled. If telepathy was one of the implants' perks, so be it. It was beautiful and scary, enticing and repellent at once. Imagine—a new human species with innate AI, all natural and organic with just a bit of code attached to it. It was like the salt in your food—just enough to enhance its taste, making it palatable and enjoyable.

She could become a node in a global mesh of brains connected to the crystal cloud, aware of her own identity. Or the AI could take over, turning her into a useful host. She wasn't sure yet which way she'd go. A chat with Ilanda, the technology's gatekeeper, would probably solve her dilemma. Cherry put her T-shirt back on and started the climb up to the house.

"Tell me more when we get into the shade," she said.

CHAPTER 4

"Ojani, you are an old customer that has always paid fairly for my blood and sweat," the tiny bold man said, "but times are changing, so you'll have to adapt to the new price."

"That's why you didn't bother answering my calls and emails, Donald, eh? Because the price went up? I had to fly all the way to South Africa and use up my business flight allowance to be told, eh?"

Ojani's voice rose while the dark-skinned man in front of him shrunk a little behind his miniature glass and metal desk. "You can't be serious, Donald. I'm your only damn client." He slammed his hand on the desk. "Don't mess with me, eh."

Ojani leaned back on the purple couch and crossed his legs. His fingers went instinctively to the small scar above his right eyebrow—a reminder of an elementary school brawl with a feisty girl, an incident over which he'd always felt embarrassed.

Ojani's assignments in South Africa, as per Ilanda's instructions, were to get a firm commitment from DeBoer as the lab's main crystal implants provider and get rid of his association with Donald Pillay, who, over the years, provided blood imprinted with his experiences as an adult movie actor for Ojani's Toronto-based crystal business, now closed down.

"I'm telling the truth," Donald said. "I have other clients. The black market went wild after hearing about that Hawaiian fella's miraculous recovery. It was bloody-well amazing! He looked cool before with all the freakish tattoos, but now? He looks like he's come from the latest sci-fi megahit. He doesn't even have to say much."

Ojani didn't like the unfazed attitude of the South African. Donald was ingenious, charming, and persistent—personality traits that showed through the cracks in the tough nut to propel him into leading roles in several blockbusters. He didn't tell Donald that he joined the very team who brought Kahuna back from the dead. Ilanda's partnership proposal, though unexpected, brought a glimmer back into his boring working days. Yes, he raised his employees' morale with gleeful smiles and loud Caribbean shirts, indulged clients with additional care, and kept in contact with those personalities whose experiences could present an interest for his sensorial crystal technology. But the routine wore on his creativity, arresting his desire to improve on a technology he intuitively knew would be part of the humanity's future. As he interacted with Ilanda's team it rekindled his intellect and allowed him to participate in engaging discussions about sound frequencies, structured water, and crystals. He was amazed at the easiness of his own decision to pack and move shop to Queen Street, in the renovated school business, not before paying his employees a six-month salary.

"Are you sure the movie deals will roll in steadily enough so you can afford the maintenance fee on this condo, seeing as how it's located in the Johannesburg's exclusive Sandown neighborhood, eh? What if your new clients go belly-up, eh?" He glanced at the artwork adorning the room. "If the tide turns on you, you might have to sell these abstract paintings and shiny wooden sculptures you're so proud of. I'll keep me close if I were you, eh."

"Maybe I'll have to scale back on the outrageous monthly parties I throw here," Donald said. "Why don't you acknowledge that there might be other entrepreneurs in the same business as yours whose budgets are able to accommodate a higher price for genius-infused blood?" Donald chuckled at his own remark.

A sheepish smile turned into a think line. His rectangular jawline and sagging cheeks were suggestive of a bulldog.

"There is no other technology out there that can even remotely mimic mine. I've stayed ahead of the pack on this one, and I intend to remain there. Such business is not sustainable without a proper clientele. And I mean exclusive ones like I have. These *entrepreneurs*," Ojani used the word sarcastically, "might pay your price for a while, but don't expect a long-term relationship as the two of us had."

"Do I look like I give a rat's? I provide blood, and I get paid. If they succeed or fail, it's not my concern. I accept their claims and nothing more."

Ojani listened to the tiny man's hollow justification. There was no point in haggling over the price. He was ready to cut the crap and be out of there and on to the next meeting.

"Fifty percent more," Donald said, repeating his previous offer.

Ojani stood up. "You know what? You're right. My business in Toronto is winding down, and there are fewer clients willing to experience the squalid actions of a porn star. I'll make you an offer: buy my leftover blood back for twenty percent more than what I paid you initially. You can still make a nice profit selling it to your new buyers."

"You want me to buy my blood back?" The actor was incredulous.

"Yep."

"My friend, I'm not bluffing," Donald said as if reading the Canadian's mind. "You don't have to pay my price increase. I'm telling you what others are willing to do. Don't worry about me—I'll be fine."

Ojani walked over to the desk and shook Donald's tiny hand, ignoring the urge to punch him in the face. "Think about my offer before it dries up."

When Ojani returned to his senses, he found himself tied to a metal chair in what seemed to be a living room on the top floor of an apartment building. He scanned his surroundings: framed paintings of stylized impala or springbok—he couldn't tell the difference—and an elephant caressing her baby hung on the wall to his left; wooden masks of various shapes and sizes were neatly arranged on a diamond shape to his right; a two-seat grey leather sofa in front of him.

The light coming from behind him was unobstructed by skyscrapers, giving him an idea of the owner's financial status. Apartments such as this one were quite pricey anywhere in downtown Johannesburg. The time that had elapsed since his blackout couldn't have been more than an hour, judging by the time of day, so he was probably still somewhere in town.

He didn't feel dizzy so he wasn't drugged, and he wasn't in pain, so no one had beaten him into unconsciousness.

Ojani licked his lips, but he tasted no blood. Whoever had taken him had done him in gently. He recalled his discussion with Donald—the odd adult movie actor, the back and forth haggling on the price, the pretense—on his part—that he hadn't cared much about forfeiting the option to buy more of Donald's blood infused with his glittery sexual experiences.

That was the last thing he remembered. He tried to hop with the chair to the three-stairs leading to the apartment's door, but the rope only cut further into his flesh, and he made no progress on moving forward. He glanced down and groaned when he saw the bolts, securing the chair to the greyish floor boards. He was pinned down, left to roast slowly in the heat that filtered through the solar wall-windows behind him. No air conditioning flowed through the duct in the ceiling. At least he was able to breathe freely, and he could yell or even sing to occupy the boring time spent in captivity.

His bound shadow forged a twisted shape on the floor to his left

—to the east—letting him assume the time of the day. The late afternoon sunlight was going down to rest, ushering in Johannesburg's nightlife and leaving him in a steadily darkening room that might not see another person until morning.

Instinctively, disregarding the additional pain it might cause, Ojani tried to escape from the chair once more. He'd read in a book a long time ago about how the mighty elephant had been tricked into thinking that his lack of strength as a child would remain the same, no matter his future size.

"Maybe the freaking bolts are only for show. If I pull at it enough times. . ." he said out loud as if to encourage himself.

Pain lashed back at him, warning him that resistance was futile. The combination of his waning hope and waxing discomfort served to rattle his short-term memory, revealing more of his last moments before the black-out.

"Crystals! Yes, I met DeBoers's VP to talk about crystals."

He forced his mind to dig up the guy's name and features.

"Corus…Corus…no…Corus. Yes, Corus Van Dent. Tallish, wire-thin frame, oversized, shaved-head, flappy ears, wry chin, brownish eyes. That's pretty good for the state I'm in."

Meeting the DeBoers executive had been, in fact, his main reason to visit the country for the first time. It was an assignment from Ilanda who had been too busy back home with all the flurry that followed Kahuna's recovery. He'd been vested with the honorific position of acquisitions manager or handler. He jokingly referred to his title as "Just get the damn quality crystals to us." Actions counted more than a nameplate stuck to a door.

Van Dent had pampered Ojani with a large glass of water, a quarter of his Toronto daily rations, and a shiny pear, grown outside of the city limits. It had a slightly fresh smell.

"We've also been hit in the last three months by drastic daily water reductions," Van Dent said, only emphasizing his largess.

The reason behind such an exquisite treat? Ojani's vote of confidence when DeBoers's offer to become exclusive crystal implants provider would turn official. The man didn't say it outright, but

Ojani could sense the intention. Ilanda let DeBoers' executive believe other alternatives were on the table for the team in Toronto, and Ojani was doing the evaluations on his worldwide trip.

"You send us the specifics of each client, and we'll cut it for you," the VP said. "We have the raw materials, the know-how, and the labor is still cheap here."

Ojani simply nodded and let the extended silence force his host to keep the conversation going.

"I assume that some of our competitors will claim they can do what we do and more, only to get your attention and sign the contract. We've been selling to Ilanda through the university for a number of years, and she's never complained."

"How is the business of precious stones these days?" Ojani shot back instead.

Van Dent nestled into the leather armchair facing his guest, his smile still large on his tanned face. "It's slower than usual. People have other priorities these days: water, food, security. Contrary to popular beliefs, these are the times when even coveted assets, such as precious metals and stones, can't buy daily necessities."

The acknowledgment was lugubrious, but the South-African maintained his light demeanor. "Diversifying is what we're looking for, and to jump on the bandwagon of an incipient industry."

"How sure are you this isn't a fad, eh? One successful implant means nothing."

The executive rubbed his palms on the fabric of his dark-brown pants—Ojani remembered, wondering if it were a twin itch or sweaty palms. "The dogs are out to paraphrase an old song. To most people, Kahuna Lapa'au's recovery was a miracle, the result of sheer prayer and deep faith. But for those of us more inclined to the scientific, the tangible explanation is that the crystals, combined with the structured water, did the job."

"You might be right, eh."

"We can turn our experience into a booming business. Slice and dice the quartz to fit any budget—or rather, almost any budget," he said.

The cell on his wide, wooden desk—an antique inherited from the founding fathers—rang, but he didn't take his attention from Ojani, who suddenly understood how serious the guy was.

"Crystal clouding," Corus Van Dent continued, "for hosting personal data and secure communications that the governments and other agencies can't touch, is in an incipient phase and controlled by Anonymous Group. They've let in only people and organizations that fit a certain profile. More companies are looking into similar technologies. The crystal prices will go up. Securing a contract with us now will lock in such variable as well."

"You guys are quite the visionaries, eh" Ojani said. He whistled admiringly.

Corus Van Dent flashed another satisfied grin, and he asked his guest if he'd like more water. Ojani refused. He gulped the remaining mouthful.

"Five or ten implants mean nothing, but envision the big picture: multiply these numbers, connect them to the crystal cloud, and you have a thriving business. One could make money from hosting, advertising, create whole virtual rooms as storage is not an issue anymore, and the connectivity device, the crystal, is with you all the time."

Ojani felt frazzled. Ilanda and her team's goal, to heal certain medical conditions for which no other remedy was in place, seemed small when compared to this intricate statement . Yes, they had talked internally about the crystals' enlarge purpose, but again, the extent was nothing as scalable as DeBoer envisioned.

"And there's more to it, which will be shared in due time," Van Dent said, his eyes glowing with pride. "Make us your exclusive crystal implants provider. We are a reputable company."

Ojani hadn't promised anything—no engagements or positive winks that might cause him grief later on. And to be sure that accepting a glass of water and a pear wasn't considered implicit consent for unconditional support, he left his cell's audio recording on.

At the end of the meeting, they'd shaken hands cordially. Ojani had promised to convey the big picture to Ilanda and arrange for a video conference right after.

He was still tied to the chair in the dimly lit room, nothing else to do but push his mind into recollecting his steps after leaving the DeBoers Building. He'd walked one block east, looking for a cab when a gorgeous blonde wearing golden-rimmed shades asked for directions, swaying provocatively.

"And that was the last thing I remember, eh" he shouted, satisfied to have finally overcome his short-lived amnesia. He got no reaction from the empty room, but that small detail couldn't put a dent in his contentment.

He couldn't make sense of his kidnapping. He hadn't fallen over DeBoers's idea to stick a piece of crystal in everyone, but he wasn't completely against it either. Was this punishment for secretly recording their conversation? If so, he thought it a bit harsh.

A blinding headache came from out of nowhere, like a late hangover.

Worrying was futile until imminent danger presented itself. He calmed his breathing, emptied his mind, and called upon the teaching he hadn't had time to practice lately. The warm, loving face of Tenzin, his Buddhist friend, materialized in his mind's eye. Any sensation of fear vanished, and he made peace with the troubling situation.

A FOUL SMELL assaulted his nostrils, waking him up. Ojani felt a dampness between his legs. In spite of being uncomfortably tied to a chair, the sweetness of his dreams had softened his inhibitions, and his bladder had released itself. His thin pants absorbed the fetid liquid, copiously darkening his pants just above the knees.

He was soaked in urine and drenched with fear. The last thread of his composure had fled along with his common sense, and without consciously acknowledging it, his brain let out a terrified scream for help. Flecks of spittle bordered his lips, and his dry mouth demanded a sip of water.

"What do you want from me, eh?"

He was certain someone was watching him, and he worried they would see his desperation, come in, and request information he didn't have, only to admit that it was a case of mistaken identity. They would let him go with a new pair of pants and his pride intact.

He tried one more time. "I'm a Canadian citizen. I have rights, eh." The citizenship trick didn't have the same weight as it did thirty years ago.

The light in the room grew brighter—it was another glorious day in Johannesburg.

These were the risks of being a crystal procurement manager, he thought, and his frustration surfaced again. "To hell with the crystal. I swear I'm retiring if I get back home in one piece. I'll buy that piece of land and become a farmer or join Tenzin at the temple, eh."

He paused for a moment. Tenzin's name, his childhood friend, lingered in his mind as did the numerous past excuses he'd come up with to avoid being a renunciate of the Riwoche Buddhist Temple, where he knew he was always welcome and where he'd learned the Buddhist way.

The need to care for his mentally deranged and physically degraded parents had vanished five months ago when their weakened hearts had collapsed. The personnel from the assisting living facility had called him twice in the same week. It was painful but a relief at the same time. And like that, any connection to the land of his parents, Jamaica, completely vanished.

"I swear, Tenzin: I'll reconsider joining the monks," he promised out loud.

Hunger nipped at his stomach. He was sure he'd lose his mind in a couple of days. The people who kidnapped him were bound to have a messy floor in about ten days.

"I hope my insides leave a permanent stain on your boards, lessening the resale value, eh." He voiced his aggravation again, thinking, for no reason, of the state of the Toronto real estate market that had yet to suffer a downturn in more than three-quarters of a century.

There was a blip. The apartment's main door unlocked, and a plump, dark-skinned woman wearing surgical gloves and a colorful bandana around her head stepped in. She looked at him with dismay as if catching a delinquent stealing from the deserted house, but he'd been forcefully placed there, and there was nothing of value to steal anyway.

Her eyes rounded, her jaw dropped, and she turned halfway as if to flee the scene frantically.

"Please, don't leave me here, eh," he begged. "I've been kidnapped. I'm a foreign citizen. Either let me go or call the police now, right there, in front of me, eh." He shivered at the thought that she might leave him there, locking the door behind her as if nothing were remiss.

She hesitated, glancing back and forth at him. Dealing with the police force could be tricky—there was always the possibility an innocent person might be incriminated. The woman definitely didn't want to call the police.

"Please, untie me . . . Please!"

The woman kept her distance, standing at the top of the three steps. She puffed in disgust when she caught a whiff of the stench.

"What's your name, eh?" Ojani asked, recalling that, in the movies, any successful hostage situation started with establishing a personal relationship with the kidnappers. This was his real-life turn to try the stratagem, even if the cleaning woman had nothing to do with him being placed in that room.

"Rosana," she muttered, still edging toward the door, ready to take off.

"I can't hurt you, eh. Look at me—I can't move, and I haven't eaten or drank anything since yesterday afternoon. Could you spare a sip of water, eh?"

She stared at him fiercely this time, as though he had spoken a magic word meant to win her over, but it had no effect in a land of cool-headed people.

"Water, mm-hmm." She smirked. "Water is money. I get paid in water."

She shuffled her feet at the top of the stairs before slowly pushing forward. She placed her foot carefully on each step as if checking for a potential trap or something that might pop out to clutch at her ankle. She came within arm's reach.

Ojani kept still and quiet, not wanting to spook her. He plastered a confident smile on his face and waited for Rosana's final decision.

"I cut you free, and you don't move until I leave," she said.

Ojani nodded. Help is on its way, he thought, praying he'd stay calm enough not to change Rosana's mind.

She cut his left leg free first and then his right with the multipurpose knife from her uniform pocket.

Ojani held his breath. The pain in his calves subsided. He wanted desperately to massage his legs or even shake them a bit but refrained from doing so.

The woman assessed him once more before finishing the work.

He could move now. "What neighborhood is this, eh?" he asked, remaining immobile, as promised.

Rosana stepped back in a hurry. "Pretoria. Where were you before this?"

Ojani understood she was implying the moment before he was kidnapped. "Close to downtown."

Rosana whistled. It wasn't a catcall, but more of one that said, "You're screwed."

"Thanks for releasing me, eh. Can we go now, just in case someone else shows up, eh? I promised I wouldn't move until you were gone."

She smiled. He'd passed the trust test.

"You stink," she stated when he whisked past her. "There's a park two blocks west of here. It has a pond. Kids splash in it all day long."

"Thank you," he said again, and he meant it.

Ojani asked her for one last favor, and she handed him her phone.

The chat with the Canadian embassy was short. A scan of his right pupil and of the chip on back of his palm over the AugReality call confirmed his identity. The official ordered a driverless cab to the address Rosana provided and paid for the fair; Ojani didn't have to wash away his misery in the pond.

He left the building right away, taking the emergency stairs from the fifteenth floor, eager to reach the safety of the embassy.

CHAPTER 5

Maahes was enjoying the view from the outdoor patio at his hideaway in Costa Rica, his morning coffee still in front of him on the patio table. He admired the palm, avocado, and mayo trees dotting the impeccably cut lawn. Their fruit was heavy on their branches, and their scent kept Maahes in an induced reverie about the world he had left behind almost two years earlier. There were no more expensive suits and ties, no expensive dinners with power-hungry individuals, or business trips to drain his energy, making people yearn for a deeper meaning in life.

The life of the "dead man" was beyond expectations. Worry-free days passed between swims in the pool, trips on the catamaran, and incursions into the jungle to spot a wild white-headed capuchin monkey, ocelot, or the three-toed sloth.

There was still an abundance of green in spite of the shrunken rainy season—it had lasted only three months, almost half of what it used to be. He glanced at the land, teeming with bountiful life around him. It sparked a darkish thought about how his Egyptian relatives had been stuck on a parched territory that was eroded and polished daily by the insatiable winds and relentless sun.

Maahes puckered his lips—a gesture that had recently begun, manifesting from his disturbed subconscious—wondering about Ilanda's whereabouts and other dear memories dating back from the refugee camps in Egypt where they first met. Even then, thirty years ago, people left their homes chased by draught and unstable weather, clustering in camps at the mercy of powers invisible to them to provide rationalized water and food. Nowadays was even worse in certain areas in Africa and the Middle East: people would simply wait for their end, void of the strength to travel to the next promised oasis.

Maahes perched his legs on the wicker chair in front of him and picked the cell up off of the table and enabled its AugReality feature.

"Dial Marian," he said.

"Dialing Marian," Siri's voice confirmed.

"Hello, boss. How are you?"

The hacker's shiny head filled the 3D image, and with light coming at him from the side, his brown sunken eyes were almost invisible. No wrinkle cracked the skin of his face, and Maahes realized how young the man still looked even in his late forties. Marian was his only connection with the world he left behind, a man with a mission, acting on behalf of Maahes on a well-detailed list of events that would manipulate the media, induce urgency into the masses, and generate the entropy for achieving his most precious goal: the crystal implants. To regain mobility and privacy was now an asset, both coveted and priceless.

"Another day in paradise. I can't complain. You should come to visit me more often. If you've used up your vacation flight allowance, I can pay for more."

"I will, Maahes, I will," Marian said. "Maybe I'll move in with you, too Mr. former CEO of Vivus Water Inc., if I can bring all my security crap over." Marian's words were slightly muffled.

Maahes chuckled, assuming Marian's remark was meant to have been considered a joke. "Come after the mango wine is done. We'll have a glass or two and smoke cigars."

He sat up taller with his feet firmly on the floor. "I've read the report on Ilanda."

"You can't make things like that up. She's kept a relatively low profile after Kahuna Lapa'au's successful revival," Marian said, almost apologetically knowing he still couldn't provide the proof Maahes expected.

"Indeed. I would have anticipated her to appear on a talk show, boasting about ushering in a new technological era in humanity's evolution. Instead, she complained about the technology's unethical use. I predicted her behavior a long time ago," Maahes said.

He stood up and walked to the edge of the patio, his back to Marian. "While I was 'still alive,' I gave her a hint about the colossal potential for the technology outside of the medical field, but she wouldn't listen."

He clenched his fingers into a fist several times. "There's a huge potential for patients being treated for paranoia, bipolar disorder, OCD, schizophrenia, and Alzheimer's. And this is the field she's interested in. But a healthy mind can do so much more when enhanced with the crystal: go deeper into one's own consciousness, connect telepathically, create virtual worlds and populate them with the characters one's want. No more limitations. We won't need an AI to tell us things we don't know. We'll be the AI ourselves. She has to let it go faster," Maahes said with an increased cadence of his words.

He turned around and addressed the hacker. "I need to get a hold of that crystal enhancement without her knowing it's me. I'd give anything for a pep-talk with her. Do you think she'd recognize me?"

Marian plastered on a grim smile. Maahes knew he could count on the truth from Marian rather than sugar-coated platitudes. "You grew a beard and cut your hair short. You don't have any crystal implants yet, since your eyes are still green, and the shade of your skin is still dark enough. Unless, by some miraculous process, you've either grown or shrunk, I don't see how Ilanda would have a hard time identifying you; she's smart."

"You're right. Lying to myself doesn't help. We have to force her out of her shell. She needs an aggressive push."

"What do you have in mind?" Marian asked, leaning forward to catch every word spoken by his highest-paying client.

CHAPTER 6

When Ilanda woke up, she acknowledged, without a doubt, she'd had no dreams, nightmares, or disturbing, swirling mind images that fit into either category. She stretched and yawned at the same time; the blue bed sheets crumpled beneath her body.

Friday was the only day of the week she had to focus on the results of her team's research fully. They were advancing at a healthy pace, matching the frequencies of a six-note micro-electric scale known as Solfeggio with the crystals' frequencies. Quartz, amethyst, and amber were the most common crystals the team had considered as the starting point in terms of availability and affordability. Ilanda was miffed by the knowledge of sound healing developed millennia ago by the mystics that put the Solffegio together and connected it to healing.

"Dr. Joseph Puleo, a naturopathic physician and herbalist in the 1970s," Octana had told her, "decoded the micro-electric frequencies from the Solffegio and matched it to chakra balancing using six-forks. This tone opens the crown chakra and resets the pineal, pituitary, and hypothalamus glands. In the end, every vibration is tied to an organ."

And now, the team associated the same healing vibration to a specific crystal.

Ilanda had a nagging feeling that no matter how close the match was between a crystal and its host, the results could still be unpredictable, seeing as how they'd be influenced by an intangible intuitive intelligence that didn't follow the rules of science.

Kahuna Lapa'au's case had had a happy ending. It had a lot to do with intangible energies that she, as a neurosurgeon, couldn't pinpoint and wasn't able to mention in a peer-review paper. The spiritual leader had had external help. She'd witnessed the water ceremony in his hospital room and experienced shivers up her spine when the healer from Hawaii came to perform the ritual. He'd invoked the water, addressed it as if he were talking to a living, intelligent entity.

"Another patient might not have had similar support," she said out loud. She turned onto her side. Her head rested on her open palm as she took in the magnificent day, which had been blessed with a blinding sun.

She couldn't shrug-off the annoying thought. It had attached itself to her mind before she'd fallen asleep, and it was still there in the morning, sluggishly chipping away at her attention, diverting it from more pressing activities.

Reviving Kahuna Lapa'au had been an enormous victory in the short-term. Moving forward, any new case would help put procedures in place, identify and address potential challenges of the medical process.

"We'll chug along and see how far we can go without killing anyone," she muttered.

Ilanda got out of bed, invigorated at the prospect of the long walk to the lab on Queen Street East. She crossed the small hallway to the bathroom without glancing at the door to Maahes's bedroom, which had remained locked since his death.

Bitterness nagged at her— his body hadn't been repatriated and had perished while away from her and before they could reconcile. It was one of the few regrets she had in life, alongside that of not being a mother. Facing his scent and the scattered belongings in his room would come later, after the bitterness had faded, and she resigned herself to accepting that terrible, uncontrollable things happened in life. Maahes had to pay for his share of the careless behavior.

It was he who had offered to get a crystal implant as soon as she'd confirmed its safety.

She'd brushed him off then, offering him not kind words, but he returned it with another rambling on his insensitivity toward water.

"Siri, the latest news," she demanded from the AI while busying herself in the bathroom.

"Ilanda, do you want local or international news first?"

"Local with international implications."

"Hundreds of people gathered downtown Toronto at the Princess Margaret and St. Michael's hospitals, demanding access to the implant technology proven successful when it worked on Kahuna Lapa'au, Hawaiian spiritual leader and one of the few survivors of the terrifying explosion that targeted the Water for All conference last year."

Ilanda's ears perked up, and she moved to the living room, still drying her hands on a large towel. "Louder, Siri."

"When asked if access to such technology would help their loved ones recover from extreme medical conditions, the demonstrators gave vague answers. An ad-hoc survey done by our reporter revealed that people are willing to get the implants not only for medical purposes but for the potential brain enhancement."

"What the hell?" Ilanda blurted in frustration, tugging at the towel. "Give me more of this."

"There are similar gatherings in Vancouver, Ottawa, New York, Washington DC, LA, and—oh, dear," Siri exclaimed, sounding like an exasperated wife, "half the European capitals and couple of cities in the Middle East. Add Tokyo and Sydney to the list. Which one do you want to play?"

"All have the same demands?"

Siri split the TV screen into twenty-four squares. She turned the sound on for each location, one at a time, as Ilanda listened and read the translated caption.

Ilanda dumped herself on a chair by the kitchen island, facing the living room. "What started this madness?"

"News agencies from all of these countries have received press releases about the Canadian government's suppression of the crystal implants. Human rights activists and other NGOs jumped at the announcement."

"This is insanity!"

She ran her fingers through her hair as she sighed deeply. "Show me the press release."

The text displayed on the top right corner in a font size big enough to read.

"Press Release

Source: undisclosed

Release date: June 22, 2057

Attn: News agencies

The world welcomed the recovery of Kahuna Lapa'au of Hawaii and acknowledged the efforts of the team of doctors and scientists that developed the technology used for such medical achievement. The potential of technology in helping others overcome their health issues is unlimited.

It was brought to our attention that for the past several months the Canadian Government has blocked the medical team from starting the legal procedure so the crystal implants could become a standard intervention at your local hospital.

It is your right to be healthy.

Say no to Government intervention."

"Where did it come from?"

It took Siri a few seconds before replying, "That information is not available. No source is mentioned."

"So, how could these media idiots run with a story without verification from multiple sources?"

"It came from three different sources, but all of them were encrypted. To quote the anchors, 'This news is too good to be discarded. It has to have a seed of truth,'" Siri said.

Ilanda felt short of breath, as if someone was trying to strangle her. "Enlarge the Tokyo crowd."

Siri obliged. Men and women, young and middle-aged, politely waved signs in-line with Japanese etiquette. "Crystal implants for all!" Siri translated. "We are the new technological society!" "Don't suppress the crystal technology!"

The participants at the other locations were more vocal on the subject.

"What's gotten into them?"

She asked Siri to dial the lab.

"Nanette, are you guys, okay?"

"Thank God you called," the young researcher said. She sounded relieved that she hadn't needed to initiate the call with her boss. "Everyone is here, but they're worried about this crazy turn of events. Did you see the spread?"

Ilanda looked at her assistants' frayed faces. "I assume you got the same info about the unreliability of the sources behind the leaked press releases?" she asked.

"Pretty much," Nanette said. "It's interesting that our real location wasn't disclosed. They either don't know about it, or they're trying to protect us."

"Any reaction from our government yet?"

"Fast and furious. As if a hot iron had burned it into their flesh like a brand. They're being called crystal inhibitors and diversity killers. The news snuck up on them as it did on us."

"Sit tight. I'm leaving now."

"Ilanda, there's more." Nanette's voice cracked.

"What?"

"The prime minister's office contacted the lab. They're the only ones aware of where we do our work. They'll keep their lips sealed, but they need to hear that you have no involvement in this leak."

The young woman bordered on tears.

"Christ! Don't answer any calls or communicate with anyone else. Complete shutdown. Understood?"

The team members with Nanette nodded furiously in agreement.

She ended the call and swore her planned walk was a write-off.

Ilanda hurried to the bedroom for the wig she kept hidden in one of the drawers. It had been a gift from Maahes that was supposed to have turned her into an inhibition-free woman, release her innate wild side, and please him. That never happened, but she was thankful she hadn't thrown the fake hair away.

She checked the black, curly locks flowing over her shoulders in the mirror.

"Good luck to us," she mumbled, still not sure how to handle this new stir. There always seemed to be something like this to push humanity from one crisis to the next. And the one regarding water hasn't even been completely addressed yet.

She stormed out of the apartment, ready for another fight.

Ilanda stepped off the subway thirty minutes later, at Queen Street Station on the Yonge line. On street level, she stopped at a convenience store, checking her reflection in every shiny surface to be sure she wasn't followed. Panic entangled in her gut like an octopus compressing its prey until it gasped its last breath.

The threats had begun to follow a pattern of two calls per day from a blocked number, and the garbled voice had a creepy metallic tinge. Each call trashed her usually calm demeanor.

What had first annoyed her as a bad joke two weeks ago had now felt like personal terrorism. She had no one to whom she might go to for advice, but then she remembered Maninov, Maahes's lawyer, who had chased her until she'd signed the will, thus closing one chapter in her life and beginning the new one as a widow.

Widow. The word sounded strange when she repeated it in her mind. She'd have preferred to have been separated, implying that her ex was still alive. The civilized terms of their divorce would have also allowed for occasional dinners or rushed coffees in the airports of the world, should their traveling schedules intersect.

Maninov suggested the most convenient solution: go to the police.

"It doesn't matter if it's a blocked number. They can still trace it back somehow," he said adamantly, which was uncharacteristic for him.

Ilanda agreed to think about it, but in the end, she took no real action. Days went by in which she was swamped with work. The nights were fraught with solitude. Not even the youthfulness of her team could fill the growing chasm. The success of the crystal implants—first on Kahuna and then on his daughter, Marinka—elated her spirit to a level she'd never experienced professionally. The scientific world was at her feet, expecting more, in spite of her scarcity of sharing research data.

She wore a disguise, frantic at the thought someone might recognize her as she snuck into the building. The dilapidated school-turned-research-lab tended to keep a low profile in the neighborhood. There was no plaque on the metal fence nor on the building to scream its designation. The flow of visitors in and out was kept at a minimum so as not to raise anyone's curiosity.

Once inside, Ilanda went directly to the basement where the operating rooms were, along with a windowless meeting space, large enough to fit a round table with eight chairs crammed around it. Each wall had been painted a different bright color to compensate for the lack of natural light and claustrophobia. It was the team's refuge space between crystal batch trials, where they jotted down the results and recorded the time slots to code crystal type.

They were huddled together, mesmerized as they watched the AugReality projection of the daily news. The women, Nanette and Octana, were seated, while the men, Mark and Raman, leaned on the wall, watching from behind.

Ilanda closed the door behind her, dropped the wig and her purse on one of the chairs, and nodded to everyone.

The CBC anchor, a skinny Asian woman, spoke loud and quickly as if trying to match the energy of the group on which she was reporting.

"It's been six hours since the simultaneous protests started all over the world, and there is no sign that the number of participants is about to subside any time soon. In fact, the opposite is happening.

Parents have brought their children along, claiming the future of the little ones would be better off if they were connected to the crystal cloud. At this time, we only have sketchy details if this new concept of crystal cloud would replace the traditional crystal data hosting available only to foundations and NGOs working on environmental sensitive projects. The storage capacity of any type of crystal, which has already been confirmed on this channel several times by both scientists and technology gurus, could be the solution for the data-intensive society we live in. Are we ready to open such technology to everyone? Could an implant like the one Kahuna Lapa'au has be compatible with the crystal cloud?" the anchor asked, rhetorically. "At least this is what the crowds gathered in various cities claim. So far, the police have cordoned off—"

Ilanda killed the feed with an abrupt gesture. Her team portrayed a mosaic of emotional states. The round-eyed girls had trouble keeping their hands steady: Nanette pushed her locks behind her ears and Octana played with the silver chain hanging around her neck.

"Crystal cloud for everyone? When did this concept enter the public discussion?"

"Right after we hung up with you. It was introduced in Berlin first," Octana said.

"The concept is being used restrictively and in parallel with the Web, and slowly, might be used less and less in the coming years. I've heard the encryption is a masterpiece," Raman, the resourceful application developer, said.

"Someone is spoon-feeding the media and the crowd with ideas that the public can't understand, let alone explain. It becomes everyone's point-of-view when it's added to the list of demands," Nanette said.

"They say it's a concept already developed, but the government's suppressing it because it follows open-source, high-encryption concepts." Raman added.

"What do you think?" Ilanda asked.

Raman pushed himself off the wall and took a seat. Ilanda fixated on his blue eyes, wondering for a split second how they might look when covered by the same color implants. Maybe the lack of contrast would diminish his weirdness.

"We've all heard about the Anonymous Group who developed stand-alone crystal-based data hosting locations. There is no confirmed number on how many of them are out there and if there is any connectivity that could turn them into a cloud-type of architecture," he said. "And if that's true, no one knows how far they've expanded the network. If they made an announcement tomorrow, it wouldn't surprise me. Anything is possible. I simply can't understand why the sudden surge on this issue now."

Octana tilted her diminutive head left and right as she always did before making a statement she thought was important. "There is no doubt about the simultaneous staging of these events. Whoever is behind it has the financial prowess and brains to drop the outrageously appealing nuggets at the right nodes on the informational Web. We need to work on the basics: who and why. As for the how, what, and when, it's right in front of us."

The cell left on the table vibrated loudly, and its enabled AugReality projection started automatically. It had been programmed to initiate the broadcast of new evidence on this, the hottest topic.

"Envisioning the near future of the crystal implants," the same anchorwoman said in dismay, "the crowds demand changes to personal and corporate insurance policies to cover such a medical expense. This is new territory for us. Our next guest from Blue Cross Insurance will be joining us shortly. We'll discuss the pros and cons, timeframe for adding clauses related to crystal implants, and financial implications for both the insurer and the insured."

Octana lowered the volume. "Look at the pattern of how these ideas are being disseminated. It's not all at once. The originator gives time for each one to sync with the masses and be discussed on live TV. It's only after all angles and implications have been discussed that another is released."

Silence followed as they mulled over Octana's statement.

"It's a well-rehearsed plan," Ilanda said. "What could be next?" She clenched her fists as if trying to squeeze out an answer.

No one dared suggest any.

"By the way, have you heard from Ojani? He landed in Johannesburg twenty-four hours ago."

Short denial nods followed.

"I really hope that he gets DeBoers's acceptance to become our main crystal supplier," Ilanda said.

"Watching the news doesn't help much," Nanette said. "You should call the premier's office. They're waiting," she reminded Ilanda, who stood up and picked up her bag.

"I'll call them from my office. Ping me if anything crazy comes up. Try reaching Ojani." She walked out of the room and up the stairs to the first floor.

CHAPTER 7

"Be careful." Cherry caught Nanette's elbow before she fell on the wet stones.

"Thanks," Nanette said.

Before starting their walk, Cherry complimented the younger woman for keeping her indigenous features unaltered by makeup, lipstick, or hair color. She loved Nanette's high cheekbones, wide nose and chin, and the dark, marble-like eyes. Her black hair was braided in a thick ponytail, swinging on her back as if helping Nanette keep her balance on the winding trail. Her square shoulders held her head high with pride.

They were the only ones taking the annual summer outdoor trip along the Humber River, northwest of Toronto, initiated by Cherry. Her finicky mood allowed no room for a larger gathering of her university students as it had in previous years, encompassing sustained planning, logistics, and coordination. She didn't have a second thought selecting Nanette, Ilanda's team's sound specialist, as her helper. A sobering whisper during one of Cherry's occasional day dreaming interludes had permeated her consciousness, hard and incisive like an epidural to the spine. *Nanette-you don't need anyone else but her.*

Nanette's First Nations Cree heritage attracted Cherry as she already had a connection with Kahuna Lapa'au in Hawaii, and she knew fairly well Chief Landing Eagle of the Navaho, who perished in the explosion in Toronto in 2055.

Nanette happily obliged and for the first part of the day, Cherry lectured her on ecosystems and aquatic ecology.

"An ecosystem is a community of living organisms and their physical and chemical environment, linked by flows of energy and nutrients. Ecosystems can be defined at a variety of scales. For example, the Humber River basin can be considered an ecosystem. Also the entire planet is an ecosystem. The boundaries of an aquatic ecosystem are somewhat arbitrary, but generally encloses a system in which inflows and outflows can be estimated. Ecosystem ecologists study how nutrients, energy, and water flow through an ecosystem," she had explained to a quiet Nanette. "And today, through our sampling, we'll look for the presence of sentinel species such as stonefly and caddisfly. They usually disappear first if there is unbalance in the environment conditions such as diminished oxygen levels."

They were negotiating a portion of last year's path along the Humber River, collecting water samples for chemical analysis, gently turning rocks upside-down, looking for visible forms of life, then placing them back in the same grooves.

"By looking at the dried marks on the edge of the river channel, we can determine the water recession levels." Cherry picked up a stick and pointed to the soil. "Over here the soil is so dry that a six-hour intensive rainfall will cause a major overflow. In the last ten years Humber River had lost half of its effluents due to longer and hotter summers that increased evaporation, diminished precipitation by thirty-five percent, and reduced underground water resources." Cherry she ran the stick along the darker line of soil.

She hunched down to examine the density of plants common to the area such as trout lily and trillium sessile. Did it match the ratio from previous years? A reduced density would have been a sign that changes in water's behavior had affected the conditions for local flora to develop normally.

"Did we collect, you know, enough samples?" Nanette asked.

"I think so," Cherry said. They had filled five glass jars with water from different locations, marked them, and safely placed them in foam compartments in a camping-style cooler. Both women held onto the wide handle on each side of the box to carry it.

"In the months after the awakening of water, you heard countless times that the molecular structure of the water in Ganges River, Jordan River, and other important bodies of water have changed to a hexagonal shape similar to the one of structured water," Cherry said, trying to get to the point of their hard work.

Nanette nodded silently.

"Usually, using structured water is a good thing, as we all know from Ilanda's research when she paired it with the crystals. In the case of 'the awakening,' the newly formed structure acted as a corrosive liquid, burning our skin. Days after the incident, scientists observed that even plants and trees along the river banks were affected, withering away. So we'll analyze this year's samples and compare it with the ones from last year for levels of nitrogen, phosphorus, and oxygen. Low levels of all these components means that the growth of algae and aquatic plants slows down and even stops."

They approached a miniature waterfall, its three-foot drop feisty and whirling, as unsettling as a bigger sister. Two half-sunken, oversized boulders functioned as stepping stones. A light foam churning at the bottom of the fall enchanted the eye only for seconds before the ebb of the shy western wind pushed it down stream. Hollow pinewood trunks with shredded edges gave shelter to a sorority of wet leaves as they gathered in their decayed interiors.

"Do you see the water vortexes at the bottom of the fall?"

Nanette stepped closer to the edge of the river.

"Spirals are the basic form of motion in nature. It's like moving the energy from one level to another," Cherry said.

"Isn't water, you know, purifying itself when going through such vortexes?" Nanette asked.

"Indeed." Cherry lifted the protective layer of leaves with the end of a bent stick, and the spiders, centipedes and worms hiding underneath went into a panic. "Life is back at the edge of the river."

She smiled, straightening her back as she gazed at the thick forest. "The crawlers sensed that water, if still in its awakening phase, has reduced her pH, hence returning their ability to thrive. People don't seem to understand that chemicals in a human body have an adverse effect on its fertility, metabolism, and locomotor functions. Similarly, the planet goes through the same ordeal of adapting to our pollution assault. The Earth's water is like our body's blood. And instead of Earth going into biological and evolutionary unconsciousness, it activates water as a defensive measure."

"So what are, you know, the new coastal measurements saying: is the water's pH lower than 7.5 as it should be for the marine life to survive?" Nanette asked.

"In the reports we received at Water for All two weeks ago, it said that the level hovered around seven right after 'the awakening,' but now is coming back to its normal level, hence the aquatic life is returning as well."

"How much farther upstream?" Nanette asked.

Cherry put her backpack down and ruffled inside for the water canister. "No more than one kilometer. There's a small pond on this side of the river I want to sample." She swallowed a healthy sip before handing the canister to Nanette, along with an energy bar.

"What made you want to study sound's vibration and frequency in college?" Cherry asked.

Nanette's gaze seemed to marvel at her surroundings, and she slowly extended her arms. She looked as if plunged in an involuntary trance. "All life, you know, permeates with energy, which has its own sound imprint. My forefathers, you know, roamed these lands showing respect to the protective spirits, carefully maintaining the necessary balance, you know." The young woman's reverence as she walked through her ancestors' natural cathedral didn't show in her voice. Only resignation and anguish.

"Grandfather, you know, is one of the few tribal elders still alive that has kept our knowledge intact—the medicine wheel, the invocation of spirits, and the classification of the medicinal herbs, among others, you know."

Cherry had questions to ask, but instead, she sat on a dry boulder, letting Nanette continue her impromptu confession. During the little time she spent with the whole team in the past, Cherry didn't notice the younger woman's speech pattern.

Nanette swallowed the last piece of the energy bar, put the wrapper in one of her backpack's pockets, and sat beside Cherry. "The decimation of indigenous peoples, you know, all around the world has followed a plan extended over centuries, you know. Land grabbing was the main drive for such extermination, you know. With not enough population left, you know, they signed treaties with the local governments and had no more standing, you know."

Cherry was familiar with the struggle of the indigenous people over civil rights and land arrangements that never had been respected by successive governments, but she said nothing. She sensed that Nanette needed to share what troubled her, and maybe justify why sometimes she felt like an outsider.

"I didn't believe my grandfather initially, you know. I thought no matter how wise and compassionate he was, you know, a level of hate and torment would still cloud his judgment, and no helping spirit, you know, could purge it from him. But I was wrong, you know."

"You're right. It happened in most of the newly discovered territories," Cherry said.

"Correct. My research, you know, on the history of Canada, the USA, Australia, and other countries revealed a similar pattern with the indigenous people's disposition." Her eyes waxed cold and sorrowful. "This humiliating and commercially-driven process, you know, has left them broken, physically, and mentally. It's diluted, you know, their identity and discredited the enhanced spiritual connection with the higher realms. Modern society, you know, couldn't accept us the way we were for generations, and they clobbered our customs, you know, leaving only lies and half-truths. That's all we mattered to them, you know."

Cherry nodded. The drama of the African people—which had come from the same source—was painted in red tears on Hayyin's wooden mask. It was the conquerors who had downplayed the truth regarding the amount of blood and suffering the assimilation of the natives had generated.

Nanette's eyes took life. "Since I was little, you know, my grandfather taught me that everything around us has its own spirit and sound, you know. We walked this forest together every time we visited from Victoria, B.C., and this is where, you know, I imprinted in my mind the sound of the leaves ruffled by the wind, the crack of a young tree pushed by a strong breeze, and the tug of the boisterous water on the silent stones, you know.

"Later on, when I was around ten-years-old, you know, my personal library of sounds was enriched by the trill of the woodpecker, loon, and moose. All of the nature's sounds, you know, soothed me on my long walks through the forest or grassy hills. I felt caressed, loved, and healed, you know. Only in my late teens I understood, that we produce our own sounds through words, you know. And our intention, sincere or not, loving or not, propagates with that sound. We can hurt or help with words, you know."

"That's why people ask for others' blessings when they are in a bad spot?"

"Precisely. But how many understand, you know, that the blessings need meaning behind it. Form the thought, you know, say the word, and mean the meaning," Nanette said, her high cheekbones pushed up by a large smile.

Cherry could only imagine the trauma and blockages haunting Nanette as it came through her broken voice, reinforcing her words.

"And nowadays, you play with crystals that are another wonder of nature," Cherry said.

"Indeed. Octana gave me some hints, you know, on what I should research further, and it's amazing to find out that, you know, encoded sound frequencies appear in the Bible's Book of Numbers. And scholars have traced, you know, its threads as far back as the pre-Egyptian mystics. These sounds, you know, are also known as the solfeggio frequencies."

"How do they correlate with crystals?"

"Not only with crystals, but with parts of the body as well. For instance, you know, musical note 're' corresponds with water, the sacral chakra, the reproductive system, and—"

An unnatural buzz forced their gaze upward. One of the drones —stamped with the Ontario Environmental Agency's logo—spotted them and drew closer.

"I thought surveillance, you know, only applied within the cities," Nanette said, her mouth twisted in disgust. She bent down to pick up a stone and clutched it in her palm.

It was Cherry's turn to prevent her disgruntled companion from committing an offense, thus ending their peaceful hike at the police station. "I got scanned twice the last time I was on one of the Humber River's tributaries. Sorry, it slipped my mind to mention it to you," Cherry said. "There is no more privacy outside our own homes, and it's awful."

Nanette placed the stone back on the ground with care, as if it were a living organism whose life depended on her. "The desecration of my peoples' lands, you know, continues to this day with this invasive presence of technology." Helplessness trailed in her voice.

"The surveillance for water traficants has extended significantly in the last couple of months," Cherry said.

"Where did they get potable water in this area?"

"From the illegally dug wells on Crown lands."

The conversation stopped and the women raised the back of their right hand to the drone. It hummed as it scanned their embedded chips. The machine blinked a green light at them from fifteen feet in the air and then flew upstream. Nanette retied her hiking boots, while Cherry secured her backpack so they could move on.

"Do you think the crystal technology, you know, will help humanity improve?"

Cherry discarded several thoughts before replying. "Depends on the angle from which one assesses its impact. A purely commercial approach, which is always a pragmatic point of view, is welcomed by the investors and the parties that benefit financially."

"Yes, it's always like that, you know. Ethics and commons sense are intentionally forgotten," Nanette said, stepping behind Cherry.

"Medically, it's a fantastic way to help people who lack the means, but I'm concerned with the more trivial uses for the implants: entertainment, virtual sex, TV binges, and the simulation of drug and alcohol abuse. People will get all that if, in the near future, they'll connect to the crystal cloud that pesters the news these days. Permanent online connectivity through the crystal hubs creeping in could morph into permanent habits."

They walked slowly, avoiding the puddles and fallen branches littering the ground.

"This obsession with trivial compensation," Cherry said, "could further remove a significant percentage of the population from the burning issues of the society and humankind." She was not shy at offering her blunt point of view to whoever was ready to listen. "Unless," she continued, "attaching the crystal performs a miracle, shifting our consciousness."

"You mean forcing a transformation, you know, of brain's neuroplasticity through crystal vibrations?"

"Maybe Ilanda had this objective in mind all along," Cherry said, "but she kept it to herself. Who would willingly embed a stone in their body to experience enhanced pleasure, then awake the next day vastly smarter and yet keep the implications to himself?"

Nanette giggled. Her eyes, like polished charcoal on her Cree features, filled with joy.

"Imagine a society in which the majority of its members live a conscious and meaningful life," Cherry continued.

"Quite creepy, you know," the younger woman said, sarcastically.

The path widened, and they walked shoulder-to-shoulder. In the bushes several yards away, a murder of crows squawked their discontent. Even more birds filled the trees nearby, issuing harsh caws. It gave Cherry reason to pause—so many birds in one place was not the norm. It looked like a dark feathery line-up waiting for a long-overdue feast.

"Let's have a look." Cherry sauntered closer. "It might be a hare or a fox they're feeding on, but then again, it might not." She pulled out a precautionary whistle and stepped off the main trail, cutting through the high grass. The high canopy fretted in the mild wind, but it wasn't loud enough to overcome the ruckus ahead.

Cherry clutched the whistle tightly. An intense whirlpool of flapping blackened the air, and coos, rattles, and clicks reverberated with deafening intensity. The women squared on the ground, and Cherry blew the whistle again and again. With Nanette watching her back, she moved forward, using the annoying sound as a weapon.

"Look at that," Cherry said loudly. "They only moved up in the trees."

"They must be feeding on a tasty meal, you know," Nanette said, looking up as if expecting an attack from the flying hoard.

The wind changed direction, and an unimaginable stench assaulted them.

"That's not the smell of a decaying rabbit or fox, you know," Nanette said, stepping out of the wind's gusts. "It has to be something bigger, you know."

They were now in front of the bush from where the smell emanated. Cherry looked over the leaves. The whistle fell from her hand, and her legs melted. Cherry turned to face her companion. "Oh, my God." She bent forward and spat on the ground. A cough hit her next. Her right arm clung to Nanette with diminished strength.

"Don't look," she said.

Nanette complied, but she pulled out her cell, lifted it, and started taking pictures of the scene behind the bush without looking directly at it.

"It's a human body," Cherry said. "Male, I think."

Layer after layer, the crows regained lost territory, swooping from the high branches, their intimidating caws intensified.

It worked. The women retreated, satisfying the determined predators who covered the body as if it were a moving carpet.

Nanette enlarged the images, one by one. He was lying on his belly, the head resting on its right side, left eye missing, though whether it had been pried out or swallowed by the feathery thieves, she couldn't tell. The flesh on the cheekbone was gone, revealing an ugly gash. The long-sleeved shirt he was wearing had prevented extensive damage to the left arm, which was extended out, palm down. Only the back of the hand had a nasty hole in it.

"Is that wound from the crows or was his chip cut out?" Cherry asked.

"I'm not sure, you know. Maybe his chip is embedded in the other palm, you know. I won't go to check, though. Seriously—it's not our problem now, you know," Nanette said, hands writhing in front of her.

The crows had done a number on his back, exposing his bloody vertebrae. Cherry moved the enlarged image to the left to see that he was wearing running shoes instead of the recommended hiking boots. "Who do we call—the police?"

"Yes. Tell them, you know, about the drone that scanned us earlier," Nanette said, her emotional balance regained. "Our coordinates, you know, should have already been sent to the central database."

Cherry called the emergency number and activated the AugReality feature for live recording.

"No, I can't step closer to where the body is. It's crawling with crows, and they're insensitive to the whistle. You send your people here," she said forcefully. "You've got the coordinates—we're leaving."

"You can't leave the site unattended before the officers arrive," the female voice said.

"The site was unattended before we got here." Cherry shook her head in disgust. The pressure of the unexpected situation, the fearless crows, and the fact that she had never seen a dead person in such a high degree of decomposition rattled her usual calm.

"I'll tie a ribbon at the edge of the path. They'll hear the noise anyway. We're going south now. If they come the same way, we'll provide a statement."

Cherry disconnected and gestured Nanette back toward the main path. "Send the pictures to your personal email account, then delete them from your cell," Cherry said, anticipating trouble at the potential future encounter with law enforcement.

"Here's another justification, you know, for cordoning off a big chunk of the forest and make it off-limits for public access, you know," Nanette said, her voice shaking. "There is a sacred indigenous site two miles west of here, you know. Grandfather and I perform a medicine wheel ceremony there once a year, you know. I hope it stays hidden. It's one of the few pieces of land we can still call sacred, you know."

The trees seemed to scratch the dome of the sun, letting its rays through. The water climbed over the rocks and sunken branches, insensitive to the drama unfolding in the thicket as she found her way to Lake Ontario. Maybe she had already recorded in her molecular structure the crime in the forest and the crows' satisfaction after claiming the large prey.

Cherry believed in water's storage properties. But water could only record and store information, letting things flow as prearranged by the universal matrix. She believed in magic ever since her father read her the Brothers Grimm fairy tales as a five-year-old, hungry to build in her head new worlds in which she was the perpetual hero. And if there was magic on Earth, it was contained in water.

After the next bend, the women saw flashlights. Barking dogs cut through the silence , and then the buzz of drones hovered above them.

"Let's wait for them here," Cherry said.

They rested their backpacks on the ground and pulled out their water canteens.

"I hope they won't force us to go back, you know," Nanette said with displeasure.

Cherry shrugged. She was exhausted and not ready to engage in a verbal hassle with the authorities. "Only if they carry us on a stretcher." She gave a nervous-ridden laugh.

"You did what?"

Ilanda shrieked at Cherry and Nanette, who were sitting on the couch in her office, their hands folded in their laps as if waiting to be reprimanded by their high school principal.

"This is serious, Ilanda. We're still shaken by what we saw. And the crows made the experience so much creepier." Cherry grimaced as if to underscore the incredulity of their story. She nodded at Nanette, who pulled out her phone, enabled the AugReality feature, and let the photos she'd taken float in the air. "Check the back of the guy's left hand and eye socket," Cherry said, indicating areas of interest. "We couldn't tell if the crows did the damage on location or if they were separated from the body ahead of time."

Ilanda got closer and started to change the angle and enlarge certain spots. She went through all of the photos before returning back to the first one.

"That's definitely a straight cut on the back of the hand," she said, still snappy. "In fact, whoever did the work had limited surgical skills." She gnashed her teeth. "The incision is a bit bigger than should have been necessary to extract the chip, but the eyeball was scooped out clean with no residue left behind. The crows would've done a dirtier job. I can't see the other side of his face, but I'd bet my license that the other eyeball is missing, too."

She shuffled back and forth. "These inhumane butchers!" Nothing else caught her professional interest.

"Bloody nightmare." Nanette let out a heavy sigh. "All I can hear in my head, you know, are the caws and clicks chasing me." Her hair flowed loosely reaching her waist, and she kept combing it with her fingers in a nervous move.

Cherry snorted. Her thoughts were also tainted by the disturbing images of the sprawled body crawling with the black and noisy plague.

"All sorted out with the police?" Ilanda asked.

They both nodded, neither of them willing to share anything more from their experience at the police station, which lasted almost two hours. The annual hike, the drone scanning, the discovery of the victim, along with the live streaming performed at the time of the call, satisfied the officers, and they were let go. There was nothing else that could have helped the investigation on their end.

"The guy was probably sacked somewhere else," Ilanda said, her voice still on a high note. "It took a lot of effort and risk dropping him off so far from the city."

"Would the police be able to identify him?" Cherry asked.

"Maybe." Ilanda peered at the enlarged photo of the hand one more time. "I can't tell if his fingerprints and dentals are still intact, but I don't see the logic in killing for the chip and eyeballs only to leave the other body part intact for identification." She swooshed the images away and sat behind her desk. Otherwise, I assume it was an enjoyable hike," she said with a maddening smile.

"The GTA is pretty much under full surveillance for illegal water and gun possession," Cherry said, disregarding her friend's sarcasm. "There is no safe place to dump a body, not even in the sewers, without being found within twenty-four hours."

"It was bad luck for the killers, you know, that we passed by. One in a million chances," Nanette said.

"Could one re-use the chip and the eyeballs?" Cherry stared at Ilanda, waiting for an answer. Ilanda's cheeks, once round and rosy, were now sunken and pale. Deep ruts had formed at the corners of her eyes. She looked aged, well beyond her forty-seven years, but the scientist and warrior inside her had kept the lights on, moving her mind and body together day after day, challenge after challenge. Cherry knew Ilanda's greatest desire was to implement crystal technology in the most ethical and sustainable way possible. Cherry loved her friend for her altruism, though she sometimes loathed her stubbornness.

"It's possible. Whoever did the extraction had to prevent the signal from sending faulty warnings to the government-supervised dashboard. Otherwise, it would trigger a trace-back and a police search."

"I assume the thieves don't want the freshly-harvested organs, you know, to get damaged," Nanette said, unable to help herself.

"A skillful technical team could maintain broadcasting the

frequency of the chip while being implanted in a different body—an exchange, if you like," Ilanda said.

"Stolen identities?"

"Yes, Cherry. Anything is possible in this upside-down world: new eyeballs plus a new chip equals a new person. High rollers trying to evade the law and infiltrate the borders have the means to do it—a facelift isn't enough anymore considering the advanced face-recognition software implemented in all major cities."

They all sat quietly for several long moments, riffling through ideas, wondering if certain disturbing questions should be asked out loud.

Cherry folded her arms. "Will this incident prevent the roll-out of the crystal technology?"

Ilanda shrugged. It seemed more an involuntary body reaction to a bothering question than a conscious acknowledgment. She squinted as if assembling an answer caused her unbearable suffering. "Only if it becomes an epidemic and the crimes are connected to stolen identity cases."

"And how, exactly, will you define that term? One hundred victims? One thousand?" Cherry asked.

The doctor shuffled in her chair, staring at the black-and-white poster of New York City hanging above the coach. "Maybe I misused the term. A virus generates an epidemic. A killing spree has a person or an organized group behind it. Any number higher than ten in a city like Toronto is enough to generate concerns and have the police force on the look-out. Unless similar cases start showing up all around the world, which is expected. The government and the police will insist on more stop-and-frisk filters, intensified drone surveillance, and potentially, additional aggressive measures as an intimidation tactic."

A sudden haze cluttered Cherry's mind. She couldn't accept the thought that stealing identities to conceal crimes could become a sport and prompt a worldwide killing spree.

Humanity was scarred by the phenomenally damaging environmental changes, but it still had issues keeping it together and staying the course of ethical behavior and compassion for one's neighbor.

Cherry had the impression that every time things were on the path for improvement, a little devil perched on the decision-makers' shoulders filled their ears with cynical thoughts, smashing their impressive work and good intentions to pieces.

She'd listen to sages and Eastern philosophers that talked about high spiritual vibrations that could shift humanity's consciousness to a positive scale many times over. That change of mindset should have created a generation capable of and willing to turn things around toward light and love to heal Mother Earth. Maybe the crystal implants would see a change in purpose from delivering pleasure to the involuntary awakening of consciousness. Such an unprecedented awareness would shift the balance so distorted by a consumer-based society.

"If the people behind the latest mass media crystal technology manipulations that have the world on puppet-strings would tone it down, then murders like these would be minimized." Ilanda muttered these words as if she were chewing on dense, tasteless grit that choked her pipes.

"I wouldn't worry too much, you know," Nanette said. "Look back at the last fifty years, to see how secondary markets and products have been generated by off-shifting technologies, you know."

"Are you implying that killing for eyeballs and chips could become a secondary market resulting from the crystal implants?" Ilanda asked.

"No, not at all, but we'll be hit with a wave of initiatives as soon as the implants become a commodity, you know. There will be requirements, you know, that we won't be able to or care to provide, and someone else will, you know."

"I feel like we are putting out the option for any psychopath to get away with murder by paying for a new chip and eyeballs as a new identity." Ilanda stared at the women in front of her, features distorted with horror.

"No, she's not saying that, Ilanda," Cherry interjected. "As a doctor, you have a responsibility to provide the best care, considering the technology is new. But it's already tested, so as long as there are zero failed cases, you're good. Anything else is police business."

Cherry put a gentle hand on Ilanda's shoulder. "Focus on the next cases and forget about the outside world."

The doctor flashed a smile, and with the vigor of a woman drawing her last breath, she said, "Okay, let's do it."

CHAPTER 8

Maahes walked along his favorite beach in Costa Rica when Marian called with updates to the plan that was moving forward on multiple fronts.

"I can report that in Johannesburg, everything happened to a T. Ojani reacted as you anticipated and will convey his criticism of the experience back to Ilanda. The team I hired through the Dark Web delivered," Marian said.

"Nice," Maahes said. He kicked at the sand, satisfied. "Ilanda was predictable, too, using her old source of crystals in South Africa. The pressure is high on everyone."

"The next step is ready," Marian reassured. "Just let me know when to release the fake news about their failed partnership with Ilanda's lab. As soon as De Boers's stock takes a nosedive, our puts are in the black, almost matured."

"What about the calls?"

"Bought those, too. We'll make a killing on the way up, as well. How fast do you expect Ilanda to react and turn things around?"

"Twenty-four to forty-eight hours, right after De Boers provides proof they're not involved in Ojani's kidnapping. Let them struggle a bit. I see no other option for Ilanda and company to back out of this deal. De Boers is the only major player able to offer the full range of services."

Maahes walked toward the palm trees randomly lining the shore and sat on one of the wooden benches. "How is the internet access in Canada? Any outages?" he asked. "Here, it's becoming a pain in the neck."

"More like power outages. At least once a day and more often in smaller towns with aged infrastructure," the bald man said.

"What I gathered through the sporadic internet access all major news agencies are now broadcasting our press release on the 'forbidden crystal implant technology.' Is that accurate?" Maahes rubbed his eyes, chasing an itch. He glanced upward at the sugar-like clouds sprinkled on the blue-icing sky, mimicking an upside-down birthday cake unevenly coated with fine, tasty icing powder. He would never tire of his version of heaven while still alive.

"It's like fireworks on New Year's Eve. They lit up one after another. Big cities on all continents are hot spots now—impossible to quiet them down."

Maahes chuckled. His years as the CEO of Vivus Water and master-puppeteer of intrigue and convoluted scenarios of divide and conquer were not spent in vain. He still had a good sense of how the markets and the crowd would react, even without the inside information he used to have. In fact, he was generating the inside scoop, and no one else—except for Marian—knew his next move.

"And the cherry on the cake? The insurance-related aspect of the crystal implants blew everyone out of the water. If you ask me, I'd bet the farm that it's a done deal. It might take six, maybe eight months, but it will be sorted out," Marian said, conveying his certainty of the success of what they'd set in motion.

Maahes tugged at his buff-colored straw hat and put his shades back on. "Or even faster if we're the ones daring to take a stab at it."

"What do you mean?"

"I've been keeping tabs on a mid-sized insurance company down in the Bahamas. Recently, the CEO's retirement triggered the loss of the main co-insurer in the US. No other company stepped in. They were on the brink of folding when I made them an offer they couldn't refuse."

"Ha, ha, ha." Marian's tiny mouth barely moving upward to form a smile.

"Yes. I had to be a step ahead of everyone. I'll send you the info for the press release that goes out tomorrow. The world has to know there is already an insurance company willing to sign policies for crystal implants." Maahes took off his sandals to let the soles of his feet rub against the hot sand. The local officials had relocated what used to be the beach, behind a concrete wall as a barrier against advancing water levels; it was a one hundred-meter area of stone-free, fine sand.

Marian's 3D AugReality image seemed to melt in the sweltering light. "I see the weather maintains the same charm as the first day you landed. How's the water?"

"Taking a dip is not prohibited. The sensors on the buoys near the shore are green, but I don't have the gumption to go full in. What if the water changes its mind suddenly because a jerk dumped acid in the river in Germany? We were told by the scientists roaming the shores every other day that the acidity level is lower than three months ago, but it's still twenty percent higher than before the water acted out . . . or before 'the awakening,' as some idiotic TV anchors have labeled it. It's not life threatening—"

"If that's the case, don't try anything silly; we haven't implemented the plan completely," Marian said. He chortled loudly.

"Don't worry. I'll keep playing in the sand, building castles and sirens with oversized breasts," he said sarcastically.

The bald man chortled loudly again, sounding as if he were almost choking.

Maahes was content that no roadblocks would jinx the plan hatched over many months of concentration and focus. He still loved and cared for Ilanda, but she had to let it go. The technology she'd developed wasn't hers to keep anymore. Maahes, the silent and mysterious investor, had congratulated her after her initial announcement and asked her what was next. He'd used the encrypted WhatsApp line Marian had provided. Ilanda's answer was evasive and far from the firm commitment for the widely-used commercial application he'd expected.

The technology belonged to everyone, and his desire to become an "enhanced" human being had raised its inquisitive head ever since she'd mentioned it over their failed dinner. At least, their chat had engaged them intellectually, which definitely influenced his decision to reform himself from a self-centered CEO to a soul that yearned for unconditional love. Even that path had changed the moment he'd "died" in Egypt, a necessary staged event to shield Ilanda and his relatives from potential repercussions. And by repercussions, he meant the peace offering in the form of returned land and underground water rights to the proper owners that had been divested through arm-twisting, political influence, or printed money whose value diminished fairly quickly.

His benevolent plan required consequences. He had to pay a high price and lead a solitary, amended life.

"Have you confirmed that Kahuna's health is stable?" Maahes asked, bouncing back from his short reverie.

"My contacts in Hawaii didn't see much of him, but I hear he was walking on his own and seemed in good spirits. There's something wrong with the island's connectivity, similar to what you mentioned about Costa Rica. I couldn't chat for too long."

"What you got is better than nothing. It proves that Ilanda got it right."

"And you desperately want to be next."

Maahes heaved a big sigh in confirmation. "You might have to wait in line. At least you won't be the second person to get an implant."

The older man pricked up his ears and straightened his back on the bench. "What do you mean?"

Marian barred his teeth as if preparing to tell a dirty joke. "If my contact wasn't flush with alcohol when he saw Kahuna's daughter, then what he saw was true—she got the implants, too, like father like daughter."

The hacker rubbed his large palm over his scalp. "Are you sure?"

"As I said, only if—"

"Yes, I heard you, but is he reliable?"

"Yes, he is," Marian said.

Maahes changed from cheerful to grim. After a moment, his expression returned to cheerful.

"What now?" Marian asked.

"I hate to do this to Ilanda, but if she insists on being stubborn, we'll release the info you recently gave me through the same channels. The people and the media know only about Kahuna."

"You expect the second implant to be kept as a secret to break the camel's back, so to speak?"

"Exactly."

The reply had an ecstatic tone to it. Maahes sensed his skin suddenly flushed as if a beautiful woman had embarrassed him by refusing his indecent proposal. His intricate plan, perused many times as he searched for brittle points, only gained strength after it had been unraveled. "I'm going to celebrate with a glass of coconut water." He raised his hand in a mock toast.

"I'll let you to it, then," Marian said, and he disconnected.

CHAPTER 9

Keeping her composure while talking to the liberal prime minister took a lot of effort on Ilanda's part. Her tongue had deep marks from her teeth bearing down on it in an attempt to prevent any mentally unfiltered words from spoiling the decent relationship she had with the people in power.

"I kept my word and didn't do any backstabbing," she said a couple of times in answer to the rhetoric question, "Did you leak the information about my government interfering into your research?'"

"I'm not in the public relations business, nor do I have the budget for such a concerted plot. Mr. Prime Minister, your advisers should have informed you that this was the job of professionals who were given a generous allowance."

"But we still need an official denial from you," the red-faced government leader demanded.

"With all due respect, sir, I should have been kept out of this mess with a strong message of support coming from your office. We run a private enterprise that happens to have a lot of public exposure these days." Ilanda held her sweaty palms under her desk to hide her obscene hand gesture of defiance. She had no chance against the political clout. They wanted her out in front of the reporters, repeating a half-page message that had been sent to her by the prime minister's speechwriter, word for word. Even if she had to dance to their music this time, it wouldn't be premeditated.

They had been taken by surprise as well and equally affected. Compliance would have won her points in the government's books. "Keep loading your physical and imaginary bank accounts with spiritually, goodwill, and positive actions," someone had once told her, "so, when there's a bump in the road, there's plenty there for a withdrawal."

It was one of those instances of making deposits in a bank that could go belly-up at any time due to unexpected geopolitical thunderstorms, or because the assets behind such deposits were volatile and few, and she couldn't liquidate when she needed it.

She never trusted those in the office, and this time was no different. She only hoped this prime minister would hold onto his cabinet long enough to pay back the emotional and public image deposits she was about to make.

"You'll read the communique from your office in Toronto in one hour. We don't have to disclose your location. You can still answer questions within the parameters we talked about," one of the advisers said. He thanked her and disconnected.

"To hell with this situation." She exhaled loudly and thrust both middle fingers in the air as suddenly as if they'd been possessed by demonic forces.

She needed comfort food. Ilanda opened a box of salty biscuits. She bit into one and kept it on her tongue for several seconds, the salt on the exterior helped to release the pressure and calm the ripping roar of fury inside her. Halfway through the package, she was completely calm and ready to face her team.

After summarizing her discussion with the prime minister, Ilanda asked again, "Did anyone call Ojani?"

"I did," Mark said. "There was no answer, but he reached out to us minutes later from the Canadian embassy in Johannesburg."

"From the embassy? Is he in trouble?"

"Not anymore. He wasn't specific, but he didn't have a phone. He either lost it or it was taken away from him. He should be back the day after tomorrow, and he'll have more details in person. That's all he said," Mark Sarafian said, concluding his report, then sat down at the table beside Octana. He had the habit of leaning on walls as if standing gave him a better vantage point.

"As long as he's safe, let's focus on what's important here," Ilanda said. She moved feverishly along the short length of the room. Everyone stayed out of her way.

"This is a staged worldwide event with a clear agenda: let the crystal implants create their own market like any other product. The deep pockets financing it have envisioned their potential, both medically and recreationally, and are forcing our hand."

"What other options do we have?" Octana asked.

"Not many. We can buy some time by claiming a number of medical cases we're working on. We should stay firm that observing and monitoring these individuals would provide indispensable data for implants in the population at large." She clenched her fists, keeping the earlier rage from spilling out again.

"Invoke the ethics, the Hippocratic Oath, and whatever plausible reasons you can think of," Octana said.

"Show me the list of candidates."

Octana touched her iPad several times, and the list appeared on the wall. On it was at least thirty-five names, broken down into phases. Not everyone on the list was critical. She didn't want to become a factory assembly-line for crystal implants, which would incur more costs, more personnel, and necessitate a larger holding capacity, especially for medical cases requiring post-surgery supervision, unless she would get local government's approval to negotiate an agreement with St. Michael's Hospital to take the less complicated cases, which only necessitated the standard monitoring equipment.

"The ten-year-old boy from Thunder Bay who was in a car accident and the seventeen-year-old from Germany who fractured his spinal column and hit his head falling during a rock-climbing session are the priorities right now. They've been put into an induced coma," Octana said, bringing clarity to the table.

"Have you determined all the parameters?" Ilanda asked.

"Yes. The younger boy resonates with quartz, the other with opal. We determined the thickness of the crystals. We have the eyes' measurements, and Raman is ready to upload the code. We just need the patients to arrive on-site," Mark said.

Ilanda scrolled through the list, looking for stats such as re-occurring incidents, age brackets, and location—there was no immediate correlation between them. "What are their chances of survival without this intervention?"

"Based on the doctors treating them? None."

"We've been chastened enough. Double-check their kin have signed the forms releasing us from any responsibility. Send the docs to our lawyer. The laws in UE might cause some unforeseen difficulties," Ilanda advised.

She took a long time reviewing the critical cases' MRI scans, tucking her hands into her pockets and clocking more mileage pacing.

"What's bothering you?" Nanette asked, interrupting the thick silence.

Ilanda stopped her frantic pacing and leaned against the wall. "I have a bad feeling about these two. Even if they're in induced comas, transporting them over a distance could generate complications. It's more likely for the one in Germany. The weather's still unpredictable. Air-born transportation can't guarantee the complete immobility of the patient."

There were limitations that precluded them from saving more lives.

"That's why we need to have a super-tight legal agreement in place," Ilanda said. "We can be the darlings today and the enemy tomorrow. Don't underestimate the manipulation of the masses."

Everyone stood in shock. Nanette seized the silence while playing with her hair, which had been gathered into a thick, wavy ponytail. "What type of structured water, you know, are we going to use to excite the crystals?"

"The same as for Kahuna. There's some leftover that's maintained its initial properties. Nothing changes until we have several successes under our belts," Ilanda said. "There's still so much work to be done before it becomes sharable with positive effects." She felt exasperated by the conundrum she and her team were facing.

"Are you afraid a new wave of fake or unqualified surgeons will jump at the opportunity like what happened a couple of years ago?" Mark asked.

"We'll see more malpractice, for sure," Ilanda said. "They might even claim they had our blessings." She stopped in mid-sentence as if an acupuncture needle had hit her speech nerve by mistake. A ferocious gaze cast on her long face, imprinted with the fine, unavoidable lines of aging.

"What?" Nanette asked, jerking forward on her chair.

"I'll read the damn script sent by the PM, but I'll make it clear that we are not giving anyone else the right to use it, improve upon it, or play with it at this time. Not until we prove that it's completely safe by monitoring several dozen cases. There is too much liability involved."

Fake claims always wound up killing people or creating chaos. The thought of the added responsibility choked her, and she knew how to avoid such a catastrophe, by playing the same channels that had spread the unverified news in the first place.

"Going back to the remaining work," she said. "The correlation of crystal and sound chart you guys put together is very useful. We need to add the third component: type of structured water."

"We all read the data you provided on mice and were amazed by the results. That type of research has to continue, you know," Nanette said on behalf of her colleagues.

"And?"

"Ilanda, none of us has the experience required for such experiments. We're talking brain surgery on mice here."

She pushed herself away from the wall and took a seat. *Yes, they were right. She would still have to lead them through the unchartered territory of noticing alterations in the brain exposed to sounds and nanobots.*

"The equipment that arrived yesterday," Ilanda said, "is a miniature replica of what we use in the OR. It comes loaded with an AI that recognizes several types of mammals and can perform several highly complex surgeries on them. Raman will have to tweak the routines to accommodate the embedding of the crystals. The manufacturer hasn't included this option yet, but they will soon."

"Is that the moment we'll play hardball with the licensing rights?" Raman asked sarcastically.

Everyone let out a puff of amusement.

"You're right. That would be our first significant *ka-ching* moment—the payoff that will generate more, but you know I'm not in it for the money," Ilanda said.

She was sure they knew she had financial safety on her own merits as well as the recipient of Maahes's will. The team was also aware that only work—hard, intense work—would keep her sane and away from solitary confinement in a condo emanating a mosaic of fond and despicable memories. She craved busyness, diverting her attention from her roaring emotional pain.

"We're creating an industry-standard, people." she drummed her fingers on the table, her brain on overload. "Everyone else's tries have been rudimentary, Ojani's included. He told you his story and why he joined us. He saw the potential then, when there was nothing else on the market, and he sees the potential now by joining the winning team. Sooner, rather than later, your names will be leaked, and you'll turn into stars and starlets."

The young men and women around the table grinned at her as if to say they rather liked that experience.

"You might like it for a while, but not for long, believe me." Ilanda's deep tone quelled their smiles. "Publicity at that level implies quasi-permanent harassment from the media and individuals that are either on your side or against you. There is no winning situation."

No bad jokes or raised voices contradicted her. She felt like a hen rounding up her newly-hatched chicks that weren't ready to face the harsh realities of life yet.

"Or another company will catch up with us and we'll be one of many. I know a consensus is important on such a small team, but there are options we haven't considered yet." Mark Sarafian said, and the situation changed, his comment wiping off the grins on their faces.

"Such as?"

"Franchising the technology. We could do it and keep tight control over how it's being implemented."

Ilanda felt her cheeks flush, and she bolted up like a spring released. "That's heresy," she said loudly but smiling as if she were joking. "It's your sweat, too, in this research. How could you propose such a ridiculous option?"

Mark shuffled in his chair and boldly glanced at his peers. His look gave the impression that he'd had no previous consideration of sharing the outrageous approach with the team—he was, nevertheless, on his own when it came to the thought.

Ilanda had to rein him back into the corral of like-minded thinkers. The uniformity of minds and opinions counted when it came to the applicability of crystal implants. Ilanda simply couldn't lose any more control than she already thought she had.

Turbulent times were impending upon their shores, battering their morale and the trust and ethics they'd built as a team. In front of everyone, Mark had asked her to choose a slow, safe pace or a fast one, prone to failure.

"In a way, it really is heresy," he admitted, his gaze holding Ilanda's. "Historically, medical franchising has had a higher rate of success than other fields. It has different dynamics as it involves human interaction and the more emphatic, personal touch of medical personnel."

Ilanda scoffed at the statement as it were old news.

"The franchise I've referred to encompasses a large number of medical services. I suggest one focused solely on implants. You all saw the public reaction," he gestured as if pointing to the outside world. "How are we going to deal with such a demand?"

"Not many could afford it," Ilanda snapped back.

"Not now, but like any other product or technology, it'll be affordable two years from now. How?" He paused and turned his head left and right, as if expecting some feedback, but they were only scientists with little business acumen. "By improving the technology and creating multiple worldwide locations."

"Common sense," Ilanda said.

"Which you are against right now."

"We're not ready yet."

"Quench the uproar by providing a twelve-month and twenty-four-month implementation plan. It'll show we're willing to share but not without safeguard measures in place," Mark pleaded in an even tone.

"It'll also take the pressure off the government and off our backs," Raman said, inserting himself between the verbal duelers. "It might work," he continued, apparently not aware he was indirectly taking sides.

Ilanda scoffed again, louder this time.

"Hear me out," Mark pushed forward, his sail swollen with the energy of a sudden gust of wind. "We keep our HQ here. All the surgeries would be monitored automatically by an application Raman will be in charge of developing." He turned toward the team's highly-skilled coder. "We need you to design a masterpiece."

Raman responded with a wide smile and a tap on the desk, indicating he was up for the challenge.

Ilanda noticed the change in tide, and she didn't like it. She surmised she still had the women on her side. "So, he develops the interface . . . then what?"

"We'll look for medical doctors who are able to assess the patients, determine a diagnostic, and load the results for us to double-check them."

"It's that simple?" Ilanda asked.

"We have to make it that simple, have several rooms equipped with surgery robots, an office manager, and one or two doctors able to pull the funds together to pay franchise fees and cover monthly expenses. We'll split the revenue. And all the data loaded onto crystals plus the actual implant surgery will be scheduled and performed remotely from this very building. We'll control how many offices are sustainable in each city."

"What do they say about the restaurant, fast-food, and real estate businesses? The better the location, you know, the higher the visibility and revenue stream," Nanette said before Mark could continue. "My father used to have one of those franchises, you know. I worked there several summers for pocket change."

"The real estate game is secondary to what I'm suggesting," Mark said. "A rented office is all we'll need. That and the right people, thoroughly checked." He looked for a reaction, but not even Ilanda could find the words to fight back.

"And one other thing," he continued. "Complex medical cases will be dealt with at major hospitals, but following the same process I just mentioned—we are in control at all times."

"The security of this app will be a real bear," Raman confirmed.

"We'll upload it to the crystal cloud and lock it with at least two vibratory signatures. Encapsulated like that, there's no way a hacker, no matter how blessed, could break-in."

"Not even when it gets downloaded to the robotic arm?" Ilanda asked, a little less sour now.

"The file reaches that stage as an executable file. No code will be exposed in any way," Raman said.

"Look—we can run all of the possible scenarios later on," Mark said, gaining control of the conversation again. "Ilanda, you gave me this amazing opportunity, and messing it up is the last thing I want. Helping as many people as possible, medically or otherwise, implies scaling-up the process."

The physical weakness that had troubled Ilanda the other day hit her again. She felt too tired to withstand the energetic flow of her younger colleagues' enthusiasm. She needed a quick way out, a delay until their hot blood cooled off. A surge of hope sprang from her heart along with the answer.

"Let's wait for Ojani," she said. "He'd be interested in hearing your proposal, Mark. For now, we'll give the crowd what the government requested of me, and the promise that our team is working on both a short- and long-term strategy."

Ilanda had fended off a *coup d'etat*. They all seemed content with the compromise, but how long would it last?

CHAPTER 10

Romana Pilb, the president of Water for All and U.N. Water, and Srinitham Maghatham, the head of the organization's Varanasi office in Uttar Pradesh, walked shoulder to shoulder along the banks of the Ganges River, kicking discarded sticks and soda cans aside every now and again, breaking their pace.

Dressed in a cotton opal sari lined with wide floral embroidery from top to bottom, Romana, tried to blend in. A scarf from the same material covered her head, framing her light chestnut skin and blue eyes.

The late afternoon heat seemed to have no intention of ebbing. The air virtually boiled in the open, subduing colors and diminishing the vitality of all forms of life. The pungent smell of burnt bodies from the upstream ghats clogged Romana's breath. She eased her air intake by using the ample sleeve of her sari to cover her mouth and nose.

Srinitham's gentle approach to the daily crises the Varanasi office had to handle smoothed her New York edgy demeanor, giving her actions a different and deeper perspective. He even helped her find a place to rent, hire a cook, and he taught her Indian customs for basic survival when on her own. She cherished the happiness of his full lips and brown eyes that sparked her day the moment he arrived in the office.

"I hope I didn't put too much pressure on you by naming you in a management position," Romana said. She had learnt to rely on Srinitham both professionally and personally.

"Not at all," Srinitham said.

"When Naia had decided to resign from this position due to medical issues, no one but you stepped up. And I'm here to share my fifteen-year experience at the helm of U.N. Water." She paused, realizing she might have given away how much older than him she was. She fancied a wry smile and kept looking up at him but aware of her step.

"I like the challenge."

"You handled yourself amazingly well two years ago when the 'awakening of water' had occurred in this very spot of the Ganges." Romana justified her decision. "I can't believe no one took the appearance of the Palmaria Palmata algae[1] in the Ganges as a warning. The reddish color of the water got a mystical interpretation by the onlookers."

"I felt the pain of those people bathing, unaware of what was going on. Their skin looked like boiled water was poured on them."

"I know you wanted to help, but your work was more important at that time. We had to know what changed in the water's molecular structure to have such devastating results," Romana said, and she looked away from the river as if afraid that the disturbing scene would repeat only by mentioning it.

"We matched the samples we collected that day to water we had exposed to feelings of hate and despair."

"Yes, I remember," Romana muttered from behind the veil. "The image of the frozen molecule looked muddy and twisted," she added.

"Someone in the team suggested that behavior was if water intentionally transitioned to a state of panic and damaging madness," Srinitham said. "The analysis showed how one water molecule gained a hydrogen atom and therefore took on a positive charge, while the other water molecule lost a hydrogen atom and became negatively charged. The newly form combination is called a hydronium ion, and it made things acidic, hence, burning the skin."

"Disturbing, indeed. The assumption that our irrational behavior vis-à-vis the environment triggered that change in water came days later. Few believed it."

"There are still non-believers today, almost two years after the fact," Srinitham said.

"Forcing U.N. to put forward a resolution on equal terms for all countries eased the pain. Interesting times, anyway."

Particles of ash suddenly dropped all around them as if snow had turned bad. Srinitham coughed and used a handkerchief to cover his mouth. They walked faster and stopped under a banyan tree, one of the few shade respite along the shore. Some of its generous branches ran almost parallel to the veins of its roots that formed braided patterns on the ground. The canopy was still as if the entire overstory had fallen asleep.

Around them, others have taken a break from the daily scorch on their destinations.

"No matter the legislation the government will implement, the ghats will never be shut down," Srinitham said, while he brushed ash off his shoulders and hair.

Romana did the same to the thin layer that covered her sari.

"It should be part of the restrictive measures related to climate change. But as you said, trying to remove all of the secular customs might trigger an acid reaction from the population," she said.

"It's a threshold too risky to pass."

Under the shade of the tree, Romana saw in him a more mature person as if his face had gathered an instant gravity and determination to deal with all the climate crises at once. Several strains of ashes still hung on the side of his head and she wanted to remove it herself. Touching him would have given her the pleasure like that of a lover too shy to express her feelings. She stepped closer to the main trunk of the banyan tree and rested her hands on its smooth bark, ready to feel the sap coursing up, carrying nutrients. The daily news arrived from miles away from its brothers through the invisible entanglement of fused roots. She closed her eyes and silently asked the old soul of the banyan tree for advice. *Should I extend my stay in India? Would I be happy here? Would Srinitham bend the local customs for me?* Her right palm pulsed with heat. Underneath her feet, the ground rumbled, while she heard the canopy fretted, quilting together sounds to form words that would make sense to her. The heat progressed through her right arm, split at the shoulder, finding its way in every part of her body. Her posture adjusted to one of a single but confident woman in a land that felt so familiar.

Srinitham's voice brought her back to the day's sultriness and the people surrounding her clustered inside the shade.

"The time we live in won't allow us, as a species, to adapt fast enough to what's happening all over the world," Srinitham said. He wiped off the perspiration running down his face and neck.

"At university, I learned about the anomalous properties of water. Imagine that! Those amazing properties should be taught in elementary school so children will get interested and understand water from an early age," Romana said, too preoccupied by her own thoughts to expand on the subject of the survival of the human species.

Srinitham nodded. "Which of those behaviors puzzled you the most?" He showed respect and consideration, and she liked that.

"There are several of them, but the one topping them all is how water defies gravity when it travels up tree trunks," she said. The process of cohesion and adhesion developed by the tree so the water molecules form a column; it's mind-boggling. We take it for granted, like the heart beating or the lungs breathing."

She smiled broadly at him as a sign of appreciation for his efforts in keeping the Water for All brand visible during and after the tragic events that happened in the same location they were walking.

The crowds that had swarmed the shores of the river in the first days after water's awakening were reduced to random clusters of ten to fifteen people each, dragging their feet on the dusty dirt edging the stoned steps leading to the water. Twenty months later and they were still debating possible theories about why the water of the Ganges had changed its molecular structure voluntarily and worked as a weapon against the Indians worshiping the river and its cleansing powers.

Back then, the expectation of witnessing the miracle of the water's red coloration for a second time eventually wore down, and only those fully taken by faith camped on the bare ground, praying and chanting continuously. The local authorities were given instruction to remove them if the level of excitement or a public disturbance threatened to affect the safety of others. Luckily, it didn't have to come to that. The police restricted the use of tents and open fires; only allowing incense to burn on the site.

"Aren't those the same old men who weren't affected by the acidity of the water when it happened?" Romana asked, pointing to two withered individuals, clad in loin-cloths and knee-deep in the muddy water. Fragments of wood, plastic, and wet, lifeless ceremonial cremation flowers bobbed alongside them. Their tanned skin stretched on their bones like a hide on a drum. It seemed as if these men had defied time and frozen in place as if waiting for her to come to them.

Srinitham pulled out his cell phone. "I'm connecting to the server where I keep the recordings I took on that day." He touched several icons and then flipped through rows of images till he found the one he was looking for— the recording of the live connection with the WFA members to which Ilanda had referred. He fast-forwarded the movie to the moment the screaming had started and checked it frame by frame. "Yes, it's them. The same yogis. It was their blood we sampled to figure out what was different with them."

Excited, Romana climbed down the stairs with Srinitham behind her, quickening his pace. "Ask them if they're willing to answer some questions. Maybe they'll recognize you."

The young man spoke slowly in Hindi and gestured toward her. Romana sat on the wet stones at the edge of the water, smiling, trying to calm her mind. Positive thoughts emerged inside her—she was somehow conscious of the fact that the yogis might read her mind even before she was able to gather the words into a sentence. Observing them soothed her as if they were intricate beings of light, manifesting their prowess in her, turning her into one of them. They weren't floating, nor were they walking on water, but this was her impression when contemplating the silly moves of the emaciated bodies. Foggy retinas veiled with saggy skin around the eyes gave the impression that these were old people enjoying their last days of life. She knew their clarity came from inside them. It was their sharp consciousness and complete awareness that made them special.

On that day of horror when the water had turned into a predator, these men hadn't succumbed to the pangs of fear like everyone else. The water hadn't bit them but embraced them with a protective shroud. Deliberately, using a steeled mental coordination, they'd maintained the molecular structure of their blood in their state of awe, sheltering them against the acidity of the water.

Now, the same yogis stood two steps away from her, gazing into her eyes, waiting.

"*Namaste*," she said, her palms held together as she bowed her head. "Thank you for allowing us to take blood samples. It's important to understand what was going on at the time."

Srinitham translated. The one to her right nodded and made a quick hand gesture as if saying, "Don't bother."

"Do you have an explanation as to why you were protected?" Romana had to be direct, asking pertinent questions to lift the veil of oddity around the water-related incidents happening all over the world. "It is my conviction," she continued, "that water had acted with impunity on us, forcing a painful and brutal awakening from a long, insensitive indulgence. Please translate," she said to Srinitham.

No matter her conviction as WFA and U.N. leader, she had an obligation to investigate the cause further, rational or not.

"Our state of being is always the same," Srinitham said after pausing to mentally check on the accuracy of his translation. "We pray to Brahman all the time. No disturbance in the energy field could cause us to digress."

The old man's words were fluent, slow, and crisp. His lips, barely visible behind his bushy mustache and beard, emitted sounds that resonated. "Our physicality is inconsistent. We don't identify ourselves with these bodies anymore. This way of thinking is inconceivable to the western mind."

"The concept of being bodiless and adopting the state of mind of pure energy has kept them alive," Romana muttered as she shifted her feet in place, grinding the stone beneath her sandals. "This is not something for everyone to do," she said out loud, switching her gaze from Srinitham to the yogi who had, voluntarily, provided such a profound explanation.

"What should we do?" Srinitham, asked.

"Water is still restless," Romana began. "The Earth is restless. Humans have swarmed above and under its skin and submerged to incredible depths in the oceans, most of the time for the wrong reasons. All of these pernicious actions have disturbed its balance. Mother Nature's panting had grown heavier and heavier with the incalculable mistakes of the very people she hosts and provides for—"

Srinitham's deep sigh broke Romana's tirade. It wasn't a disrespectful response to her diatribe, but a natural display of concurrence.

"I know I sound preachy. The politicians came to the same conclusion after my United Nations speech."

"Mother Nature won't succumb to fright and desperation," the yogi said, his scrawny fingers combing the foam framing his face. He raised his gaze upward as if expecting an important download from his invisible protectors.

Attracted by the chance of being in the holy person's energy field, a sizeable crowd had formed behind Romana, out of her sight.

"So, what should we do?" Romana said, repeating her earlier question.

Srinitham translated once again. She knew there was no quick fix. The radical shift in humanity's mentality—cooperation instead of senseless competition—was the only pertinent way out.

"Ignorance and egotism on our part have blinded us into thinking we could mold the Earth to suit our needs," the yogi said, delivering the speech to everyone who was listening. His eyes, touched with a hue of anger, seemed to clear the mist of his cataract for a moment.

Someone on the shore gasped loudly. Strident yelling soared through the heavy air.

Romana looked in the same direction and saw a naked body floating in the water face-down, bobbing gently up and down with the water's soft undulation.

No police were in sight. Two men jumped on a battered boat tied to a metal ring on the shore. They rowed downstream toward the corpse before the current could push it out of their grasp.

Romana stood charged with electricity from the excitement of the surrounding people. Her cells became electrified, communicating as if preparing for a fight or flight situation.

The crowd along the river bank thickened, drawn by the additional yelling and finger-pointing. One-hundred meters south from where Romana was, another boat left the shore, and the two men inside paddled furiously while the third held a long stick with a metal hook attached at one end. Romana intuitively knew they were driven by an innate fear the water might 'awaken' again, having interpreted the corpse as a gesture underscoring defiance for the previous human casualties she had caused.

Srinitham maneuvered in front of her body like a protective shield.

"A dreadful rumor has spread that Mother Ganga is disturbed by our continuous desecration of her waters," the young man explained when she gazed at him inquisitively.

"Dumping of any kind ceased after the first incidents," he continued. "Businesses, compensated by the newly-implemented evaluation program, are at a standstill while investing in revamping their manufacturing processes. Neighbor is spying on neighbor, so illegal disposals are immediately reported."

"Are you telling me an environmental issue has been clothed in religious rhetoric?" she asked.

He asserted, "Involuntarily, yes. It's the most efficient way. Science doesn't hold much credibility with the masses. They need a language they understand."

Romana sensed the crowd heaving like the belly of a great beast giving birth. It moaned, shrieked, and sweated at once. Cells linked together with the threads of emotional energy and the frantic desire to see the happy-ending of the rudimentary chase through the water.

A tree trunk resurfaced abruptly through a forceful vortex near the first boat and headed for it. The crowd howled, but it wasn't enough to draw the attention of the men determined to intercept the corpse. Wood hit wood with a thud, spinning one of the boats, changing its course.

The men wobbled in the wooden shell, but none of them fell over. A sudden ebb grasped the floating body, pushing it toward the second boat whose crew seemed more aware of its surroundings.

Another ripple of emotions shivered through the crowd when it understood the first crew of rescuers were out of reach.

Romana gasped at the scene, and the body odor from the crowd almost choked her. She grabbed Srinitham's hand for support, ready to escape the compact masses, though it seemed impassible. Romana used her sari's generous sleeve as a breathing mask. It was a futile defense against the persistent odor being released by the boiling pot of humans.

Throngs of people held mobile phones in the air, aiming to catch the moment when the body would be hooked and hoisted into the boat.

Srinitham used his body to push through the tight labyrinth between the roused mob.

Romana barely kept her breakfast down as they make their escape. She held onto the man's hand like a baby elephant clutching her mother's tail. They reached an open area near a row of deserted fruit stalls, their owners at a distance, keeping an eye on potential customers or thieves. Those in the crowd without a means of recording the events watched over the shoulders of those broadcasting live.

The mob released an enormous roar when the body was finally hauled in. From the fringes of the crowd, Romana pulled out her own device to watch the streaming feed of the boats approaching the shore. She magnified the image of the victim's head as it leaned against one of its rescuer's legs.

The corpse's eyes were missing. His skin formed a grotesque mask scarred with reddish marks.

Several police cars and ambulances blocked the street, boxing in the horde that parted to let them through.

"Are those wounds on his head and hands?" Srinitham asked.

She looked at him, barely recognizing his features. The familiar sharp nose, narrow forehead, bushy eyebrows, and entangled black hair slithering down his slender shoulders forged a distorted, Picasso-esqe painting. The mélange of heat, desultory smells, and fright pushed her into a state of nausea.

Romana once more reached for Srinitham's hand to gain balance.

He welcomed her weight and led her to the shade of a nearby cottonwood tree. Then, he called a street vendor over and bought two bottles of papaya juice.

Romana scavenged feverishly through her remaining energy in an attempt to dissipate her foggy vision and the weakness threatening to crumble her middle-aged legs. She took a sip of the papaya juice. It was sweetness tinged with cinnamon—heavenly. Short moments later she was able to regain her energy.

Srinitham's face became familiar again, and she smiled at him. "Thank you for taking care of me."

His eyes smiled in return.

It was then she remembered his question about the wounds on the victim's body. "His eyes were missing and I think I saw a cut on the back of his hand where the chip was. With so much live broadcasting happening at the same time, the world at large will provide an answer soon—I'm sure it will top the daily news, at least here in India."

Srinitham helped her stand. With measured steps to conserve her recently gained energy, she headed with him to the WFA's air-conditioned office.

. . .

THE EVENING's mellow arrival didn't even bring a drop of coolness to the sizzling city, but rather, a torrid heaviness, that slowed the pace of life. Even the locals, Romana noticed from the WFA office windows—those who were used to the high summer temperatures—had to wear a medical mask over their mouth and nose as protection from dust, ash, or clusters of polluted air from other parts of the province brought in by high winds. Srinitham mentioned to her how the wet relief granted not long ago by the dip in the sacred Ganga River was now intangible and stretched everyone's senses and patience.

"Social media is buzzing with posts about a praying session scheduled for tonight," Srinitham said, shuffling through the AugReality news projected from his cell. "TV channels in the provinces along the Ganga are broadcasting the details, encouraging people to participate."

"Pray for what?" Romana asked, moving from the window to the only other wooden chair available in the austerely furnished room. A metal shelf and an antique cottonwood desk, donated by the previous office head, rounded out the furniture in the room.

In the years preceding her presidency, a significant percentage of India's administrative funds had been used to migrate paper documents into electronic records. The outdated equipment was now gone, leaving behind a barebones, three-room office, but its members had better connectivity and communication devices than ever before.

"For forgiveness," the man retorted, his tone conveying the message she should have known.

"Oh!" Romana improvised an excuse. "Praying to Ganga for forgiveness, especially for what happened today with the dead body."

He nodded.

"Expecting a big number?"

"At least fifteen million people on both shores. More will participate from home, imparting their message of humbleness and love to water all over the world." He leaned back on the cheap but sturdy chairs, staring at Romana with candor.

"Both you and that doctor friend of yours from Toronto said we should develop a language for water to bridge the evolutionary gap." His raised eyebrows hinting he was expecting an answer.

Romana almost gasped upon hearing her words repeated back to her. She had played that card at the important U.N. gathering, having borrowed it from Ilanda Mazandir, the now-famous neurosurgeon who had brought Kahuna Lapa'au back from the dead.

"I do believe in that approach. Dr. Mazandir expanded on research done by other scientists, and I also know of similar groups who accept the concept of storage capability of water. Obtaining funding to further the research proving that water has memory is still a challenge." She shuffled in her chair and looked uneasily toward the street as if waiting for a reasonable distraction that would change the subject. She was not sure anymore if Ilanda, after having so much success with the crystal implants, would pursue the creation of a water language, translatable into easy to understand terms. Maybe she had passed the relay to someone else.

"Do you think the development of such language would adjust our powerful beliefs based on dogma? Would it show us a simpler way of evolving consciously?" he asked.

"What do you mean?" Romana took the risk of looking ignorant.

Now, it was Srinitham's turn to pause and gaze outside.

Romana's familiarity with the Indian culture didn't mean she was aware of subtleties that would have been obvious to a native.

"Through love and gratitude. A universal language taught by the Vedas," the man said, still fixating on the clouds hanging on the sky like dirty laundry.

Romana felt idiotic and embarrassed of not making the effort to think of an answer to Srinitham's question.

In his self-induced trance, Srinitham either didn't notice, or he pretended not to. "Your Bible teaches of the power of love and compassion—they all do, all of the sacred texts—but we only take away whatever is convenient for us."

He's right, she thought, searching her mind for an answer that would seem like common sense. "The message comes from the heart. In fact, it comes from so many hearts, it's impossible for water to misinterpret it. Didn't she receive our love before she felt our betrayal?" Romana said. "The language I referred to is much more technical and direct. The scientific community, money-makers, and non-believers who signed off the U.N. resolution all agreed on the message of peace to the water by stopping harmful activities," she continued. "This time, we're all in—no more dangerous margin bets."

Srinitham mulled over her statement, then asked with a smooth voice, "Are you implying that we need both languages to work in tandem?"

"Yes. The heartfelt along with the more abstract interpretation of our message has to be delivered at the same time."

She stretched her arms out as if searching for another comparison on the shelves of her mind, something that might get her idea across easier. "Think of the constant fracture between the masses and their elected representatives. During the election campaign, they vouched for a permanent link to the pulse and voice of the people. They swear no law to encumber their liberties or social rights will ever pass through their vigilance, and the moment they're officially elected, a brainwashing takes place, and they succumb to the pull and pressure of the corporations, forgetting about us and our needs."

Srinitham nodded and scratched an itchy patch under his right ear. "They work more against us than for us."

"Exactly, but this time is different. Water's awakening has proven, even to the hardest deniers, that she learned all of our tricks, and she won't step back unless there's full participation on our side," Romana concluded.

"Would you join me tonight? I'm going to attend the outdoor prayers," the man said.

She could only imagine the immense vortex of energy that

would be released by all of the minds linked toward a common goal, and a cold shiver spiked through her body as she thought of that experience.

"Pick me up on your way there," she said. "I'll be here, catching up on several calls back home."

He smiled and pointed to the kitchen. "Vegetarian food and a one-day water ration in the fridge." He walked out of the room.

Romana's gaze lingered on the void created by Srinitham's exit. She yearned for love and attention, intangible assets her life had always lacked. It felt like a permanent drought in a land of abundance, fueled either by having grossly misjudged the character of the men who had populated her adult existence, or by the bundle of work that seemed to crave her unswerving attention the moment the potentially right partner had materialized.

No matter how much she desired the warmth and loving touch of a man, surrendering to Srinitham would be a monstrous mistake in a country still subdued by millennia of customs and prejudice. Forgetting the age difference would be the easiest of all the hurdles and inconveniences. That she was his boss would complicate the love affair that had formed in her mind.

Romana hadn't wanted to fantasize about being caressed in a world that was crumbling around her until two years ago. She'd step down from the helm of the two organizations that kept her mind, body, and soul firmly planted in reality if true passion was what she truly needed, especially if it meant her heart's desires and the man's would vibrate on the same frequency.

Ardor, wisdom, and honesty would have to compensate for her aged beauty. She hoped that a younger suitor like Srinitham would appreciate these qualities without running a comparison test against his previous romantic encounters.

CHAPTER 11

It was late August and Cherry had two more weeks of self-imposed relaxation before the start of the new university year. The trip to Hawaii had shielded her from the surge of pain and depression on full display during commemoration services in Toronto. The two-year anniversary of the explosion would have exposed her still open wounds to further grief and to the collective hatred that most of the survivors' relatives seemed to find hard to let go. She had made peace with the loss of human life along with the event precipitating it.

Forgiveness. It was the principle brought forward by Chief Landing Eagle—now returned to his ancestors in the astral plane—and Kahuna Lapa'au, still alive and aware of his responsibility to prepare Marinka as his successor and spiritual representative for the people on the islands.

What else was left to do if not forgive? Why bottle up hatred and allow it to poison our minds and souls? Why imprint such damaging feelings in one's body water? That was the wrong way to pay it forward.

She would have told them to celebrate instead. Having recovered from their injuries, the WFA had become stronger as an organization due to the significant number of new members and volunteers that signed-up for active projects. The U.N. had managed to gain a remarkable consensus on the water resolution triggered by the 'awakening of the water,' and the new rules had ripped through humanity's consciousness like a tree splitting a car in two on a head-on collision.

Stripping the radio and TV interviews on this subject, off their scientific terminology of viscosity, osmolarity, resonance, frequency, and levels of oxygen left Cherry with an unavoidable certainty: the atmospheric phenomenon could barely be predicted for more than 48-hours. Tornadoes, storms, and ruthless rain behaved like pop-up shoe stores: brisk set-up and dismantling, leaving behind submerged subdivisions, downtowns struggling with chaotic traffic and damaged property, or uprooted trees dumped on brittle bridges that succumbed to the blazing wind. Cherry had the impression that water in its various forms followed a guerilla practice: attack, destroy, disappear, caring little about the trail of destruction. If its main goal was to demoralize the world's society, it was successful.

Laying on her living room couch, Cherry glanced at the carry-on, still half-unpacked from the trip. She saw a smooth, black edge through a blue T-shirt, and she jumped onto her feet as if she had been electrocuted. She kneeled down to pick up the lava stone that Marinka pointed to during one of the walks on the beach. Its spirit had agreed to be removed from the ancient land of the island.

"When you get home," Marinka had said, "hold it in your hands and ask the spirit silently where you should place the stone."

"Silently?" Cherry had asked.

"Yes. Ask it with your heart, and the answer will emerge. Be patient."

And so, she did. It weighted approximatively three kilos and looked like a stylized pyramid with a small, triangular base and soft edges from being battered by the water. One side remained rugged. It was a natural sculpture that still held captive the sound of the waves within it, the deep whisper of the ocean, and encrypted knowledge from the middle of the earth. The stone, belched from a volcano, encapsulated the wisdom and healing power that had been gifted by its spirit.

Cherry couldn't decode any of that, but she asked the question as she was told, her heart swollen with love and acceptance. It was how her brain translated the situation as she had never had a conversation with a stone before. She had, however, had conversations with water before—rivers, lakes, and oceans—though she often questioned the hierarchy of spirits in the water world.

In the garden by the dead cherry tree, facing east. She felt—more than heard—the answer, remembering, at the age of five, her father telling her the occasion for planting the tree: her birth.

With her slippers on, she walked outside to the wooden skeleton of a tree that had been stripped of its fecundity and pride years ago, soon after water restrictions for outdoor activities such as pools and lawns came into full force. She poured out her heart's love while making illustrations in her mind of a young, restless girl hanging from its branches like a wild monkey, happily eating ripe cherries then spitting out the seeds in an imaginary game of acrobatics. She fully revealed her jubilant memories of a lost ingredient of her childhood for the stone's spirit.

She placed the stone facing east, two palms away from the tree trunk. Her parents would have been proud of her. Cherry thanked the energy field she communicated with before going back into the house.

CHAPTER 12

Over the next two days, Cherry caught up with Romana Pilb at the U.N., learning the latest updates on the entities and countries conforming with the agreement, checked with her faculty coordinator to obtain the number of students registered for her limnology class, and contacted several *Water for All* members.

Ilanda Mazandir was also on her list, but the call from the neurosurgeon came in before Cherry reached out to her. "Hey, girl!" Ilanda said. "Welcome back from paradise!" On the enlarged augmented reality image from her office, the grooves around the older woman's eyes seemed deeper, her cheeks droopy. The tension of the last few days had had a palpable effect on her.

Ilanda grinned painfully at her friend.

"Paradise, indeed. Kahuna and Marinka send their warmest hugs and kisses," Cherry said.

"I'm so pleased they're both well."

"They're enjoying their re-gained lives, even if they're aware that the fight against the multinationals isn't over yet. I heard what happened here while I was away—was it hell for you and the team?"

"Still is." Ilanda brusquely shoved her hair behind her ears.

Cherry expected to see her munching on salty biscuits, her favorite comfort food, anytime now.

"They made a mockery of me," Ilanda said. "Fake claims about the government who got irritated by the news and jumped on my case."

"Really?"

"What else do you expect from bureaucrats—responsibility? Not in our lifetime. I was forced to read a statement confirming that the officials hadn't interjected themselves in our research in any shape or form."

"That went well," Cherry said, giving her assessment of what she saw as a reaction to the five-day-old recordings. "But did you get the sense if the government is going to interfere in any way?"

Ilanda massaged her forehead for several seconds before replying. "Couldn't get a read. If we screw up and someone dies, they'll shut us down and take over the technology, making it theirs."

"I've only heard from a handful of entities that argue against the benefits of the crystal implants," Cherry said. "The church is one of them."

"And the most vocal of all," Ilanda said. "These self-entitled righteous people will deny Jesus of his Second Coming if the man will have the wrong skin color, or manners, or he will be slightly off the scripture in order to adapt to this century' realities." She puffed and rolled her eyes.

"The next-step strategies you threw out there," Cherry said, "ignited a bit of a giddy atmosphere. Everyone is content."

Ilanda chortled. It was a spasmodic sound, as if her body had contracted around Cherry's positive assessment of the situation.

"What's wrong?" Cherry asked.

"We have a Maverick in the team: Mark Sarafian. He spoke out against me in front of the other team members."

"What, exactly, did he say?"

"He wants us to franchise the technology," Ilanda said, round-eyed, as if she'd confessed being a Christian-sympathizer to a fellow atheist.

"Was his proposal logically sound?"

"Maybe . . . I don't know. This isn't a fast-food business."

"Was anyone else in favor?" Cherry asked.

"At least one: Raman. I cut it short before the others had something to say. I want Ojani to weigh in."

"When is he back?"

"Tomorrow. Why don't you come by, too?"

"I will," Cherry confirmed. She was ready to disconnect when a last thought came to her. "Ilanda, how is your funding going? You haven't generated any revenue yet."

It took the doctor several seconds to change mental gears. "It's all good. We got a pat on the shoulder from our elusive silent partner. The gesture told me that we are not forgotten. The team already assessed that the revenue would—"

"Sorry, Ilanda," Cherry said, cutting her short. "You said that the investor contacted you?"

"Yes. I assume it's the same guy or group of individuals that donated to WFA, and those funds were diverted, as per your instructions, to build the lab. Why do you ask?"

Cherry felt her cheeks flush. At that very moment, she wished she had Hayyin's mask on. She stuttered several times before intelligible words came from her mouth. "I…I'm…I'm glad that he—or they—are pleased with your achievements, and they can make some or all of their investment back. See you tomorrow." Cherry hung up.

"How is that possible?" Cherry said out loud. "Maahes is dead. He's been dead for more than a year. Did he have partners?" Ilanda had confessed to Cherry that Vivus Water Inc.'s shares had been sold quietly, and the funds were gone. Maybe his death wasn't unpredictable, after all. Had Maahes had been a part of a group of investors that had hedged their bets from water to crystals. Had he been their representative?

As with other similar instances, the Anonymous Group had delivered on the task and identified the donor funding the lab. The insidious trap the hackers had planted on her cell had worked beautifully. Once the integrity of the façade had fallen, Cherry and

Anonymous had been equally fazed—why would Maahes Mazandir fund Ilanda's research?

At the time, Cherry couldn't muster the fortitude for a confrontation with Ilanda. She ran a number of scenarios through her mind that could have played out, but she knew, instinctively, that Ilanda would stop the research if it were revealed to her that the donated funds had indirectly come from a business she despised.

She had kept quiet. Then, five months later, Maahes, the CEO of the third-largest water bottling company in the world, had perished in Egypt. The ensuing scandal after his death had ripped the company apart.

Nevertheless, Cherry still held a burning secret, but her guilty conscience had found an intelligent loop in the thinking process, and she shelved it in a dark nook. She hoped she'd never have to retrieve the memory again, but she was wrong in that assumption.

CHAPTER 13

Ilanda, Ojani, and Cherry, talked in the doctor's office on the main floor of the research building in Toronto. It was the same design as the office she had at the St. Michaels' hospital: minimal furniture, only a chair and a couch. She also brought over the two photos of New York City's Twin Towers, one in black-and-white and the other in color.

"I adhere to both approaches, Ilanda," Ojani said in a conciliatory tone after hearing the cause of her disagreement with Mark Sarafian. He was leaning on the wall beside the couch, his fingers patting the scar above his right eyebrow. "The technology has to induce enhancement, not death. Safety is my main concern, too—it always was—but once that hurdle is done with, franchising it the way Mark explained might work very well. It will be less capital intensive, and we will have minimum responsibility and maximum profit, eh."

"But—"

"Don't forget that insurance companies will pay for the surgery—that's free money for us, eh" Ojani continued.

"Code can do anything these days. Raman is very confident when it comes to the app he plans to develop. If Anonymous trusts hosting on crystals, why shouldn't we? Controlled surgeries for any location in the world—this is what appealed to you initially."

Only then did Cherry witness the sway Ojani had with the neurosurgeon. He used facts and common sense, not embellished words and evasive verbal tactics as Cherry had heard so many times at the *Water for All* meetings. Aside from his experience in the crystals business, Ojani brought a flicker of color to the team, not only through his blazingly bright shirts but through his open, worry-free attitude. Every time Cherry met him, he kept to himself, almost too shy to boast about his sharp mind that turned a Canadian-born kid of Jamaican descent into a millionaire at such a young age. He fit right in with the eclectic group of young scientists, and his feedback commanded almost as much weight as Ilanda's.

"Cherry, what do *you* think?" the doctor asked.

Why do you clench so desperately to the idea that the crystal revolution you started has to slow down? Cherry asked herself. And you were so proud of it, too. The smoldering path to the future wouldn't be traversed by taking baby steps. Instead, it would gobble up the old and decrepit, roaring with incredible fury at those who tried to stop it, and admonishing them and unleashing the power of crowds all over the world. She couldn't say all that out loud without embarrassing Ilanda in front of Ojani.

"The genie is out of the bottle, Ilanda," Cherry said instead. "You can fake that releasing the technology is what you want, for a while, but it won't take long before someone figures out that you're just treading water in order to protect it from getting into the wrong hands. If one person voices such concern and has the right platform to spread it the same way as the press release that ignited the madness with the government in the first place, then the backlash and the pressure will multiply a hundred-fold."

So much for my support, Cherry thought. She was only following her instincts, the ones that matched Ojani's, that the technology belongs to everyone.

Ilanda tossed her hair over her shoulder, and her hand moved toward the drawer to the right, but it paused half-way.

"People marveled at Kahuna Lapa'au's incredible recovery. It's an achievement you should be proud of. That and the entire team," Ojani said, defending his position.

Cherry blistered another silent thought to herself. "It's also helps with a shift in our consciousness."

While in Hawaii, Marinka's confession, honest and revealing, had brought an additional degree of complexity to the whole crystal implant debate about how ethical it is to alter one's God-given mind and body.

"It happened during a joint meditation session, two weeks after we returned home," Marinka had said. "I felt *a...thing* probing at my mind, disturbing my peace. My first thought," Marinka had paused to giggle while telling Cherry the story, "was that I was at a level of consciousness where spirits could talk to me, but it was only my father, exploring a realm he thought he knew. Unaware, he stumbled onto a new energy path, a boundary formed by the crystal's vibrations. It felt like a gentle flutter—no one had ever entered the intimacy of that space before."

A secrets keeper. That's what Cherry had become in the process of connecting with so many people. She didn't want the added responsibility of watching what she'd say around them, nor did she want the emotional charge attached to the classified information.

Divulging the telepathic sensitivity between father and daughter remained Marinka's decision after they would explore the entanglement of their minds deeper.

This time, Cherry didn't feel the burden was hers, in particular, and she observed the verbal toss between Ilanda and Ojani patiently. It reminded her of a lovers' conversation, sweet and checkered with carefully chosen words, leaving no room for misinterpretation. Neither party had the desire to upset, and a firm position had to be maintained with very little wiggling room when it came to retreat.

"Ilanda," Ojani said, "I'm with you on this one—we have to control who gets access to the crystal implants. The regular Joe wants it for enhanced fantasies—whatever they may be, including better brain-processing power for playing multi-user games on what everyone predicts to turn into the crystal cloud in the near future.

It's cool and didn't require him to sit immobile for hours in a room that smelled awful."

Ojani quickened his tone when he intuited that Ilanda wanted to cut him short. "I have an understanding with my old clients. It's a part of the agreement between you and me as a condition for me to pack up my business and move over here as a supply manager." He chuckled when he mentioned his title. "Do you remember that clause?" he asked.

Cherry hoped Ilanda would oblige the request and answer as she wasn't privy of its content.

"We agreed," Ilanda said. "In fact, I agreed that your clients would have priority to the crystal implants if they decide to do it, for no more than ten percent of what they paid for the experience you used to offer." Ilanda seemed to force the words out of her mouth in a jerky cadence, reminiscent of the clickety-clack of a train crossing a bridge. She crossed her legs under the table and her arms across her chest like a miffed kid whose parents had given away her favorite toy.

"That's right. I have to honor that agreement. My reputation's at stake, here. It means more than money to me. These aren't military or industrial complex entities able to change its use for destructive objectives."

Ojani seemed sincere in his pleading for fewer restrictions, and his paranoia when it came to accessing the implants.

"Did any of them contact you?" the neurosurgeon asked.

"Not yet. They know I'm a man of my word, and I'll call them when the technology, the crystals, and the structured water I've been using so far are all in place and safe to integrate with the human body."

He straightened, massaged the shoulder that had been taking his weight on the wall, and sat on the couch beside Cherry. "My list is pretty long, but I can shake it down to about three hundred people who are willing to get the implants and afford to pay. If we bring them over here and do them one at a time, it'll take several months of non-stop procedures, considering the 'insignificant' detail," he said this with pointed sarcasm, "that we won't be able to offer any consistent post-surgical supervision. We only have five recuperation rooms."

"Do they need supervision for more than two days if the medical procedure becomes standard?" Cherry asked without trying to take sides.

"About thirty-five percent of them will do it due to health issues and not to enhance their brains for enhancement's sake. They'll need supervision," Ojani clarified, showing how well he knew his customers.

Ilanda and Ojani stared at each other for a long moment. Neither of them was angry, nor did they throw oblique gazes, but they absorbed the contradictory interpretations of what the other had so passionately explained.

Cherry thought that only the compelling age difference kept the two of them from having a passionate affair—Ojani was thirteen years younger. That and maybe Maahes's handsome face appearing in Ilanda's dreams.

"Protecting the technology from those you're afraid might misuse it requires precautions that aren't in place," Cherry said. "The Canadian government could step in to shield this as a private entity—which is you guys—with a special set of laws that, in the future, could be applied to similar ventures—"

"Or they can shut us down," Ilanda said, "as the two of us talked about it."

"Correct, but unless you go to them hat-in-hand, I don't see the bureaucrats making the first move. Go to Ottawa with a clear development strategy and a clear request. As I said, it should give them the impression that this package of laws will solve problems with prospective companies or technologies of a similar caliber."

She read despair on Ilanda's sagging face; the support she must've expected from Cherry had disappeared in a puff of thin air.

"There is nothing to be disappointed about," Cherry continued. "Such a large number of patients is better taken care of at their respective locations. I can't find any hole in Mark's suggestion. You can have another huddle with the team and toss more knives at the approach, but overall, I guess it's a pretty air-tight one. It all comes down to implementation."

Cherry had firmly blocked any of Ilanda's unnecessary excuses. Even Ojani seemed uncomfortable with the two-to-one situation in his favor.

"Let's go out for a bite and I'll tell you about my South African adventures, eh" Ojani proposed, his dark face breaking into a generous smile. "You don't want to miss it." He added this last bit as a spin when it seemed Ilanda didn't appear to be too enthusiastic about the suggestion.

"I'm in." Cherry stood up, ready to go. "I'll share more about my trip to Hawaii and the discussion I had with Kahuna and Marinka."

Ilanda smirked—the distraction must have thrown her—but then she opened one of the drawers, and instead of taking out the salty biscuits as Cherry had expected, she held up a black wig.

"What's that?" Cherry asked.

"My alter-ego. Did you know I created a new personality for myself recently?"

Cherry wasn't sure to what the neurosurgeon referred.

"How do I look?" The curly locks covered Ilanda's shoulders completely, making her appear to be ten years younger.

"People could hunt me down, you know?" she added, still adjusting the false hair. "I don't want to lead them to the lab. We won't be safe anymore."

Ojani opened the door for them, and then he followed them out.

Once outside, they walked briskly toward Parliament Street and turned right onto Ontario Street, honoring a new Thai joint that had scored high marks with the city's foodies with their presence. None of them used their palm-sized air filter masks. The weatherman had proudly announced there would be no dust turbulence in the morning to disturb breathing conditions for the rest of the day, and they'd taken their chances.

The after-lunch crowd had dwindled to a trickle, and they sat by the now-common semi-translucent windows that had been tinted with light-gathering paint.

The server, a petite Asian woman with square bangs, scanned the backs of their hands for the embedded chips when they ordered three cups of green tea. They were still within the daily water allowances. Smells wafted over from the kitchen, enhancing their hunger and prompting them to order too many dishes.

"Were you really kidnapped in Johannesburg?" Cherry asked, helping herself to some greens from the cold, fresh, salad roll platter.

"Uh-huh." Ojani swallowed the food and wiped his mouth. "That was my impression when I came back to my senses and realized that I was tied to a chair that had been bolted to the floor, eh."

"I'm pretty sure I'd have had a similar impression," Cherry said. They both laughed.

"That's not funny," Ilanda said over their giggles, her mouth forming a tight, tense line. "What would've happened if that woman had left you in there?" She was playing with the curls on her wig, which had no intention of loosening.

"I was scared, too. Way too scared that I'd die on that chair, eh" Ojani said, slowly chewing a piece of tofu.

"Who do you suspect? DeBoers?" Cherry asked.

"It would be counter-intuitive if it was them. They want a partnership, and my feeling is that they want it badly."

"Could it be a warning?" Cherry asked. "Do it with us and do it quickly, otherwise . . ."

The vegetarian Bangkok dumplings arrived, and they all went silent as they munched on them.

"Van Dent briefly mentioned crystals for the masses and other revolutionary strategies that would make their shareholders happy."

"I almost get sick to my stomach when I hear the word, shareholders, as a scapegoat for greed. Maahes drove me crazy with it." Ilanda paused brusquely. She hadn't mentioned her dead husband's name in a long time, but it came to her so naturally now. "It's such a conflicting concept."

"Which one?" Ojani asked. His chopsticks were at the side of the plate while he eyed the crispy morning glory dish, a combination of lightly battered Thai spinach and wheat topped with sweet chili tamarind palm sugar.

"Pleasing the shareholders of any company means making them more money. Sometimes—or most of the time—these profits are generated without consideration for sustainability," Ilanda scooped up a morsel of food.

"The selfishness driving this approach will change under the U.N. agreement. The freezing of stock exchanges all over the world was a wise thing to do," Cherry said, then took a sip of tea.

"It's never happened before. Never around the world at the same time," Ojani said, pleased to have witnessed such a significant event.

"How much longer before they re-open?" Ilanda, who was the least interested in the financial world, asked.

"Not until the compensation program is in place for all companies listed on the exchanges. They're the priority, so their stocks won't plummet at the opening bell."

"If you asked me—"

Ojani waved Ilanda off. "Yes, we know: close down the shenanigans contributing to the crises."

"Or load them on a one-way shuttle to nowhere. They can have their trading in space—a mini exchange for their bloated egos." Ilanda couldn't help saying out loud.

"I'll suggest that to the U.N. representatives as a Plan B if the negotiations trail," Cherry added, jokingly.

Finally, Ilanda broke into a smile at her friend's joke, though it was shy and short-lived. The lemongrass créme brûlée elated the doctor from the slumps of her depression to participate in the conversation at a decent level. She shared edgy ideas on how to confront DeBoers about Ojani's kidnapping that had to be gently adjusted so that diplomacy and not hotheads would prevail.

"Going back to the incident in Johannesburg—I don't have a

high degree of confidence in DeBoers being a long-term partner." Ilanda had directed them back to what concerned her. "We put all of our eggs into one basket, and at full speed, they pull a fast one on us by increasing the price like your actor friend did." She licked the spoon of its remaining sweet spots and finished her tea.

"It's the only reliable source for crystals with international reach and guaranteed delivery," the man said, justifying his preliminary vote for DeBoers.

"Aren't they equally affected by the flight restrictions?" Cherry asked, half-way turned toward the screen broadcasting the local news.

"Everyone is. That's why synchronizing implant surgeries at all locations within a matter of days is crucial. We need at least twenty of them per site to make it cost-effective. Transportation will be a significant factor in the cost."

They sat quietly for a few moments before Ojani added, "The potential clients, at least those in need of implants for medical purposes, would have flight limitations, too."

"I get it, I get it." Ilanda waved her hands as if testing the air's consistency before getting out of her seat. "We're all in agreement with the franchising concept. "See? You've given me a bit of time to think about it, and I've come around."

"Seriously?" Ojani exclaimed.

Ilanda nodded a couple of times. The man smiled largely and bounced in his chair as if it were a miniature trampoline.

Cherry had the impression that he'd been chasing a break in their conversation, and she was right. He confessed that the promised he had made to the Divinity after the distressing situation in Johannesburg would call for his retreat from business life to a farm in northern Ontario. He found it disturbing that left unchecked, his mind rushed to that memory like a child toward an ice-cream truck on a sweltering summer day. It might also have been God pushing the same guilty thought over and over again, forcing him to save himself from a world he was responsible for changing by developing crystal technology in the first place. Of what polarity that change was, he couldn't tell anymore, as individuals and corporations were bound to use it for egotistic purposes, claiming it a righteousness act.

Ojani's admission didn't elicit pushback from either woman. They both acknowledged the pressure and the commitment he needed to stay alive. He concurred that life on a farm might provide him an honorable release from public life. Cherry thanked him for having let her witness such an admission.

"Be sure it has enough guest rooms," Ilanda commented, her eyes lingering on him. "We might come to visit if this mess reaches unbearable levels here in the civilized world."

Cherry wasn't sure if there were signs to be read in Ilanda's persistent gaze or the fact that Ojani liked her beyond any comprehension, considering the age gap, or the infatuation infiltrated his imagination like moss covering an aspen tree.

Ojani fumbled with his napkin, almost dropping it under the table. He waved at the server to bring the bill, retrieved the napkin, and headed to the washroom.

Left alone with her friend, Cherry asked a question she had about the silent investor. "The other day, you mentioned a call or text from the investor."

Ilanda leaned back in her chair, picked up the spoon, and used it to create an abstract drawing in the medium of melted crème brûlée spots. She'd managed a series of thin brownish smudges, interrupted by the cup's white bottom.

"Did he say anything else other than congratulating you and the team?" Cherry asked.

"Not really. He didn't say it, but I bet he was wondering if his investment was ripe enough to cash in. I expect another communication as soon as we announce the franchise strategy."

"He believed in your work." Cherry's fingers wrapped around her own empty crème brûlée cup, twisting the bottom against the table.

Ilanda scoffed at Cherry's remark. "Who—the investor? No way. It was mainly you and partially WFA. Don't you remember the first time we met, when I told you that you have more confidence in my research than I did?"

"But still, he dashed more money later on." The limnologist envisioned that it was Maahes who was behind the initial funding, but Maahes was gone now. Who was behind the recent message? Did Maahes have any partners for which he'd played the frontman? Cherry would have to tap into Anonymous's un-exhausted resources again to find out.

"Ladies, are you ready to go?" Ojani didn't bother to sit.

The women nodded, and they all went back to the lab.

"WOULD you really turn yourself into a farm boy simply because a potential punishment from God might drop on you at any time?" Ilanda asked Ojani as soon as they got back from lunch that day. There were only the two of them in her office as Cherry left for her evening classes at the university.

"A promise. It's a promise, no matter if I made it to myself, to God, or to anyone else who might hold me responsible," Ojani said, surprised that Ilanda was willing to continue the conversation he thought he'd finished after the acceptance he'd witnessed earlier.

"What a character!" Ilanda said.

There was a tinge of admiration in her voice that briefly inflated Ojani's ego. He'd recently been looking to her for consent, more than he should, like a first-grader trying hard to become the teacher's favorite. He'd also made her another promise, an impulsive one, based on the innate feeling that she would reciprocate his honesty when the time was right—he planned to take her to the Buddhist temple, introduce her to Tenzin, his childhood friend, and let her roam through the tiny library and interior garden. He never had anyone else as his guest in the space made sacred by the instruction and understanding he'd received from the monks.

She accepted with a glimmer in her eyes, giving Ojani the hope that a more intimate relationship might mushroom from their professional interaction. He learned that disruptive events, those artificially created from innocent daily synergy, might impede on his intention and his ability to keep his promise.

Discreet inquiries to the team about the weekend's schedule had proven that Ilanda was not planning in joining them at the lab to review results, so the coming Sunday would be the day of visitation. Ojani didn't ask Ilanda if she had anything else arranged outside of the office, but he firmly announced that he would pick her up in the early afternoon.

"The monks had a hard time adjusting to the water rations, eh" Ojani explained while in the electric cab taking them to the temple.

"How much history do you have with them?"

"Enough to be considered family, eh."

There was a twist of the wheel and their bodies were tossed around to fill the space between, touching on the arms and thighs. Shy smiles bloomed on both faces, and Ojani felt as if he were a lapidary who had just removed a stubborn-cut to reveal a diamond in hiding. Ilanda irradiated energy, which he sensed when he placed his hand closer to her.

"Are you going to tell me the whole story after you retire to the farm?" she teased.

He laughed sparklingly, feeling muzzled by her words. Maybe she'd implied a message she hadn't intended to give, but he was keen to enjoy the fantasy with Ilanda in it until he received confirmation that her interest didn't go further than the professional.

"Some of the monks scattered to other provinces or flew to sustainable communities in South East Asia, eh."

Ilanda cringed. Her face turned the color of the pewter clouds that threatened the city with sleet that had yet to come. "Who's left, then?"

"The abbot, three senior monks, and no more than five students, all of them cramped into the building we're about to visit."

"Is there anything we can do for them?"

"Nothing more than I've already done. But, hey, they're all healthy, and a minimized existence is what they've trained for, eh. As long as their daily routine isn't brutally disturbed and their inner-peace was in synch with the universe, they considered it a meaningful day."

Ilanda's eyebrows arched with excitement. Ojani bet she'd inched closer to him in the backseat.

The two-story brick building had aged under the layers of dust and the bite of the sizzling wind. Restoring it wasn't feasible as money was short, and the future was bleak. Ojani offered some financial help, but no persuasion could convince the abbot to accept his generosity, and Tenzin knew better than to intervene on his behalf.

The wooden door opened at the first knock, and Ilanda stepped into a world foreign to her, that of spirituality through meditation and observance of moral discipline.

Tenzin was waiting at the top of the stairs.

They removed their shoes and joined him.

Ojani bowed slightly in front of his friend, and then they hugged, their eyes glistening with tears.

Ilanda bowed as well. It was a simple gesture of surrender to the protocol.

Ojani helped her to step into this parallel world of serenity and inner-reconciliation, free from the worry of the abysmally long to-do lists that pinned her down to the office late into the night.

Tenzin whispered in Ilanda's ear so as not to disturb the Buddha and the *rinpoche* statues of magnificent detail. The stilled figures were enhanced with dramatically vivid color, to reveal the significant milestones commemorated on the historic quilt of the temple. The story was punctuated with frowns and smirks on both of their faces.

Ojani sat on one of the low benches at the end of the room, taking in the familiar view. The masterfully mixed paint that had been applied to the wooden statues of venerated masters was still an eye-catcher. In several places close to the ceiling, the yellowish wall paint slinked down as if heavy with memories. From his angle, the exposed bricks seemed to laugh back at him with the bewildered expression of being caught naked.

The corner to the right of the door proudly displayed its age by the slanted boards that could no longer be pushed into its original rut. The wood had acted out, impervious to where it might end up beyond these walls if they were somehow replaced.

Maybe it could no longer take the chanting and the prayers. Ojani grinned at himself. Small repairs could turn into expensive restorations if not taken care of in a timely fashion.

He closed his eyes, shutting down his mental highway until a tap on the shoulder restored his awareness.

"It's time." Tenzin gestured at Ilanda, who was already in the hallway.

They repeated the arrival protocol in reverse. Few words were spoken, and those that were spoken were mainly hushed as if the ancestors were present, hanging from the intricately carved boards, eavesdropping on their conversation.

The men stood for a long moment in awe of each other, searching for any visible physical changes since they had last met, long before Ojani's trip to South Africa.

"The farm up north I'm planning on buying might be the only escape if all of this shatters to pieces," Ojani said.

"Unless I go down with the ship," Tenzin said in the same faint tone.

As always, the monk seemed to irradiate a light tenacious enough to reach out to those close by. Ojani knew how hard it would be to sway his friend. It would be even harder than trying to convince Ojani to join the monastic ranks over the years.

"We'll build a temple there, wherever that may be. You could all come." It was a statement that he only half-believed. The implants, the crystal cloud, the franchises, the politics—all braided a sturdy net around his life's mobility, but when pee was running down one's legs, and tie-wraps cut into one's flesh, the perspective and the alternatives were so much clearer.

Ojani would have to go to that darn farm no matter if it was turned into a home, or, in time, uninhabited and ill-maintained, become a refuge for critters and climbing vines which squeezed through the cracks in the walls.

Ojani nodded. He had the impulse to salute Tenzin like the captain he thought himself to be. He led Ilanda outside to a frenzy of cars and passersby on the main road only feet away from the dead-end street. He felt disoriented, like he'd been awakened suddenly from a charming dream, and Ilanda grabbed his arm for balance. The locks of her wig fluttered in the wind, asking for the sun's attention, and it obliged immediately. Sparkles danced in its coal-like color, bringing some life back into it. The light caught Ojani's eyes, and he joyfully laugh.

"You're beautiful," he said without thinking. He'd witnessed fire igniting behind the blue of her eyes, compelling an allure and lust inside. Maahes's death and the lab that demanded work came to his mind abruptly, and his feelings of lust crumbled.

Her grip on his hand tightened, indicating his fortuitous compliment had been well-received. "I'm hungry," she said.

Ojani tapped their coordinates into the app to hail a cab. He was hungry himself, but not for food. It was a hunger that kept eating at him from the inside, diverting his attention from the insignificant stuff. Ojani felt as if he had awakened from a dream at the same time as Ilanda, and they shared the same vibration of heart and mind, a synchronized superposition that would make them whole.

Their behavior remained decent on the drive to the Eaton Centre, steps away from the office. Remnants of the lunch crowd still lingered in the food court, munching on muffins or mulling over cups of coffee. Their brains, switched to siesta position, hadn't given the command to return to their jobs yet.

The Friendly Greek called out to them: chicken skewers, rice, and steamed vegetables. Ojani hadn't taken his third mouthful when a notification sounded on his cell, and Ilanda's, too.

"It has to be the office," he muttered.

"Anonymous is making an announcement?" the neurosurgeon exclaimed. "They haven't surfaced in a while."

Ojani moved to the same side of the table as Ilanda and activated the live AugReality broadcast.

Anonymous's white mask with the black painted mustache that arched up and the thin line bridging the lower lip at the bottom of the chin spiked like bristles of paintbrush. Anonymous wore a hood and gloves on his/her hands, exposing no skin. There was no indication if Anonymous was a man or a woman, nor were there any markers of identity or ego. He was just a judiciary arm, forcing a righteous choice on the world's decision-makers that wouldn't cease spewing platitudes, even in times of crises.

"He hasn't aged a bit," Ojani said, joking. He fiddled with the fork on the anthill of rice he'd built on his plate. The interruption had spoiled the aura of intimacy between him and Ilanda like footprints of an ill-intended person on a freshly-paved sidewalk.

Ilanda leaned back in her chair, hands in her pockets, displaying an attitude of serenity that seemed to say, let it come—what else could be worse than it is right now.

"Let's hear what they're up to this time. Maybe it will help our cause," she said.

The workers and those standing in line at the various food court places froze in unison as if Anonymous were announcing the second coming of the Messiah.

"We've been working on improved crystal cloud technology for a while—two-point-oh, if you'd like. We created the first quartz crystal cloud generation to replace the webhosting providers prone to government interference under made-out privacy laws. We offered that data hosting service for free to most of the not-for-profit, NGOs, and foundations that promoted our values. The implants are starting to creep into the portrait of our daily lives as enhancements, but they could also become a tool for manipulation if used by wrong entities."

Ilanda threw Ojani a queasy look as if saying, I told you: it's about us.

"Shungite crystal," Anonymous continued, "is what we've identified as the best crystal on which to store the information. It's composed of nearly all of the elements on the Periodic Table, which speaks to its rarity."

Ilanda swiveled in her chair and made a call.

Ojani's right ear cued into the audio thread.

"Nanette, are you guys watching the broadcast?" Ilanda said

into her phone. "Good! Record it. I'm on my way back." She punched the screen, ending the transmission.

"I thought you wanted to listen to it," Ojani said, puzzled by her quirky behavior. The lack of interaction with women older than him would turn into a somatic experience only the crystals could match.

"I do, but we need the team around us."

She focused back on the food and nodded at him. "Let's not waste it."

They were in the lab fifteen minutes later. "Play it again," Ilanda said. The whole team gathered around the conference desk, their iPads out, typing notes.

"A surprising feature of this gemstone is that its health-giving components are absorbed by water, which makes shungite a great filter to clean water," Anonymous continued. "Shungite, with its antibacterial properties, can clean water of almost all of organic compounds, metals, bacteria, and harmful micro-organisms. It also removes chlorine compounds and fluoride, while increasing the levels of potassium and its anti-oxidant power."

"Now, is the crazy part," Octana said, and she was hushed immediately by everyone else.

"Our scientists have devised a way to aerate the crystals. Once in that state, another unique property for the stone's residue is that they become magnetized when within mere millimeters of water or any source of moisture."

Ojani didn't have a full scientific understanding, but he watched the team, who were in awe.

"The dust is given replicating properties, and each speck has been programmed with compartmental capabilities to hold and store a massive amount of data, up to one hundred kilobytes per speck. We decided to use high sound frequencies to dismantle the crystals naturally to form a superfine powder, one-thousand times smaller than a speck of sand."

The team cheered as if it were their personal discovery that had been made public.

"The next step is to deploy the crystal powder using high-altitude drones. Once the powder is delivered, it will bond with the moisture-rich air to solidify as a crystal again. The speck can be manipulated with a paired application that moves and shifts to allow water to pass through them or relocate the cloud."

There were more giggles and strident exclamations. It was the sound of scientists in love with unadulterated ingenuity without a trace of jealousy or envy. It was pure, professional bliss.

"The cloud can be as small or as large as we choose to make it. Our paired remote system can receive and send data as requested and can even cloud-hop the data with other crystal clouds in different locations. If struck by lightning, the clouds can store the energy bursts for later use."

"That's really magnificent." Mark Sarafian couldn't hold back the remark.

"Through personal implants, one will be able to store information on the cloud and mentally connect with others with similar crystal grade implants. We are working on an interface that we'll allow us to pair the AugReality feature of our cells with the implant. Do you want to record your dreams and review them next day? Now you got it! Anarchy is coming, people, swiftly and peacefully. I will keep you posted," the mask said, and the transmission stopped.

Ilanda fretted on her chair for several seconds. Everyone gave her the time to think. "How is this going to affect us?" she asked.

"It will have no impact on the medical aspect of what we're trying to achieve," Ojani said, taking the lead, hashing out his understanding of what Anonymous had said. "There's no reason to alter our strategy. We have a solid arrangement with DeBoers. If they want to branch out into this new shungite crystal cloud business, good luck to them!"

No one reacted immediately.

"I agree," Mark Sarafian, a proponent of the franchise approach, said to break the silence between them. "Anonymous's actions might have taken the limelight off of us for a while, which will let us concentrate on the cases we already have on the go."

"I'm still not clear what the heck the 2.0 means," Octana said with a burst of unobstructed fury. "We've discussed about using the quartz crystal cloud to host our clients' medical data. Are they going to trash it? Is it compatible with the shungite cloud?" She arched her eyebrows and twisted her mouth in a display that no one had seen from her before. She grabbed the mug in front of her, and for a second, Ojani thought she would smash it against the wall.

Where had the scientific admiration gone?

Ilanda was still mulling over her thoughts, disregarding Octana's reaction.

"I'm talking practicality here, nothing else," Octana said, fiddling with the mug nervously.

"And why are you pissed?" Ojani asked. "He didn't say anything about discontinuing the quartz cloud."

The young woman puffed at the silliness of his question. "But if they do, I might have to spend time to configure the data to a slightly different vibration to fit that of the shungite crystal. It takes time to do that. Time I don't have with all the crap coming at us from all directions."

She stood up, mug in hand, and walked out for a coffee refill.

"We need answers, and that's a fact; many answers," Ilanda said, her fingers wrestling with each other as if in competition.

"Why change now?" Nanette said, voicing her concern. She glanced quickly around the table as if searching for the right pretender to answer. She focused her gaze on Ojani, and he played along.

"I'm less qualified to justify Anonymous' actions. It could be the unheard-of properties of the shungite and its versatility at changing sizes, and potentially, even shape—"

"Or the simple fact that they've secured a great deal of shungite in Karelia, Russia," Raman said. "I guess they've offered the government top-notch cybersecurity against outside hacking in return for the crystals. Russia needs such a service now."

"It's definitely something specific in their proprietary process that can't be replicated that makes them bold enough to step into the lion's den," Sarafian said, throwing another idea into the pit for the lions to chew on.

Octana returned, balancing the mug, which was filled to the

brim. It was a habit that always left dried rings on the desks as if it were her personal brand.

"What if they keep 1.0 and 2.0 running in parallel?" Ilanda said, raising her voice over the cross-table chatter. "If I am correct, they used quartz for version 1.0 of the cloud. It's widely found everywhere on Earth. We know that initially they offered 1.0 only to non-government organizations, not-for-profit, and to teams like ours. A cloud pilot of the sorts, but also to show their discontent with the governments and those controlling them. What if Anonymous migrates all of the above to 2.0, the shungite version, opening 1.0 to the public?"

"It does make sense," Octana said. "If the shungite's vibration signature includes the quartz's signature, then, later on, a microscopic layer of shungite applied over the quartz implant could make the two compatible while maintaining the privacy and data integrity."

"Should I go buy shungite bracelets and pendants from the jewelry store across the street before everyone else wakes up to this idea?" Octana asked, much more composed.

Ojani let out a breath as if about to burst at the seams. Others copied him wholeheartedly. It sounded as if a fail-safe valve had reached a near-dangerous threshold. The brief respite from the animated chatter seemed to blow the dust from the looking glass, refreshing their perspective.

"Octana is right," Ilanda said, wiping tears from her cheeks. "Even if the retail pieces aren't of a high-quality grade, at least we can slice it and learn about its geometric patterns and how much energetic information it contains."

There were unanimous nods around the table.

Ilanda continued. "We follow the same approach as per the previous cases, but with a different crystal. At this stage, we won't bother to replicate the aerating process."

There were more nods.

"Do you want to hear a crazy idea?' Ojani asked. His question was met with warm laughter, encouraging Ojani. He was also stimulated by the intellectual challenge put in front of him. "Why not blow the same microscopic layer of shungite dust Octana mentioned onto the white crystals DeBoers plans to produce—"

"That would result in a better decoding of the structured water, and it would also connect with the crystal cloud 2.0 at the same time, potentially turning them into the artificial version of the quartz implants," Mark Sarafian said, snatching Ojani's conclusion away from him in another attempt to prove his sharpness.

Ojani didn't mind the repeated interruptions. He valued their presence more than he would a quarrel over mind power.

"I expect Corus Van Dent to call tomorrow," Ilanda said. "I'll be able to tell right away if they've secured a shungite source in Russia or if they're still scrambling for one. His ears always blush when he's panicked. He just can't help it."

Nanette was the first to walk toward the door. "Are we shelving the language of water research, you know?" She blocked it as if trying to prevent anyone from escaping before getting the answer she desired.

The sudden reminder of one of the team's purposes for having been brought together froze the side conversations.

Several pairs of eyes focused on Ilanda, like magnifying glasses. Their look was intent enough to almost leave burns on her skin.

"Let's consider it a forced shift due to more urgent matters, but I'm open to suggestions. As Octana said, there's no time for anything else right now. I can guide, but I can't do the work anymore," she said apologetically.

"Maybe we can train the guys who handled the water samples for us. They don't have to interpret the results—all they have to do is run the tests in a specific sequence," Octana said.

"And each of us could alternate supervising them, you know," Nanette said, encouraged by the invisible peremptory hand that helped to change the mood of her team members.

"Talk to them, and let me know what they said. It's above their pay grade, but we can improve on that, as well," Ilanda said. "We can also ask Cherry to help. She's qualified." She moved toward the door. The look in her eyes seemed powerful enough to break through Nanette's barricade.

CHAPTER 14

Ilanda and Ojani discussed how Canada could use four franchise locations to start: Toronto, Montreal, Calgary, and Vancouver.

Other selected cities in the US and Europe would only have two licenses to start. He would be in charge of checking the individual applications.

After the public announcement went out, Ojani couldn't contain his laugh when the CEO of Tim Hortons approached them with a sweet offer: his company was already in the franchise business, and it could help by selecting the locations and doctors in return for a small fee. He had to admire the guy's gumption, but he turned him down politely with no hard feelings. The coffee and donut business was not as thriving as it used to, and new sources of revenue would be needed.

The team's personal network of friends and acquaintances working in the medical field had expressed an incredible interest in holding a franchise license for the crystal technology. Ophthalmologists, pediatricians, dentists, and even gynecologists had submitted their names through an AugReality video.

Egos riffed through the revamped resumes, dusting off credentials like artists working with highly volatile substances to bring back forgotten painting found under a dull layer of mud.

Ojani and Ilanda threw wry glances at each other while watching the recorded interviews. They sometimes burst into laughter at the falsity and insincerity of the doctors who, based on their profession, were still supposed to have traces of decency left in them. Their involuntary outburst served as a sign of rejection.

At other times, a nod was enough to qualify the pretender for the next step.

The workload drew them closer, and neither of them minded as their apartments were not accommodating for such a task. Ilanda confessed to Ojani that since Maahes's death in parched Egypt, she used her condo no more than three times a week to grab a quick shower and a clean change of clothing. She still had some motivation back then, a reason to wait for her husband to return from one of his extended trips around the world after chasing the water rights for Water Vivus Inc., now a defunct company.

"Our intellectual tussle," she had confessed, "had usually trumped our domestic fights, and only in you, Ojani, have I found some of Maahes's passion for striving for what I believed in."

Ojani had almost blushed when she'd confided in him. He'd kept quiet but nodded in appreciation of the comparison with the man she'd loved.

Ojani's two-bedroom apartment was also a pit stop for bare necessities and not a place to which he attached himself. He became its owner as a result of a trade-in for his uptown penthouse along with the rights for first row seats for an entire run of Toronto Raptors championship games.

He valued more what the walls sheltered than the place itself—vintage Buddhist books, several African masks, and a small collection of contemporary artwork, made primarily by Ontario-based artists he'd gathered at national and international exhibitions.

Spending time with Ilanda and the research team had freed him up from other insignificant preoccupations.

"So, what do you think of the location?" The forceful tone of the question jostled Ojani from his lengthy day-dream. He looked at the oversized sixty-year-old man strapped with suspenders for keeping his pants up and a snake-like belt to contain his round belly. The potential franchisee for the Toronto Downtown location also had bushy sideburns, a monocle fixed in his right eye, and tumble-weed-like black hair.

"When the Chinese construction companies won the air rights over the railway tracks at Union Station, everyone thought they were nuts, but I'm telling you, those guys can smell money from continents away," the potential franchisee said.

Ojani wasn't sure if the verbal barrage was supposed to have distracted his attention from something that hadn't quite fit the requirements or if the man was being himself.

"I pulled in funds with another six doctors and bought two floors before they even broke ground."

"Do you still have them as partners?"

"No, no. I bought out the last of them a couple of years ago. They all got tired of being landlords, but not me. My father, God rest his soul, taught me a lot about real estate investments and passive income—never lost a penny."

The man's right eyebrow and cheek twitched in an attempt to keep the monocle in its place.

"I hope you don't mind that the outside view is obstructed by the other buildings. I know it feels like entering a glass canyon when you drive down there," he said, and he pointed his chin at the portions of the highway, barely visible between the towers. "It's the same view up until the fifty-second floor. Only above that can one enjoy the view of the lake or lower downtown. Honestly, it was too expensive to purchase higher at the time."

The man seemed to have been embarrassed by the confession, and he shuffled his feet like a shy little girl waiting to sing in the school's Christmas concert.

"It shouldn't be a problem," Ojani said automatically, in an attempt to make conversation.

"The voice-activated plasma TV windows allow the patient or his family members to create the necessary ambiance. This floor will host the administration office, lounge, kitchen, and five operating rooms. Initially, this area had a medical designation, and we kept it. It also came with a private elevator," the owner said.

Ojani opened several doors in the main hallway and peeked inside at the virtual images of furniture, surgical equipment, and interior design that had been prepared for his visit.

"If anything has to be moved around, please let me know," the man almost implored.

Ojani pursed his full lips, undecided if he should have some fun with his host by showing him contempt. "It looks great," he said after inspecting the last room on the floor. "Do you have any comments about the contract?"

He knew that the franchisee had no wiggle-room when it came to changing the terms, but he'd asked anyway to show consideration.

"No, no concerns," the man said. "You order the equipment, and I'll pay for it and have it installed within the week. If, for any reason, our deal is dissolved, you will have the right to buy the equipment back at fair market value."

Ojani nodded.

"You make all of the arrangements with the patients, I receive the crystals through secure mail, and the surgery details get uploaded from your end."

"Correct," Ojani said. "I haven't checked if an UpLink connection to the crystal is available in the building. If not, we'll have to take care of that, too. That alone might take about a week to activate. And the connection stays under our name for as long you run our franchise."

As discussed internally, the connection to the crystal cloud was one way to maintain the monopoly of crystal implant technology through enhanced encryption.

"Did you get any official assurances from the government as to keeping your monopoly in place for a while?" the man asked. He used his belly to direct Ojani toward the elevator to the upper floor.

"The Canadian government will play along and let us be the only game in the country . . . for now!" Ojani said. "We have a head start, but nothing will stop the competition from hiring lobbyists, paying politicians, and forcing a vote contrary to what we have now. They'll start to play the same old game of influence."

The elevator doors opened onto a large space, a former reception area, now gutted and showing fifteen virtual rooms, fully equipped for post-intervention monitoring.

"Impressive," Ojani exclaimed. His first in-person interview was going better than expected.

"But you have control of the crystal manufacturer, don't you?" the old man asked. It was a subtle question, designed to test how safe his investment would be in the long-term.

"The guys in South Africa are pretty solid, and we have an exclusive arrangement with them," Ojani answered after he dismissed his initial impulse to ignore the question. There was no point in raising any doubt about a business model that no one was one hundred-percent sure would work. The ten-year exclusive deal didn't mean much, but it was enough for them to push ahead of any competitors and give them a breather in which to build a market that might evolve exponentially in a matter of years.

DeBoers could sell unmarked crystals, a cheaper version than the white grade, meant for entertainment purposes. No one could stop or control them as long as it didn't match the features included in the contract. Their part of the deal had no loose ends, no loopholes which might allow patients to get implants without paying or being included in the monitoring database.

"If the demand is as high as the number of participants in a flash mob, you'll need some security measures."

"Such as?" the man asked. He'd hooked his thumbs into his waistband. It made him look like a plantation manager Ojani had seen in the books his grandfather had brought back from Jamaica.

"A security guard downstairs by the elevator. Patients won't be able to come upstairs unless their eye scan checks out, no matter if the case is medical or for pleasure. It means the individual isn't in our database, and no prep work was done."

"Understood."

They began to walk back to the elevator.

"I should let you know of our decision in a couple of days, but . . . what can I say? I'm impressed. You're ready to go." Ojani out stretched his hand and received a vigorous answer.

CHAPTER 15

"Wakey, wakey!" Maahes approached Marian holding a coconut in each hand. His slippers made a funny sound when they hit his heels, like a fly-swatter slapping against a hard surface. Marian was lying on a large wicker beach chair, covered with a blue towel.

"Got some tonic for you." Maahes merrily sat on the adjacent chair. "I dropped in a little bit of brandy from a stash I saved from before my 'death'." He laughed at his own joke, then leaned back and put his legs up.

"Free coconut water." Marian pursed his lips as if participating in a wine-tasting session.

"Nothing is free these days, my friend. But because I'm a steady customer with a fat disposable income, I get a discount." Maahes sucked on the bamboo straw piercing the top of the coconut and took off his straw hat. He slapped his belly gently and said, "I've lost thirty-two pounds since I landed in this paradise two years ago. Salads, fruit, coconut water, and fresh fish every so often, but mainly the lack of the stress from running a corrupt company really helped shed the pounds."

The out-of-season crowd was almost non-existent on the private, narrow, arched ribbon of sand. A thirty-inch high concrete wall separated them from the sea. Raised sea levels had mischievously gorged on the natural beauty. The sand, saved from the original beach, was tossed generously over pebbles and leveled shoreline, mimicking what used to be one of the most-visited vacation spots in Costa Rica.

Several locals carrying cheap trinkets had a hard time convincing a handful of tourists that no trip was worth coming back from without a souvenir, but they were all a fair distance from their normal spots. Maahes felt safe speaking freely, without having to use hushed tones or look over his shoulder to see if anyone was listening.

"You couldn't have selected a better place for retirement, boss," Marian acknowledged, slurping from the coconut.

Maahes smirked back. Up in the mountains, twenty minutes away, his hunkered-down, self-contained property had a tinge of elegance to it while blending into the lush landscape. The short drive to the beach using an electric cart only served to pump more adrenaline into his aged veins, making him appreciate the simpler lifestyle. Having Marian as a guest was a real boon for Maahes's social life, which was usually limited to the gardener, his wife, and the five local women who ran the vegetable and fruit stands at the open market with whom he sporadically engaged in barebones conversation, limited by his broken Spanish. He didn't count on the security guards rotating every three months from Asia, Europe, or the odd African country. Those guys valued their mission above a personal relationship with clients.

There was no one outside of Costa Rica he would have entrusted with the knowledge of his staged disappearance. The hacker had been in with him way before his "death wish," and slowly became a trusted extension of himself. Yes, sometimes Marian's manners and comments were too much like sandpaper for Maahes's taste; nevertheless, the remnants of his previous flamboyant and excessive lifestyle needed the "in-your-face," harsh, honest remarks.

Maahes's longing for Ilanda's company came and went like a

sunburn from the kiss of the celestial king on bare skin. The self-imposed low profile in his adopted country had tempered his habit of flirting with other women when given the opportunity. It was more of an assessment of his seductive charm and level of attracting interest from the opposite sex rather than a conscious decision to conclude a light discussion with passionate physical interaction.

The beard he'd shaved for his new identification photo had grown back rougher and grayer than before, showing his age.

"The statement you made last time we talked nagged at me," Marian said while pulling up the top of the beach chair to a higher angle.

"Which one? I don't keep track of minutes from our conversations."

Marian's tiny mouth rounded to form the perfect letter "o," which he meant as a smile. "You were wondering if Ilanda would recognize your features if you went for a crystal implant."

"So?"

"They're opening offices all over the world." Marian slurped again. "It's going to be controlled from Toronto, but there's a certain flexibility to getting on the list. For you, money is not an issue." Marian spoke his words slowly as if he were spitting marbles that would collide with others to break into countless shards.

Maahes didn't rush his friend. Costa Rica, the beach, and the ever-present sun sucked most of the urgency from his daily activities. Time was plenty.

"A facelift will do it. I did some research in this area, and there are a couple of reputable clinics. They're very private in terms of protecting their patients' records." Marian looked sheepishly at Maahes, whose lips puckered around the straw.

"I thought you were against suggesting a hack to their database, which to me, is a much simpler approach," Maahes said.

"Not for this one. Ilanda's team went crystal cloud hosting. They've announced recently."

"Crystal cloud?"

"Yes."

Maahes remembered that Ilanda had mentioned that a certain group—he couldn't remember which one—had developed such technology to increase online security and to keep private information out of the government's hands.

"My beautiful green eyes, superbly soft creole skin, and strong cheekbones don't inspire you anymore?" Maahes asked.

Marian smiled with his eyes this time, forming thin blades on his round face. "Your cheekbones might stay even if a slight structural change is recommended, but the beautiful green eyes definitely have to go. There has to be an exchange of some sort."

"Why?" The tone of Maahes's voice was a mix of sarcasm and whining as if he were seriously looking for justification.

"The eyes are the gate to the brain enhancement. Faking your retinas won't qualify you for the implant. The identity won't match, and a warning will be triggered in Big Brother's database."

"But that's a place you can hack, isn't it?" the older man asked hopefully.

"I'm not sure yet where they are pulling the identity information from. It could be from the embedded chip or the social security database owned by the government," Marian said. "While you were stuck here, the world has evolved into a more controlled entity."

"Yes, I know. The airport and border security checks were a nuisance," Maahes said, frustrated by the "going-in-circle" approach.

"Moving forward, the agreed-upon method of personal identification will be the retina scan. You can fake passports, fingerprints, and so on, but not this one," Marian said.

"So, I'm screwed!" Maahes brushed a spot of sand off his thigh with a brusque gesture. A pattern of palm tree leaves danced on their tanned bodies like snakes hypnotized by the sweet sound of a flute. A hole in the sand drew his attention. He picked up one of his slippers and looked around for a stick. "At least, as you said, I live in paradise," he said resentfully without raising his gaze off the hole.

"There is one option that could re-establish your complete freedom."

"Do you want me to beg you to share it?"

Marian put the empty coconut on the sand and whispered, "Switch eyeballs with a person who hasn't been tagged yet."

"You want me to scoop my eyes out?" He straightened in the beach chair as if needles had poked up through the fabric, but continued to stared at the hole. The sand on the edges poured in slowly stirred by movements inside. The claws of a crab came out first.

"I thought you understood the statement I made minutes ago, the one about the 'exchange.' I wasn't kidding." The bald man pushed sand left and right with his foot, avoiding Maahes's gaze.

"Most of the Central and South American countries are lagging behind when it comes to chipping their people. If you're going to do the switch, now is the time."

Marian stood his ground. His tensed upper body and pressed lips were signs of how serious the situation was. The crab was in the open. With a quick swap, Maahes covered the hole with one slipper and pinned down on the hard shell with the stick, incapacitating the creature from digging himself back to safety.

"What about the chip?" he asked. "I don't have one anymore. We left it back in Egypt for appearances".

"A new one has to be embedded. You'll have a clean database entry, here in Costa Rica or Panama—it's your choice. It all depends on where we do the switch. And this operation will require bribing the right people."

Looking toward the ocean to take in its relentless energy was all Maahes could do. Thoughts that didn't belong to him spattered against his skull like the waves smashing against the protection wall. Sins resurfaced cynically, an avalanche of black soot clogging at the back of his mind.

The balance of his positive actions as Water Vivus Inc.'s ex-CEO couldn't outweigh the squalid ones that had destroyed companies, communities, and individuals while exercising his position of power. Directly or not, in the end, the hired-hands had acted on his command. His armor-like conscience had given in almost three years ago, besieged by a positive light and the realization of the pain humanity was inflicting on the Earth.

Maahes reverted his attention back to the crab that stopped moving his legs as if waiting for a breach on the pressure on his shell.

"A stash of cash has to exchange hands, too. It's unavoidable," Marian said as if to be sure Maahes had understood the meaning of the word bribe.

A soft and warm wind pushed west and the scent of coconut sugar and cinnamon from the bakery edging the beach lobbed in their nostrils.

Maahes recognized the high voices of the kids who were paid a small percentage of the sales they made while walking up and down the sandy shores. The sound of pure, pristine, youthful energy, along with the silky taste of home-made delicacies were recent and enjoyable experiences he wanted to keep as memories.

"Let me treat you to a marvel of pastry subtlety that you won't find in Toronto." He stood up and lean his weight on the stick, piercing the crab's shell. The victim remained impaled as a testimony of Maahes's past behavior: cruel and selfish. He gave Marian a nudge to stand up.

He was not ready to compromise on the decision that would mark his remaining years: have his eyes replaced. He could, at least, sweeten the decision period with a couple of cheese pies. The burning sand turned the men into hilarious dancers as they quickly advanced toward the loudly advertised pies.

CHAPTER 16

"Hey, Ilanda," Marinka said, greeting the doctor's AugReality image from her father's living room in Hawaii. Her father sat beside her on the sofa, letting her do most of the talking during their monthly remote health checks, as usual.

The AugReality image showed a sleep-deprived woman who was juggling issues that she felt no one else but she could handle.

Marinka could see herself what Cherry had confessed about Ilanda during her short visit to Hawaii.

"Hey, you two—how are your energy levels?" the doctor asked.

"Pumping wildly through our veins," Marinka replied to the question that always began their calls. She glanced at her father for reassurance and to show Ilanda that they were both in sync.

"Got the results of the bloodwork you did the other day. The numbers are excellent, from iron to hemoglobin to B12, pH, protein, cholesterol, and glucose," the doctor said, using the usual medical terms in which neither of the Hawaiians was interested. It confirmed what they intuitively knew in plain language, but Ilanda's emotions erupted over her dam of self-control once more.

"Other vitals are also within the limits of a twenty-eight-year-old person," she said, her voice imbued with disbelief. "It's better than last month—what are you guys eating?" Ilanda chortled. She pushed forward, not expecting an answer. "I didn't notice any highs or lows in the vibration of the crystal implants. Though this type of monitoring is still new to me, I wasn't expecting any significant rollercoasters."

"We're fine, Ilanda," Marinka said, trying to calm her down.

"How's your eyesight? Still seeing things in shades of light blue?"

"It's getting better. After being colorblind after the implants, I'm slowly adjusting to what I was able to see before. Same for my father."

"The brain is adapting its neural networks to visual stimuli and nanobots. It might take a while before you're one hundred percent back to full-spectrum," Ilanda said. "This is a sticky point on the path to recovery. I can't guarantee there'll be full recovery of the entire color palette. I'll have to tell the lawyers to include a non-liability clause in the base contract. It's better to be protected."

"Are these check-ups still necessary?" Marinka asked.

The doctor's face pulsed with a nuance of red as if invisible hands had pinched both of her cheeks at the same time. She stood up and came around her desk, giving Marinka the impression that she was trying to be intimidating.

"Don't be silly," Ilanda said. Her voice was staccato, as if she were barely able to contain herself from giving a scolding answer. "I need this data. The team needs it to improve the algorithmic downloaded into your implants." She looked down for a moment, displaying a quirky, self-destructive side of her personality Marinka hadn't noticed before.

"Since we've internally decided on the franchising model, many potential candidates have been evaluated and selected for medical procedures similar to yours. Maybe you don't remember what I told you in Toronto, that monitoring the crystals is part of our deal. The chips embedded in the back of your hand don't ever take breaks from transmitting your heartbeats to the government-owned database. The same goes for the implants."

"And this data is for your use only?" Marinka asked.

"Yes. At least, for now."

"Could they ever force you to hand it over?"

Marinka felt Ilanda's gaze on her skin like sandpaper brushing against a rough wooden surface, and she shivered; it was almost painful.

"Raman, our application developer, had explained to me that they might, but I have no intention of letting them. Raman also said that access to the application backend rather than just the data could be much more dangerous."

"What do you mean?" Kahuna asked as if the heavy veil of silence shrouding him had been lifted.

Ilanda paused a bit longer after the elder's interjection. "My understanding is that data mining won't hurt anyone," she finally said, "but playing with the parameters of each crystal is a totally different ball game. And if the government or some other ill-intended agency gains access to a crystal hub, interfering with the host's brain is the next natural step."

"We'd be on remote control, then," Marinka said.

"Like zombies on a leash, to be more precise," Ilanda said. "But let's cross that bridge when we get there."

"Is it true that the insurance companies are warming up to the idea of covering the implants, albeit slowly?" Marinka asked.

Kahuna fell back into his deep silence, but she knew he was fully aware of the discussion and would interrupt if necessary.

More composed now, Ilanda put her palms behind her and leaned against her desk. "Yes. It was enough for one mid-size insurer to step forward and make the courageous—or insane—announcement. A handful of others followed. I expect none to stay away from such opportunity. We've checked with a local law firm and no additional legislation is required in order for the insurance companies to include new policy terms in their offering."

"I'm glad your dream came true," Marinka said with as much warmth as she could.

Ilanda nodded. Her eyes averted making contact with Marinka's, looking, instead, beyond the thin layer of light surrounding the father and daughter.

"What's wrong?"

The doctor scratched her palms on the edge of the desk. "I'm overwhelmed. The whole team is overwhelmed."

Marinka thought Ilanda might break down and start crying in front of them, but she regained her equanimity after a short pause.

"We can't bring more people in to help us, especially now, when trust is such a rare asset. I, personally, can't vouch for anyone anymore. God forbid there's ever a mole. It's all we'd need for it to take us down completely."

Kahuna's elbow touched hers as he shuffled on the couch. "Don't give in to the pressure." His voice had a metallic twang to it. He waited for a reaction, but none materialized. "I can't imagine what it was like having the world's eyes on you while trying to bring me back from the dead."

Ilanda nodded.

"Just be sure to pace yourself and the team. I assume the franchise locations don't have a firm deadline for being active."

The doctor nodded her silent confirmation again.

"You've started the process to make the implants as commonplace as the AugReality technology. A little stalling might go unnoticed." Kahuna smiled broadly, as proud of himself as if he'd just found a forgotten Polynesian code able to decipher a path to a parallel universe. "Slow down. Breathe more often. The issues of the world can wait another day."

Ilanda's body slumped as if the tension keeping her frame straight had vanished, leaving a limp ragdoll in her place. The deflation shrank her size on the AugReality image, and Marinka's eyes welled, sensing their savior's turmoil. There was nothing she could do to ease the pressure. She had no other advice but that which her father had offered. The distance from the craziness witnessed and experienced by Ilanda provided the necessary focus for taking care of their community.

Marinka was willing to work alongside her father to restore the energetic balance of the island, critically disturbed since the 1990s when the first GMO crops were tested by the mainland corporations.

The foreigners had bludgeoned the Polynesian culture and the area's pristine nature, turning a deaf ear to all attempts on the part of the indigenous peoples to maintain reason and respect. Marinka had witnessed some aspects of the degradation of lifestyle on the islands, but more accounts had come from stories shared by her father as a part of her upbringing as a future leader.

Finally, water had awakened, stirring a commotion worldwide, heard by all decision-makers. This time, they had listened, frightful but obedient and ready to comply—at least, publicly.

The beauty of the ancestral volcanic island would blossom under the supervision of a loving crowd of gods and goddesses once more. Water would save them. It would save them all, even if the simple act of admitting it didn't come easy.

Ilanda breathed in deeply several times as Kahuna advised, and Marinka saw her doctor's frame miraculously reshaped back into the fearless neurosurgeon who had developed a technology that would prompt a shift in human interaction and evolution. A long term shift, she hoped. She would welcome more individuals being transformed like her, building invisible communication bridges over shungite crystal clouds.

The influencers, Cherry had told Marinka during her visit on the island, should be enticed to get the crystal implants. The creative class with a hoard of followers, and even the popular political figures, could drive the spike in demand and the acceptance of drastic human alteration. They could think at the implants as the new fad, an add-on, similar to an app on their cell phones that needs to be upgraded several times a year. Maybe her father's worldwide fans, emboldened by his miraculous revival, will tally their names to the waiting list.

She wished the attitude at the other tribal leaders would have been warmer during the several meetings she attended in the presence of her father. They were glad he was back home. None of them had the international reach and recognition her father had, and the islands, even with the turning of events in their favor, needed the additional media exposure.

"I'll see you two again next month," she said, then, as she always did, she added, "let me know right away if you notice any secondary effects."

Father and daughter nodded, smiled, and hung up.

CHAPTER 17

"Who the hell released the information that we put forward a partnership offer, and you rejected it?" Corus Van Dent said. His face was red, a marked contrast to his white shirt.

His diminished body on the AugReality transmission paced back and forth inside his Johannesburg office. The sleeves of his custom-made shirt had been pulled up above his elbows, and his light blue tie was undone.

"The share's price is in free fall, and the board threatened to fire me. I'm the only one who negotiated . . . sorry . . . had talks with Ojani about a potential partnership. Then, one week later, this damn leak happens, blowing everything up.".

"Corus," Ilanda said, "you listen to me. None of us is the source of the leak. We're still in damage control over rumors the Canadian government has interfered in our research, forbidding mass implementation." She could barely keep her tone in check while replying to the South-African's accusations. "After Kahuna's recovery, the government's goons came crashing down on us for more details as they smelled the opportunity of making money, but never threatened to shut us down."

She was sitting beside Ojani on the couch in her office, her hands in her lap and tight-clad legs almost touching his. She rolled her eyes and looked at Ojani who also seemed annoyed with the conversation. They knew they had to confront DeBoers's VP over the alleged Torontonian's kidnapping, but his call had come in first, and he had the upper hand.

"I'm tired of being accused of all sorts of things. My team and I have to spend time defending ourselves instead of focusing on our research—"

"So, who's behind the leak?" Van Dent said, refusing to let Ilanda take control of the tussle.

"We don't know. It's a concentrated, well-funded, and well-organized plan. We are the target, for sure. They used information I haven't discussed with my team, so an inside leak is out of the question."

"There must be something you can do—another public statement of sorts," Van Dent said. He leaned on the aged-wooden desk, almost begging confirmation from Ilanda.

She swallowed a smile at the businessman's scarecrow-like posture. Tall, scrawny body, like crossed twigs, tied together with frail vines, but dressed in expensive clothing.

"It'll mean nothing, eh," Ojani said, giving Ilanda a break. "Too many denials would only confirm there's something else going on, and the pundits and the media will believe the opposite. But before we even discuss releasing a statement, I want to know why you had me kidnapped in Johannesburg after I left your office, eh." He watched Van Dent's reaction closely.

"Are you trying to divert the focus of my question with ludicrous accusations?" His voice didn't pitch, his arms didn't wave if imitating a mad opera conductor, nor did he avoid Ojani's stare.

Ilanda also recognized the signs of an honest admission, and she mentally acknowledged what Ojani had told her right after his arrival, that it hadn't made any sense for their potential future partner to kidnap him.

"I was held captive in a high-rise apartment in Pretoria for twenty-four hours. Tied to a chair with no water or food. Just an empty room with native artwork hanging on the walls. A cleaning lady released me. Pure luck, eh?" Ojani said, providing the details with an uncanny detachment as if he were talking about somebody else.

"I had no idea. I'm glad you're okay." Van Dent moved behind his desk and sat down. He pulled his shirt sleeves even higher on his arm in a nervous gesture and scratched his left eyebrow. His upper lip twitched visibly, as if whispering wise advises to himself. Ilanda had the impression he would clear the top of his desk with a swoop of his hand like she had seen so many times in the movies. But he only pulled slightly on his loosened tie and said, "Now, I understand your hesitance to prop up an entity you couldn't trust. Trust is everything in business. I'll inform the board it's not you who leaked the information and let them decide the next step."

He looked around his office as if assessing which belongings were worth taking with him after he'd been fired. "Did anyone look into who owns the apartment?" Van Dent asked. "If you want, I can have a private-eye investigate."

"We had the Canadian Embassy do that. The owner is an evasive individual or group of people hidden behind an entanglement of shell corporations in the Cayman Island. No chance of finding their real identity, eh," Ojani said.

"Corus." Ilanda said his name slowly, and she pushed herself forward, closer to the AugReality image. "Ojani didn't think your company was behind his ordeal. You have his vote of confidence. As I said, another statement will do little to equal the rumors and stop the plunging of your company's stock."

"What we can do, eh," Ojani intervened, "is to announce that we signed the deal, and the leak is a criminal act concocted by market fixers who missed their play and profits while the stock-exchanges were closed. Let's throw the ball in somebody else's backyard, eh."

"Really! I'm in your debt," Van Dent said enthusiastically, his brown eyes nearly glowing.

"We know what we want from this partnership. Ojani will send you the details right after this call. Incorporate them and send the document back. We should sign it by the end of the day tomorrow."

"Amazingly easy doing business with you two," the South African said, obviously empowered by the reversal of the situation. "Before I let you go, I want to be sure that Ilanda's in agreement with the production of lower-quality crystals that will be more affordable."

Ilanda turned toward Ojani as to confirm that he already informed her about the discussion the two men had had in Johannesburg.

"I understand that they'll be a lower quality-grade resulting in an attractive price point for the masses. Are they geared toward entertainment?"

"Correct," Van Dent said. "Such as in multi-user online gaming, web surfing, virtual world creation, instant news and communication, and over-all connectivity to various apps. Pretty much the trivial stuff."

"Why would anyone implement the crystals now? There is no infrastructure in place yet. The quartz crystal cloud offered by invitation only by Anonymous is not available to individuals," Ilanda said. She crossed her legs and leaned forward, startled by what Van Dent and his management company envisioned as the enlarged scope for crystal usage.

"Correct," Van Dent said. "It's only a matter of time before such crystal-based infrastructure will be put in place. It could be DeBoers or some other company that will lay the foundation. It doesn't matter."

"What do you mean?" Ilanda asked.

"Once put in place, the network of crystal hubs has a predetermined number of nodes. But the number of users, the billions of them, is where the money is. Or Anonymous could allow everyone access on one point or as soon as the shungite cloud is up and running." Van Dent smiled, but not the sly, dangerous version of an unscrupulous, cut-throat businessman. Ilanda sensed a degree of compassion matching her care for her patients.

"We'll only have," he continued, "one artificial grade: white, mimicking the quartz—for the purpose I just mentioned. Our scientists told us it could be upgraded through software to monitor vital signs and generate medical alerts, but they won't heal their owners." He brushed his large palm against his bald head while staring at Ilanda and Ojani as to see if anything was missed. "Ah, something else they said: a higher vibration is necessary to induce the healing process. Only the natural stones are capable of such a feat. We also based this conclusion on the partial report you shared with us. Your team did an amazing job. "

Ilanda nodded in response to the compliment.

"And just to summarize what we'll see included in the agreement: DeBoers will mass-produce white crystals, customizing real ones for medical cases or for individuals able to afford the price, no matter the intent of use. The code and the intervention itself will be performed by us in the Toronto lab," Ilanda said, looking intensely at Van Dent, who couldn't wipe the satisfaction from his face once she confirmed the deal was solid.

"I agree. We also want to suggest an alternative for those in need of medical care, but who can't afford permanent quality crystals."

"Go on," Ojani said when the South African, who had been pacing inside the office, stopped to wait for their reaction.

"Short-term rent of a high-grade, fully-loaded stone."

"What?" Ilanda jerked back in her seat on the couch. She tried to speak, but none of the answers forming in her mind seemed appropriate as an answer. She glanced at Ojani whose face hung a similar puzzled expression.

"In fact, it's a humanitarian gesture," Van Dent said. "The intervention is performed, but the last step of sealing the crystals in place is omitted. After we bring them back from a coma or whatever medical challenge they might have, we clear the crystal programing using a bulk demagnetizer, then, we take back what's ours. The crystal is wiped clean and we can reuse it on another compatible patient."

Ilana stared at him, dumbfounded. "Corus, we haven't tested yet the rollback process of disconnecting the nanobots that attach the crystal implants with the pineal gland. It might create certain damages. We always thought of this process as a permanent one."

"I understand. But, look." Corus Van Dent leaned forward, almost piercing the AugReality image. "We are envisioning the uptick potential of an incipient market. Our company hired its own team of sound and frequency specialists. We want to be sure what we produce is thoroughly tested. We can't be the cause of any failure."

"Why do you think people will rent the crystals, eh?" Ojani asked.

"The fear that the medical condition could resurface is what I count on," the vice-president said. "Once healthy, they want to stay that way. No matter the cost. And if between the surgery and the moment of recovery, the family comes up with the dough we can leave it in for good." He got closer, if that was even possible, Ilanda thought, and whispered, "Once healed, people don't have the mental strength to keep a positive image about themselves. In the back of their mind, the fear that the disease could return stays palpable. Over time, it will become reality."

"And with the crystal embedded permanently, that fear is gone. This is what you are getting to, eh?" Ojani asked.

"Correct."

"Yes, very humanitarian, indeed," Ilanda added, sarcastically.

Van Dent's wry chin trembled imperceptibly, or that is what Ilanda read through the AugReality vibrations.

"The clause will be included in the legal agreement. I didn't want to surprise you. It's optional. If everything else goes as planned, it shouldn't be a deal-breaker." He almost whispered the last sentence while Ilanda pierced him with a fiery gaze meant to leave some scars on his skin.

"You can include it, but until we gather enough research on potential side-effects on removing the crystals, we are not going to honor it. Anything else we should be aware of, eh?" Ojani asked, ready to hang up.

"The news about more quartz crystals hubs coming online every other month is a positive sign for us, even if we don't know yet how

Anonymous will allocate the access," Van Dent said, disregarding Ojani's intention to conclude their discussion. "We'll ramp-up production of the white crystals, assuming there will be a high demand."

"Don't get ahead of yourself. The franchise model hasn't been made public yet." Ilanda noticed that Ojani's reply had been tinged with worry. Then he continued, "Don't put indirect pressure on us. We started a word-of-mouth campaign among people we trust around the world who meet the criteria to become a part of the franchise—"

"Nice. I knew you guys would move fast," Van Dent said with a broad smile.

Ilanda felt Ojani fretting beside her at the interruption, but he refrained from making a nasty comment.

"What I mean, Corus, is that there are still tons of work to be done on our end, and breathing down our necks like a moose in heat won't help. The production of nanobots is being worked out with a technology company in London, Ontario, and they also have to scale up for the quantities required. An ETA has not been provided yet."

"I understand," said a straight-faced Van Dent. "I'll set-up the expectations with the board. Also, we can help identify local franchisees. There is a percentage of the middle class that will be interested in the implants, and I'd bet that the high society will sign up—they can afford it, and they'll do it just to prove it."

"We'll let you know if we need your help, Corus, eh" Ojani said.

"You can count on us—"

Now, it was the Torontonian's turn to interrupt. "I got it. In the meanwhile, we need to apply for hosting on the crystal cloud. We're already a client on the first version of the crystal cloud, so we expect to be accepted for the shungite upgrade by the Anonymous Group. The moment the encryption between the lab and the cloud is tested, we'll be able to securely transmit code to any franchise," Ojani had revealed the significant step needed before the whole procedure could become fully operational.

"Here's another idea that might streamline the process and

reduce the amount of data sent to various locations," the South African said, suddenly energized, as if he'd replaced the battery powering him.

Ilanda and Ojani let him speak.

"The base code for the white crystals should be uploaded at the source, right after production. You'll still have control from the head office over the release of the nanobots and the intervention per se, and we could perform additional functionality tests to confirm that the product shipping out isn't faulty."

He leaned against his desk, legs stretched out in front of him. Dots of focused white light punctuated his shirt and face as if he were the target for a hidden squad attempting to his life; it was the pattern of light reflected off the solar panels in the floor-to-ceiling windows.

"It should work," Ilanda said. She stood up and looked at her watch with purpose.

"So, it's settled—each party knows what has to be done," Van Dent concluded. "Thank you for your time."

They both hung up at the same time.

CHAPTER 18

Cherry watched the livestreaming news in her living room. Over the stretch of one week, the evening news showed the precise trajectory of the water dousing all continents, striking with surgical precision and laser intensity. For Cherry it didn't make sense anymore. The main oil and gas polluters had brought their activities to a hum, some of them even ceased them completely; the mining operations and lumber cutting on all continents followed suit on the basis of healthy financial compensations.

Almost every night, amateur videos showed white flares stroking the darkened sky, ripping the skin that had been holding the water back. It came down, hurried and furious like the flood of old. Though it knew it couldn't replicate the apocalyptic deluge, it was relentless at wiping across the ground, bending aged trees as if they were wisps of willows. The rain let itself be guided by the wind, bending to its will as they were lovers that hadn't felt each other's tender touch in countless years and were only too happy to experience the attention, even if it were a tad abusive.

All this apocalyptic fury should have been tuned-down if water understood that measures were put in place by the society to halt and reverse Earth's degradation.

Instead, people hid in terror. Subway tunnels were turned into modern day cenotes.

It was a fury that lasted long enough to remind those harboring the sneaky thought of conquering water that she remained vigilant and had her own undercover spies.

Cherry mapped the cities that became the main targets of extreme weather, looking for patterns or clues to why the intensity affected them. The chase and the quarrel was—and always had been—with the leaders of either the countries or of corporations who put a price on everything, no matter if it were for sale or not. Cherry was puzzled by how insurance company gurus, perched on the rooftops of their glass towers still standing in most downtown cities, had decided to eradicate any mention of natural disasters from their policies in a sudden switch to survival mode. The dire circumstances called for the elimination of the assets that had turned to liabilities.

The daily destruction of property due to weather calamities was no longer breaking news, like famine in Africa or Palestinians being exterminated in the Middle East.

Teaching limnology courses at the university and going for long hikes through the patches of forest in and around Toronto that were still open to the public made her days bearable. The seasons always seemed to blend into each other in Ontario, which had an extended summer sandwiched between a tiny spring and a protracted winter that was lately snowless but still doled out random spikes of biting cold.

The west riverbank of the East Humber River, going downstream, was still her favorite route. She could notice with each passing year the erosion of the depression storage capacity of the land and an advanced exposure of the stream channel due to lack of precipitations. There was no moisture in the embankment. She could tell by just brushing her hand against the parched soil. Any rainfall would barely wash the surface and flow into the stream as if the unpredicted weather played a game of kiss-and-go with the battered dust.

The disfigurement of the land was laid bare to Cherry's expert eyes. The tree-line receded thirty feet from the river's rut, while the black walnut, shagbark hickory, and sugar maple bargained for the resources of the depleted patch of soil. She noticed an adaptation of the leaf granulation on the trees with a lighter-colored bark and in the brush that collared the trunks on the ground. The local ecosystem complied with the scarcity of water that couldn't find ways to feed the underground pools and reinvigorate the adjacent weak vegetation.

Hayyin, Cherry's hidden identity, was dormant for now, and she had no internal itch to revive the mask that carried so many scars as a result of the Earth's suffering. Over the years, any spill of crude oil in the streams of North Dakota, or in the Niger delta; any intentional chemical sludge dumped in the oceans, or in the rivers close to municipal water sources, drew invisible scars on her psyche. Sometimes Cherry wondered if her involvement with Water for All had been worthless, as the organization's actions could barely keep up with the illicit activities against the environment.

Now and then, desperation from witnessing the shrinking of old growth to insignificant green patches, boastfully called parks, heavily cloaked her for days. It limited her energy to short grocery trips, justifying last minute virtual classes with her limnology students.

The Anonymous Group had let her be Cherry Mortinger, one entity, one mind, for the longest time since they'd first reached out to her seven years ago. Back then, she had been a hobby-driven, green, online journalist, easily lured with a meaty story. It was that first assignment that had put her into the group's friendly clutches. There had been no blackmail or mind-corroding threats—only a sense of duty driving her to continue what the government and corporations had labeled as pernicious behavior that could have landed her in prison for the long-term if caught. Aside from the weather drama unfolding on the world stage in which water played so many characters at once, Cherry kept abreast of the developments Ilanda's team was achieving where the crystal technology was concerned.

Cherry was surprised by what Marinka and Kahuna had accomplished in less than one year through the crystals activated by water, structured by the monks' prayers. It led her to believe that further similar experiences would gather the critical mass of successful interventions and be revealed publicly when those living through them were ready.

Marinka confessed to Cherry how Kahuna, through mental concentration, captured his accumulated knowledge in a water sample brought to him from a pristine spring on the island. Then, the information decoded by the crystal had trickled into her mind. "Ancestral Polynesian wisdom enriched me as the next keeper of our peoples' customs. Saving my father . . . it meant the entire downloading process resumed, but faster this time and more efficient."

Cherry treasured the memory of her trip to Hawaii. Maybe she would take seriously Marinka's offer to move to the island someday. By then, the farmlands damaged by the foreign corporations' farming chemical trials would be restored to their original bloom, and the ocean would sing happily on the notes of its waves, having received a clean bill of health from Mother Nature.

The happiness of potentially moving to paradise made her remember the volcanic rock she had brought back and placed in the backyard near the scaffolding of what used to be her beloved cherry tree.

She lifted her body off of the couch and peeked outside through the open windows. "Superpowers," she said.

Marinka had revealed how the mystery behind each rock oozed from the active mountain under the direct supervision of Pelé, its god. There had been no shuddering changes to the organic configuration of the deserted backyard the last time Cherry had checked. Now, unless the angled flares of the sun were playing a nasty trick on her eyesight, she noticed the timid blades of grass surrounding the black stone. They resembled a beard being emancipated from a teenager boy's face.

She gasped and rushed outside barefoot. The sun's fiery blaze had done little to heat the stone, which was still cold to her touch, like a black hole specialized in sucking up the sun's energy while leaving all matter untouched. It was a phenomenon Cherry wanted to believe had come—as Marinka had said—from the island's god. It was a stone that was conscious and embedded with the gift to offer a second chance.

Along the western wooden fence slightly inclined inward, the once dried bushes of raspberry and parsley planted by her father when he still had the energy and the preoccupation for gardening blossomed in colors reminiscent of a carnival. The greens and reds and the attitude of the stems denoted their health, not to mention a statement of indignation against those who considered them goners.

She let out a long whoop, and her feet danced on invisible notes released by Nature. Cherry snapped several pictures with her phone, so Marinka, Kahuna, and Ilanda could marvel at the wonders within her reach once more, and she went back inside, charged with potentiality.

Would she be able to record her thoughts on the crystal implant? She wondered after settling on the couch with a bowl of coconut ice-cream in her lap. That would be cool! And if she could record the dreams, it would be even better.

Excitement jerked her body straight. Ilanda had no idea yet how many applications her technology might have. The market, as usual, would dictate its use, be it health, entertainment, commercial, or personal.

The implants could transform the humans into a new breed. The alteration, Cherry assessed, would take place publicly, not under military or government restrictive supervision.

Knowing the military sharks were always on the fence and exultant at the prospect of how much they could enhance the project by applying their bottomless funding was enough to force Cherry into panic gear. Real justification for the army's actions was barely questioned by governments. They had a tacit understanding of supporting each other against any public inquiry.

For now, Ilanda and the team had the advantage of being the only ones so advanced on the path of crystal implants, a monopoly of sorts, supported by the Canadian government. And it would stay that way until the weaker politicians were bound to break under pressure of powerful interests to the south or from the world community.

Her cell rang.

"Hey, girl!" Ilanda's AugReality image hailed her from the lab.

"Hi. I see that you don't go home much these days," Cherry said. "It's Sunday, for God's sake!"

"I know, but I couldn't help it. Blame Anonymous this time."

"Really?" Cherry dropped the bowl on the coffee table covered with books and checked her notifications while Ilanda's image hovered over her device. "Damn! I turned it off and forgot about it. How bad is it?"

The neurosurgeon leaned back on her chair and put her feet on her desk.

Cherry paused, examining Ilanda's demeanor. She looked content, for once. The panic was divested of her still, attractive features, and an aura of feminine appeal shone through. Somehow, she must have banished the slander entering her conscious and subconscious minds, and she had surrendered to positive thoughts and motivating choices, influencing her disposition. It took Cherry by surprise.

"You can watch the broadcast later. I can only stay five minutes. What's with the photos?"

"That's the result of a potent volcanic rock I brought back with me from Hawaii. I didn't say anything as it seemed silly. I wanted to see results first, as Marinka had indicated."

"What did it do?"

"Revived the grass, the raspberries, and the parsley. It brought life back into the garden."

"In other words, folklore's stories are true."

"Indeed, the stone accepted its trip to Canada to seed more faith in us. Everything has a soul and purpose."

"And we have to learn how to speak that language or interpret the signs." Ilanda smiled.

Cherry hunched over the device, trying to glean a summary of what Anonymous had unleashed.

"They're about to launch crystal cloud 2.0 based on shungite crystal," Ilanda announced.

Cherry stared back, aware her eyes were open in awe, and her hands frozen in the air in the posture of a child about to play an invisible piano. Would she do the implants? She was questioning herself more often these days, and she still wasn't sure if the enhancement would have the same effect on her as it had on the Hawaiians. Connecting to the shungite crystal cloud, or any crystal cloud for that matter, was appealing, quirky, and beautiful. Scary, exotic, and unsettling at the same time. Setting expectations would have been unwise as she preferred to surrender to the experience. Like during her meditation sessions. She would rather let herself be surprised while discovering unexplored sides of her life and personality.

"The shungite crystal is more versatile than anything we tested before. It pairs beautifully with water," Ilanda said.

"This is one crystal you never experimented with, correct?" Cherry asked.

Ilanda nodded. "Busted. In a follow-up broadcast, Anonymous explained that anyone implanting a shungite crystal would need to bring the frequency of his pineal gland and the one of the implant together. It comes with practice. But when that goal is achieved, one will feel and connect to the frequency of the shungite cloud through the ether, no matter the distance."

Cherry knew this challenge was not for everyone. It required qualities that most people shied away from: persistence and determination.

"The shungite's extraction source," Ilanda continued, "is located in a volatile region, and only someone with Anonymous's virtual reach could have cut a deal with Russia without jeopardizing their personal safety—many of them hiding behind one face."

Cherry sensed her cheeks blossom at the thought of her association with the group. For a moment, she felt left out, but relief overcame her judgment—she didn't have to be their spokesperson for that specific announcement.

"Anyway, the process they came up with . . . it's pretty amazing. I won't spoil the story for you."

"Could you use their approach?" Cherry asked.

"If what they claim is true, only shungite has the right structure to be grated into powder. I doubt they'll share the process. But what my team confirmed is that shungite's filtration process is able to structure water to a purified state with minimal micro-mineral composition and a highly bio-available structure, helping with the coherence between the crystal and the pineal gland."

"That's encouraging," Cherry said. "Maybe DeBoers could get samples based on your specifications. It might not be too late for another trial."

"Are you referring to the medical implants we've lined up?"

"Yes."

"Who will want to wear blackish implants?" Ilanda asked.

"I think they're cool. We could entice Anonymous into a technological swap," Cherry said. She propped her legs on the couch. "Their approach is commercial, as you said: crystal cloud 2.0. Yours is also commercial with a humanitarian component, serving those with medical needs and no financial means. Crystals are expensive, and the end-user or the insurance companies have to pay for it."

"We'll offer Anonymous a cut of the profit!" Ilanda said, finally cracking the riddle Cherry had posed to her.

"Exactly! I'm confident that no persuasion will be necessary—it's a straight-up business transaction."

"All we need is the powder and some middleware software to communicate between our applications and theirs." The neurosurgeon blazed through the words with regained energy.

Ilanda stood up from her desk, looking beyond the 3D transmission, but Cherry couldn't see any one stepping into the virtual image.

"Together with Anonymous, we'll create the crystal cloud 2.0 nation." Cherry beamed. It earned an authentic smile from her friend, who looked up again.

"I have to go now. We'll continue the discussion tomorrow," Ilanda said, and she hung up.

CHAPTER 19

The wind seemed to recognize Maahes's scent—lavender with a whiff of alcohol—and the swag in his walk. It slowed its race to the other end of the narrow, stony beach and stilled itself as if obeying an invisible red traffic light on a deserted street put in place for the safety of just-born breezes that needed room and encouragement to grow in speed, intensity, and direction.

Surprised by the hot yet loving embrace like that of a lover from a distant realm, Maahes broke his walk, closed his eyes, and inhaled deeply. There were no more waves beating the cement levee, no desperate caws of seagulls searching for their nests on the moonless night. There was only the candid grasp of Ilanda's impetuous appetite for caring for him while they were still running their lives from one refugee camp to the next.

Would she forgive him if he ever appeared to her, bearded, and spitting the excuse that he had staged his death to protect her and his extended family in Egypt from the repercussions of destroying Water Vivus Inc.? Maybe not. She was too feisty to let go of what she would see as a sinister joke.

Maahes kissed Ilanda's cheeks in his imagination. That and her forehead and narrow chin. His puckered lips awaited a reciprocal response, but his imagination fell short of creating it. He smiled instead of showing disappointment, convinced that his intentions—or the vibration of them—would soon reach her in Toronto, propelled by the wind that had decided to let go of him and continue on its way.

Maahes didn't need an encryption key for his immaterial message of love, nor did he worry that malware installed on his former wife's cell would intercept the subtle declaration that only she would sense.

The night walk comforted him. It kept him away from seeing his new look reflected in shiny surfaces. Life's perspective had added a new degree of mobility since the *emeralds* had been swapped for the *brownies*. What had attracted most of his lovers to him like a tongue glued to a frozen metal pole had been the intensity of his green eyes, and they were now destroyed. Had they been *re-used*, they would have triggered an alert of magnificent proportions, divulging his well-planned stratagem.

He should have been elated now that the first stride on the thorny path of assuming a new identity had been achieved, but there were still jittery moments when he visualized himself transformed, an enhanced version of what Ilanda thought had been buried in Egypt almost two years before.

Doubt that he wouldn't get the implants had vanished from his daily worries the moment a local contact had confirmed his name was on the list of the critically ill. And the *brownies* would match the ID, providing access to the crystals and connection to the cloud, be it 1.0 or 2.0. He didn't care much about which version he would be compatible with. The news on 2.0 had sent tremors of excitement throughout the world and bets on the crystals' vibrational affinity with one another took over social media chatter. He had even grown bolder, opting to lease a more potent crystal in favor of the white ones. Buying it outright would have potentially raised questions up the chain of command, as his ID portrait was of a farmer with financial limitations.

Travel restrictions would still apply to his fresh identity, though threading closer to Ilanda remained on his mind despite the added risks of being exposed.

Next on his to-do list was to have Marian begin a pressure campaign, targeting Ilanda's confidence to get an implant herself. That additional burden might crack her composure and ambition for her to join the cloud to use as their virtual meeting place—safe and private.

Technicalities of such an environment escaped Maahes's understanding, and he counted on Marian for details clarifying if an avatar or its real identity might be used in the cloud. The debates he heard around concerns of safety, addiction to the permanent umbilical-like connection, and societal discrepancies between the haves and have-nots didn't change his desire for enhancement. The same stern discussions and panels subjected psychologists, politicians, spiritual leaders, and empaths to contradictory opinions, similar to those disseminated on issues far less essential than crystal implants.

Using an avatar would provide the necessary privacy, functioning like a veil covering the face of a Scheherazade courtesan—mysterious and enticing, leaving people yearning for the features cloaked behind the delicate fabric.

Reconnecting with Ilanda while impersonating a re-birthed Maahes was the only strategy his reclusive mind could fathom. He wanted her presence more than anything material he had possessed in his past life. He missed the tussle of words, the ardent love of their marriage that had faded with age and the ambition of a higher social status, and the indirect education she provided each time water—and most recently, crystals—stumbled into their conversation.

Following Maahes's advice, Marian hadn't found proof of Ilanda's being romantically involved with anyone, and that lack of evidence fueled a blaze inside him. It would make her ferocious inside when he opened up about the insidious manipulation he had choreographed for her: faking his death as CEO of Water Vivus Inc., the lab funding, the media leak about the Canadian government interfering with the crystal technology, the first insurance company to back the implants, and even his latest trap, the one that would push her into the crystal cloud.

Revealing these misdeeds could lose her for a second time. It might also bring them together if love and desire still smoldered in her heart. Maahes had divested her of a partner. Though he wasn't completely reliable, he was her husband, and she had had no say in the matter.

The lack of an avatar would make him more cautious, and the fear of being identified through familiar gestures might spoil an otherwise flawless performance.

Random waves, too weak to remove even the pebbles beneath his feet, grazed his toes like a subservient sidekick asking for forgiveness. Close to the huts of the open market at the end of the beach, the bonfires crackled in countless sparks, enchanted by the drumming of near-possessed singers. Burnt incense filtered through his nostrils, overpowering the wet, salty smell of the ocean. In the movies, the murderer always wound up going back to the crime scene. This seemed counter-intuitive and ended in the most unexpected ways.

He was playing that character now, incapable of controlling the thoughts nudging him to the brink of his own crime scene. He was heading for an obvious ambush, carefully devised in his mind as he waited meekly for the undeniable result: a failed rekindled romance with Ilanda and shameful exposure.

Water had brought them together the first time in a rich, fluid relationship as a couple. She had stored the memories, jubilant and bitter, of each of their dramas like a court reporter recording depositions from all parties involved.

This time, it was the crystals' turn to facilitate their reunion with their wonderful, amazing storage capabilities. Another one of Earth's miracles that had originated over billions of years, its pristine structure recording the cycles of evolution as a backup plan that water was charged to document.

The ink of night blurred the swing of his hand as it held his shoes, and Maahes, saturated with thoughts of worry and the overlapping scents in the air, confined his steps toward the parking lot. The exciting near-future he anticipated had its drawbacks, but courage and grit should help extinguish them.

CHAPTER 20

They were at Ojani's apartment after a night of torrid romantic engagement. The platonic interaction they had both enjoyed had suddenly and passionately erupted like a jolt to a junkie's vein.

Imperceptible signs of her age presented themselves a shy second later—the flesh on the back of her arms, and breasts whose firmness was mostly a thing of the past. It wasn't her physical aspects that aroused Ojani so intensely, but her undeterred devotion for science through water and crystals, a combination that had ignited a unique perception in the medical field. He was a visionary, too, one that had never found his match.

Ilanda's head rested in Ojani's wide-open palm. He used his index finger as a writing tool on her naked body. She giggled at his jokes like a teenage girl impressed by an older partner. Only the roles had switched: Ojani was the younger one in this romantic relationship that had grown unexpectedly out of their love for crystals and from a reciprocal fondness that neither of them could or wanted to explain.

Intense and consuming she was, and Ojani marveled at the lowlands, gorges, and flat plains that gave shape to her body. The same naughty finger pushed gently toward her legs and turned left, avoiding giving her pleasure again. No ink escaped from his ebony finger on the blankness of her pearly skin, but Ojani's imagination was already writing a love story that would remain embossed on that noteworthy page until the end of his days.

The exploration trip, his first after that passionate night, moved down to her left calf. Muscles tensed, tickled by the soft touch. He went lower, deep to her sole. She could no longer stay still for his probing.

She covered his lips with hers, leeches hungry for blood pouncing on his mouth. Ilanda moaned when he pressed against her, and she relaxed unconditionally.

Ojani pushed Ilanda onto her back again, and their lips welded together as if obeying a mental vow. Regret that the moment hadn't come earlier to them was futile. It had been organic, explosive, and it had manifested at a juncture in the fabric of time where their needs aligned. Because of this, it might last either in the open for the team to marvel at or in the privacy they would build on their own terms.

There is no shame in honest love, Ojani had always thought. The bottom part of the wall-sized, red-tinted windows in his apartment changed their nuance as the intensity of the sun increased, absorbing the energy to satisfy a percentage of his apartment's electricity needs. The unobstructed light bloomed on Ilanda's features, making the fractals of her capillaries more visible, a faint gradation of her intense blue eyes.

"Don't let yourself be blackmailed, eh" Ojani said, lost in the glow she emanated.

"What do you mean?"

"Getting the implants. You don't have to prove anything. It's just irritating noise, eh."

She pulled him closer, her legs tangling around him like a carnivorous flower securing her prey. Her languorous smile did nothing to capture the tension he knew she was under.

Media reports, government declarations in public, and staged or impromptu gatherings across the world targeted Ilanda and her team as the only gatekeepers of the desired technology.

"I'm tougher than you think," she said, and she bit his chin with her lips as if it was a ripe pear.

Her breasts squished against his chest, filling him with warmth and boiling blood.

For a moment, he couldn't remember what he had been worried about. Their bodies lying side by side on the checkered bedsheet seemed like opposite pawns waiting to be moved by superior forces.

"This is all you love about me: my eyes?" she inquired.

"Yes," he replied, his lips puckered to tease her a bit.

"I'll implant an agate or an apatite[11], so you won't be able to tell the difference."

He smiled in spite of himself. "I always will, eh" Ojani said, somehow knowing that, pressured or not, Ilanda would eventually have to comply with the trend she had initiated.

"Shungite is the best. You heard Anonymous," she said. "It's versatile, scalable, and water-friendly, as far as atmospheric humidity is concerned."

"Black goes well with your complexion," he said, giving in. "You've tested my primitive crystal technology and didn't fall over what you experienced—"

"I never told you what I—"

"I sensed that your expectations were high, eh. At that time, you had your own theory about how the crystal implants should work and wanted to try the crude version of the technology I was using, eh."

"It wasn't like that," Ilanda muttered, unconvincingly.

"A neurosurgeon of your caliber needs to be thrilled by such an experience, and . . . your eyes said otherwise after the session was over, eh."

"But most of your clients got a kick out of it," she said. "You don't have to mind an insignificant percentage of those like me."

Ojani assumed she'd meant it as a justification, but it sounded more like an excuse. "I provided tangible experiences. I never thought that a handful of my clients would cross into realms of increased consciousness. Is this what you were looking for, eh?" he asked.

Ilanda entangled her fingers in his chest hair; it was a form of play he let her enjoy. "Definitely something stronger than what I got," she said, coming clean. "I wasn't expecting to break the barrier on my first try, anyway." She paused, her gaze locked onto his.

"You were about to say something hurtful, and you're not sure if you should do it, correct, eh?"

Ilanda nodded.

"Go ahead. I'm over what that aged technology stood for. We both know its limitations."

"You love me too much to get offended; I understand that. And I love you back, so I'll keep my mouth shut. It's all in the past."

"Are Marinka or Kahuna experiencing changes of any kind, eh?" he asked.

"They look content every time I call. They're stingy with words. Kahuna barely addresses me. He speaks only when I ask him questions he can't avoid. Is he aware of the awkwardness of his altered voice, eh?"

"Maybe, but there is something else I can't figure out," she said, hitting her thigh gently as if simulating frustration.

"Could that be the increased level of consciousness you so much wanted to achieve, eh?"

"Maybe," she said. "Consciousness is energetic information stored in the molecular structure of the water inside our bodies. The transfer between consciousness and water happens with a high degree of coherence and no loss of data. The structured water we used to activate the crystals that brought back most of his brain and body functionality could have triggered certain areas in the brain. His brain's readings show a wave pattern of emotional stability, reduced anxiety, coherence of the heart rate, and a strong immune system."

Ilanda kissed his shoulder. The skin there burned as if she were branding him, claiming him as hers forever.

Morning light reflected on the thin layer of perspiration, turning the woman into a mermaid, smelling of salt and the desire to be possessed.

"Is the team working this weekend, eh?" Ojani asked. He was focused on memorizing the fine details of her body. Lingering in Ilanda's embrace was soothing, as if she were a loving cradle he'd missed viscerally since his grandparents had passed away. Deep affection and empathy had so far been lacking from the brief romantic encounters in which he'd engaged.

"No, everyone is taking this Saturday off. We crammed additional shungite experiments in a three-week timeframe, and we are pretty burnt."

"Don't we need more people to run tests on crystal compatibility and post-intervention monitoring, now that we expect the patients from Germany and North Bay? You can't do this work on your own. You have to let it go, eh."

Ilanda changed her position, and the sun's rays shone on her breasts instead of her face. "I've decided to reach out to my former hospital interns. They've agreed to fulfill that task. There's no more conflict of interest, since I've left both the hospital and the university, and they can claim it as an internship job."

He nodded, glad that she'd finally thought about delegating a significant burden from her daily list. He thought of putting in a bid for some of that freed time.

"Security clearance has been initiated, and Nanette helped me finalize the post-intervention proceedings," Ilanda said.

Ojani's stomach growled like thunder triggered by a faraway approaching storm. They both giggled at the same time, and Ilanda patted his belly to calm the hidden beast.

"Omlet with veggies, bread and butter, cereal with mixed nuts, and of course, you can have my coffee, eh," Ojani said, listing items on his preferred breakfast menu.

He straightened his back, ready to get out of bed to prepare the meal for them, but Ilanda pulled him back, her ardent kiss sending a spike of energy through his body. He was malleable in her embrace, like a piece of plasticine in the hands of a child. He wasn't sure what she would knead out. He hoped for a better version of himself, one that would fully understand her needs and match her frequency.

"Let's do the implants together," she blurted as if an invisible adviser perched on her shoulder had waited for the exact moment to drop the thought on her.

Ojani stared at his newfound love, knowing that a quick reply was desirable before the moment turned awkward. "You name the time and place, and I'll be there, eh," he half-joked.

What she suggested wasn't child's play but a consequential life change that would last until the end of his days. Marinka and Kahuna had done it out of mutual love, respect, and support. It was a blood-bond between them. Ilanda and he would do it based on shared values—love was the leading reason on the ballot.

"Bread and butter with veggies on the side," Ilanda said, propping herself up higher against the metal headboard. "And I gladly accept your sacrifice . . . your coffee." She let out a round of boisterous laughter.

Seeing her glow made him happy. Ilanda's words floated toward him as if on an incandescent wave of energy that was almost palpable. His skin tingled when it made contact with her words, and he shuddered to maintain his composure.

Ojani was halfway off the bed, his left leg hanging over the edge, not sure if he should turn himself back into the dutiful plasticine and mold to the muscular body lying beside him or march toward the kitchen. His mind scrambled to find a little bit of 'me-time.'

"I'll be feeding you in less than ten minutes. Don't get a sunburn, eh," he said, and he pulled the bedsheet over her naked body.

Ilanda purred like an overly-spoiled cat, the only child to a bachelor who would put his life on hold to tend to her needs.

Ojani wrapped himself in the plush robe hanging on the chair.

When Ilanda's cell vibrated on the nightstand, she peeked at the display. "'Would you share the next steps? Is the gov still on-board with the

exclusivity?'" she read out loud. "It's from the silent investor. It's the second message in a week. I can't ignore it anymore, even if additional funding isn't required."

"Take care of it until I'm done," Ojani said, and he went to the kitchen. "Do you think the investor will even show his face at the lab to meet you, eh?" he called to her while gathering the ingredients.

He cleaned the tomatoes and the cucumbers in the air jet device, then sliced them on a large plate. "He's anxious for a healthy return on his investment. I've been in those shoes, as well, eh," he said over the low noise of the brewing coffee. He coated the toasted bread with a thick layer of butter and loaded everything on a metal tray decorated with Buddhist symbols, a gift from Tenzin.

He found her dictating a reply to her benefactor.

"It's done," she said, and she extended her arms to receive the breakfast, shamelessly keeping her upper-body exposed. It was a boldness Ojani savored like the whiff of his favorite vegan dish, crusted fried tofu on a layer of spinach, tomatoes, and avocado.

"What did you tell the investor, eh?"

She placed the tray on the bed next to her and gestured for Ojani to sit on the other side as if they were following the custom of a long-time marriage.

He felt content and quite happy to oblige.

"I repeated whatever is already in the public domain and added an update on the franchise locations and DeBoers's production status."

"That should fuel his imagination on how healthy the returns on his money will be and it will keep him happy for a while," Ojani said.

He pulled up his pillow and leaned against the headboard, almost touching Ilanda's shoulder. "You didn't hear me from the kitchen when I asked if you expect the investor to show up at the lab for a tour, eh."

"Why would he reveal his identity now?" She forced the words while chewing on a slice of bread. "But if the guy's an eccentric, who knows? He might come over to pick up his check in person."

The vegetables and toast disappeared fast. When she was done, Ilanda moved the tray to the floor by the door, returned to bed, and crawled over him like water on a fractured rock—possessive, relentless, and determined to find its way to the other side.

She disrobed him gently. Ojani had the impression that he was melting under a rash of pleasure when she touched his lips and the inside of his leg. It was smooth and with a tinge of orange, which is why some people called him Orange, the nickname he had while in school.

"We need to find a way to Anonymous," Ilanda said, curled over half of his naked body.

"Why?"

"I'm done with wasting time on more shungite tests. They have to share some of their research with us."

"Are you thinking about our commitment to getting the implants, eh?" Ojani asked, his hand caressing her neck.

"It's selfish, I know, but I want the right stuff for us and others, too."

"There's no rush, dear."

Her gaze seemed to implode with love and gratitude. "Cherry suggested a commercial transaction benefiting both sides. It could work."

Ojani perceived her body swelling with emotion from the thought of that achievement. "Nothing could stop you, eh. I'm here to provide whatever support you might need."

Ilanda moaned faintly. He could tell she felt safe in his arms by what her unconditional surrender. Protecting her gave him purpose, the same way caring for his parents had while they were still alive.

He let her nap on his chest as if she were a newborn secure in the cradle of her mother's arms.

CHERRY WOULDN'T TAKE NO for an answer when she invited Ilanda for a walk at the Harbourfront Centre by Lake Ontario. Water relaxed her, and the ripples smashing onto the cemented shore camouflaged the sound of traffic running one hundred feet behind her.

The strange behavior of water that started almost two years ago that some associated with an awakening had interfered intimately with the city life. The potable water restrictions dipped by ten percent on the fear that any harmful molecular changes in Lake Ontario won't be reversed at the water treatment plant level through the known processes and filtration phases, thus affecting the population. As a limnologist, Cherry joined the team that spent months of careful monitoring of the effluents and the lake itself, revealing only minimal increase in the water's pH, density, and heavy metals concentration, below the harmful levels. Even after the scientists and the professionals had confirmed the safety of water sources, the municipality locked the restrictions in with no explanation. Everyone adjusted. Cherry had too. And like most of the other city dwellers, she feared the sudden thunderstorms that grew into tornadoes in the vicinity of downtown and the prolonged weeks of sand blast brought in from Africa by the changing winds. Usually, an official announcement in weather respite would fill in the parks, the sports fields, and the forest trails still open to the public.

As a protection measure, the University of Toronto had agreed to virtual classes. Cherry missed the in-person interaction with her limnology students and their energy that fed hers more than she thought.

Water was still feared. That fact stayed drilled in everyone's mind like a dormant virus with no antidote. The ferries had halted their thirteen-minute trip to the park on Toronto Island and its beaches. The yacht club on the island had closed down as well. Its sleek glass and metal building looked over the empty slips at the marina through the scandalous growth of vegetation, freed from the gardener's daily trim. Monthly online video postings taken by police drones provided proof that the place had not been vandalized by an illegal crossing. Tight monitoring of the shoreline prevented boats from being launched on the water, no matter the reason.

The entanglement of the vines and branches crept closer to the wooden deck that had hosted the club's summer social parties, and

Cherry had heard in the news that the board of directors was ready to helicopter in a landscaping company over the stretch of water to reclaim the property from the wild. For some, the image and status of the club remained paramount, no matter if the world was in a time of crisis.

"Found you!"

Cherry got off the bench and embraced Ilanda, who was still wearing the black wig. A beaming smile, like a colorized black and white photograph, gave her an aura of confidence lost shortly after social media had pestered her with fake news fed by anonymous interests.

"You look fabulous!" Cherry said. "Have you found an elixir in the structured water you're dealing with? You should tell me which sample it is."

Ilanda chortled and sat down.

"An elixir, yes, but not in the water—it's called love."

Cherry's mouth made an odd sound like it had been covered with duct tape to prevent the spilling of invectives or trade secrets, and someone had pulled it away.

"What? Do you think I'm not capable of falling in love again? Or maybe it's that I can't be loved." Ilanda's tone was serious, but the smile stuck on her lips, stubborn, as if it had been drawn on with a permanent marker.

"No doubt about that!"

"I still miss Maahes, you know? But I need a tinge of happiness in my life."

Cherry nodded, her vocal cords stunned to silence by the confession. She wasn't sure who the new man in Ilanda's life was, and a blunder on her part might have spoiled her positive attitude.

"I'd dry up on my own. Without a social life or a warm body to wake up with, I'd wither away. It's not what I imagined for myself."

Ilanda gazed across the water, lingering on the couples pushing strollers, their toddlers hanging onto their mothers' hips. Reality passed by, a reality so foreign to both of them. Ilanda was childless and a widow. The sheen of her public persona as a result of her medical titles and the experience she'd accumulated were her biggest achievements thus far.

Cherry had almost followed suit with a couple of exceptions of her own: she'd never married or intended to, and only her hidden identity as Hayyin, if revealed, could have come closer to her friend's public recognition.

Now's not the time to be a downer.

"Who's the honey?" Cherry asked.

Ilanda yanked jokingly at Cherry's hand as a punishment for the direct question.

"No more foreplay? Yay!" The striking grin reappeared on her face.

Cherry inhaled the scent of the water. It was as if it had sent a fine mist to eavesdrop on their conversation. T*he discussion was being recorded by the water and stored away*. Where are you taking our words? How can you sustain the pronounced dualism of our lives? Don't you get tired of witnessing the humans' same evolutionary cycles? Ilanda moved her lips, but Cherry couldn't make out any words as if water read her thoughts and blocked any interference. How can we unlock your memory? We need your long-term memory, she almost begged silently.

"I really feel great these days." Ilanda's voice penetrated the haze of her mind.

Cherry stroke her friend's left hand, hoping for a full confession without much effort on her part. She wasn't snooping around for details about how fantastic the sex was or how gentle and attentive the man had pretended to be the next day. A clean, straight, out-of-the-box statement would suffice—name, occupation, age—data to feed a graph of desirability Cherry had created for herself as an amusing initiative.

A passing cloud masked the sun for a few seconds. Cyclist's bells pierced their ears as they passed. The throng of people traveling in both directions parted like metal fillings under the pull of a magnet. The cyclists were organized into smaller family groups with father, mother, sons, and daughters. The children's helmets made them look like hardheaded ducklings following their parents, bells chirping. That wasn't her reality, either.

"It's Ojani."

That was all the data Cherry needed, encapsulated into a single word. Could she prevent any further details from coming? For once, she regretted her status as confidant as with each new revelation her burden grew heavier turned into another burden, conflicting with her own. She couldn't open up to anyone about Hayyin, his mission, his achievements, and how it encumbered on her persona.

"Popcorn?" Cherry said, stopping Ilanda's potential flow of information, pointing to a teenager carrying a tray of popcorn-filled paper bags. She snapped her fingers to draw his attention, scanned her chip of his portable reading device, and snatched two bags from his tray. "It's probably GMO-ed, but let's celebrate." She took a mouthful.

Ilanda hovered her fingers over the top layer, undecided. "Surprised?" she asked.

Cherry chewed harder and tried to line up her words. "Retrospectively? No. I've noticed him looking at you in that way, but I can't imagine it's love," she finally said. "I'm happy the romantic drought is over for you."

Ilanda placed a kernel in her mouth gently, as if afraid of how it might taste. "It's an intellectual match. We're both crystal and water lovers. In a nutshell, it's what brought us together."

"Water brought you and Maahes together, too," Cherry said without thinking. She choked when trying to apologize, sputtering out half-chewed kernels on the ground, like ripped flower petals in a game of "He Loves Me, He Loves Me Not." None of them carried any water, so Cherry struggled with the cough for another minute, feeling disoriented and lightheaded. She bent forward, ready for another bout to fire up her lungs. Kernels from the bag had spilled all around them, and seagulls surrounded the area as they fought over them. The irate squabbling drew everyone's attention. Toddlers ran from their parents, trying to catch the flapping birds. A boy with curly hair picked up a kernel, put it in his palm, and waited. A white flurry of birds stormed over the little guy like he was holding the last scrap they would ever eat.

"No need to apologize," Ilanda said. "Take it easy."

Passersby kicked the popcorn, tossing it around, sending it farther away from their bench.

"Look, I'm aware he's much younger, and infatuation might play a big part in this romance," the neurosurgeon continued, checking for a reaction.

"There's no judging on my part. And by the way, I don't think Ojani is infatuated with you—he really loves you." With the cough gone, Cherry had brought herself back to a slow talk, filtering her words through mental coding she hoped would choose wisely on her behalf. *Maybe the crystal implants would, indeed, turn them into AI entities to better guide their physical bodies.*

"So, this isn't just in my mind? Could it possibly work between the two of us?"

"Age is irrelevant, my dear. Happiness evades most of us, and when we find it, we question if we deserve it."

"Lack of confidence, I assume."

"Yes, among other things. Lack of confidence and self-esteem are somehow ingrained in our DNA—unchanged, unapologetic, and freakishly stubborn in accepting any change," Cherry said. She stood up and went to trash the partially empty bag of popcorn.

Ilanda cocked her head to the side as if trying to hide her eyeglass-covered face from the sun.

"There is no happiness in hiding it," Cherry continued in a bolder tone, crafting a subliminal message for her friend who picked up on it immediately.

"Rule number one: don't get romantically involved with a work colleague. I've already trashed that one."

"Did you really enforce that rule with the team?"

"No, it's common sense. At the hospital, the university—they all know it," Ilanda said. She turned toward the water where police drones hovered, scanning the crowd.

For a moment, Cherry fancied the opposite of what Ilanda had on display in the torrid, late summer day, her straight body frame, proudly fashioning a wide-open, white silk blouse through which her unapologetically Hokuto-apple-sized breasts pushed forward.

"Good for you. I mean, Ojani. Don't doubt it, not even for a second. Short- or long-term, it could be the solid relationship that both of you need," Cherry said.

She followed Ilanda's gaze over the water toward the island and the Billy Bishop Airport, deserted if it weren't for the limited flights still allowed to land and take off on a weekly basis.

"You suggest an open-book approach, then? And only with the team, correct?"

"Yes. The team deserves to be aware of your relationship. It's not an encouragement for them to mingle romantically, but it shows trust on your part." After seeing Ilanda look down, Cherry continued, "And yes, you tell Ojani that this is the smart thing to do."

"So, he has no say?" Ilanda asked with a hue of disappointment in her voice. "We're also business partners."

"This was your team first. It's more yours than his," Cherry said bluntly, but her voice carried the affection of a friend. She put her handbag down, a colorful sack she had bought from a Colombian craftsman at a flea market, and moved closer to Ilanda in a gesture that was unthreatening but meant to make her point heard.

"This is the type of delicate situation in which the woman's reputation is more important than the man's ego. Repeat that mentally."

She received a nod back, timid, like the head of a snowdrop flower peeking through the snow at the end of winter.

"Your privacy won't be jeopardized. The team is as tight as a small T-shirt on a bodybuilder."

Ilanda cracked a melodious laugh and tilted her head high as if she had made her decision. She wavered between gloom and gushing with such ease. It was an emotional roller coaster that, though it wasn't necessarily a measure of her health, Cherry decided to check on her friend in the days to come.

"There's more," Ilanda said.

"You're getting married!"

"We're not *that* crazy," the doctor blurted. "In love, yes, but we're still responsible."

They looked up at the wave of seagulls circling overhead again, looking for another easy bounty. The flock flew toward the street where food carts lined up for an annual multi-cultural festival.

"We're getting the implants. The shungites."

Shock embraced Cherry like a cold, wet blanket forgotten overnight after being left outside to dry. It gave her shivers that only the thought of a world without water could do. "Why the rush?"

"I'm the doctor who created the trend for Pete's sake!" Ilanda flared back defensively. "Do I really need a reason?"

"No, you don't need one. It's only that I was expecting you'd hold on a bit longer."

"If I do it now, all the rumors, the attacks on the team, might cease. It'll show my confidence in the technology."

In the middle of the hustle around them, Ilanda put her head on her knees. "Don't start crying on me," Cherry said, trying a soft joke while patting Ilanda on the back. It hadn't been intended to help her to burp up gases, but to release her anxiety and frustration that had built-up in multiple layers like the soil in an ancient forest—pine needles, leaves, nuts, and the broken branches that formed the same sandwich over and over again, a humus of high-quality feeding on the under- and over-story alike. Her friend was the perfect example of a professionally-accomplished, spirituality-starved, socially-deprived human being who felt pulled in all directions, spinning in place, and being tossed around like a fuzz ball in the wind.

Ilanda was a speck in the collective trauma, characterizing the level of society's consciousness—wars, famine, water scarcity, and climate pollution were permanent blisters and bruises on the face of the Earth that could not be removed, even with a proper diet and the occasional meditation session.

"I haven't tried happiness in a while," Ilanda mumbled from her folded position, "and getting the implants isn't a condition, you know. I . . . I feel like it's the right thing to do."

"Honestly, it crossed my mind the other day that I should be enrolled, too."

"Really?" Ilanda raised her head, the black locks of her wig pressing against her reddened cheeks as if she were just awakened from a mesmerizing dream.

"The government forced the chips on us, but this time it has to be my decision, and for the right reasons," Cherry said. "Kahuna was an inspiration for me, before and after the explosion. And you know how much I respect Marinka."

"The shungite, as well?"

"Yes. Its versatility in moisture-rich air convinced me," Cherry said. It would have been ungracious for her to mention a list of cons, so she let it pass. In her mind, the statement was non-committal. It was nothing but an intention, an option she might exercise—or not—in the near future.

"Have you set a date yet?" she asked.

"For the implants?"

Cherry shrugged in confirmation as if exhausted by the effort she had put into consoling her friend.

"Not yet. It's been less than two days since we agreed that we'd do it. Details have yet to be ironed out," Ilanda said, spacing out her last words like a spoiled child asking for forbidden candies.

It was a necessary breather for Cherry, who was facing her first body alteration, and an irreversible one, at that. It wasn't like a dragon tattoo that might fade into a blotch of paint, resembling a birthmark over time. Would she perceive water in the same way? Would her crystal implant take away her ability to decide at the fork in the road between the evolution of consciousness and stagnation? Would she really turn into an AI with human personality, a transhuman? Will this transformation ever allow her borrow Hayyin's identity? That second identity had its own scars and nightmares from battles fought by previous owners in times long forgotten. Cherry had taken on the burden of the fight symbolized by Hayyin's mask. Now, the fight was for water, environment, and survival. Later on, who knows? What else would be left to fight for? The world had faith in Hayyin's intentions and his sources of information, and that was motivation enough for Cherry to jump back into that skin at any time, even after the crystal implants would settle in.

"Who's providing the shungite crystals?" she asked.

"I spoke with DeBoers in South Africa today," Ilanda said. "They've never anticipated that shungite would become such a desirable commodity. No one had. They're scrambling for a back door contact in Russia."

"If they succeed, the price tag will be astronomical. It's not worth it."

"What's the alternative?"

"Anonymous, as we discussed last week. Let me put some feelers out to them." Cherry would fill the ranks of the artificially altered contingent of people for which skin color, political affinity, place of birth, and sexual orientation were irrelevant. You want it, you can afford it, you got it. That was how fortunes were amassed in previous centuries.

Cherry imagined herself picketing the insurance company's office, the one that offered her benefits package through the university, and pressuring them into adding coverage for crystal implants to its policies. Maybe the lack of affordability would be justification enough for a prolonged postponement. She didn't want to call in any favors with Ilanda and the team. At least, not on this one, anyway.

She might even move to Hawaii for a while after the implants were in to train with Marinka and Kahuna on telepathy and other mind games they might have discovered since she met them.

"That would be an awesome achievement," Ilanda said. "Getting an answer from Anonymous." She pushed the locks of her wig behind her ears.

"Why did you ask me here?"

Cherry was taken aback by her friend's radiant look and had forgotten that she was the one who had initiated the call. She might have said, "*I want to know if Maahes has contacted you lately. I think he's still alive*," under different circumstances, but she didn't want to spoil the romance upon which Ilanda had stumbled. She needed a divergent strategy to lure Maahes or his replacement out, and Cherry had to think of what that might be.

"Water for All never stopped looking for donations," she said instead. "Even if the major polluters have ceased operations, the cleanup has to be done, and the policies through which they have contributed financially are still works in progress. We can't wait for them any longer."

"How can I help?" Ilanda asked.

"I was thinking that when the partnership was stinking rich—which would happen soon—it could give back a little," Cherry said. She extended her arms laterally, letting the wind enter the openings of her T-shirt and play on her skin—what a liberating feeling.

Ilanda imitated the gesture. Her body reminded Cherry of the mast of a sixteenth-century galleon with sails unfurled.

"Ojani and I will be happy to show our generosity. Without WFA's initial contribution, things wouldn't have happened so fast."

"Don't you have to check with the silent investor as well?"

"No. He gets his share. What we do with ours is none of his business," Ilanda said, and she brought her arms back to her knees. "I'm glad you used the pretense of discussing a delicate question to force me out of the lab. It's nice out here when the weather cooperates. They've announced strong winds tomorrow." She inhaled several times. The street performers throwing balls in the air while balancing on unicycles caught her attention.

Ilanda's eyes lowered to the circle of kids, watching them in awe.

"Do you want to get closer and learn a juggling trick?" Cherry asked. She sparked a laugh at her own suggestion.

"Why not? We might need to perform them in the lab to keep our sanity," Ilanda said, but she didn't move, her body only half-turned toward the action.

A couple with arched backs and silvery hair approached them on the bench. Small steps followed the cadence of the metal canes, giving them the confidence of a secure walk. Pergamentose skin stretched on their compressed faces beneath eyeglasses made from thin metal wire. Cherry caught the man looking at them and nudged Ilanda with her elbow.

"It's time to go," she said and stood up. "Others need a warm seat."

They waited until the old couple had reached them, securing the bench from being snatched by more agile bodies.

The man nodded at them and helped his wife to sit.

"I'll let the team know about Ojani and me, and our decision to get the implants," Ilanda said.

"That's the right thing to do," Cherry said, reiterating her earlier statement. "I'll ping you as soon as Anonymous shows any interest in our offer."

They walked north toward the glass canyon of downtown towers. Only skinny, intense ribbons of light touched the pavement, forcing the rare passerby into the shade of the buildings. It was an elegant city, pelted day and night by capricious weather. A two-day stretch was all the weatherman could report on, making his job security precarious.

The women parted ways at the entrance to the PATH[21], the tunnels running under the city's core.

CHAPTER 21

"This fundraising campaign is going places," Octana said. She raised her gaze briefly from her tablet to see if Nanette followed. She clucked her tongue a couple of times, a tick that annoyed the team when things got tense in the lab, but now, in the bustle of their favorite coffee shop at King and Parliament, Nanette barely took stock of it.

"What campaign?"

"A YouTuber chick, Crazy Velvet, is raising money for her crystal implants—three hundred and fifty G's!"

"What? It doesn't cost that much. How does she justify that request?" Nanette moved her chair to the same side of the table as Octana. Her hair, left untangled from the usual ponytail that reached her waist, floated behind her.

"She's going to draw two names from her followers' list and use the money to pay for their implants plus expenses for post-implant recovery. It includes living expenses, a shrink, additional medical intervention if required, insurance premiums, and the list goes on. She will pay for her implants herself."

"What does she do on YouTube?"

"Records intimate scenes in a green-room studio and matches

them with special AugReality algorithms to customize backgrounds, partners, and any other flavor of kinkiness one might want. It looks darn exceptional."

"Four million seven hundred and forty-six thousand followers—why did I go to university?" Nanette scratched her head.

"It's a subscription-based channel. Five bucks per month. These numbers are too big for me," Octana said.

"Click on the promo video."

Octana did, and the video started to play. *"I'm Crazy Velvet," the woman said, "and I've decided to enhance myself with a pair of quality crystal implants. This fundraising campaign will pay for two lucky fans to have similar work done on them, and then we can connect our minds on the cloud for a threesome experience."*

"She's pretty clean looking, you know," Nanette said over the harsh voice of the YouTube star. She wore no tattoos or piercings of any kind other than dark purple, elephant-shaped earrings that matched the color of her inch-long hair. She had an aura that sucked people into her fantasies, heightened by the purple contact lenses and harshly contoured lips in her signature color.

Crazy Velvet continued, "I'm willing to pay double if I'm allowed to broadcast the whole process live—"

"Did you know about this?" Nanette asked, her face on fire.

"No. I've only been following the numbers. She might have come up with this idea recently, after she saw that her financial goal had been reached."

"Ilanda might remove her from the list. She doesn't like to be pressured, you know."

"On what grounds?" Octana took a bite from the croissant at the side of her tablet and scrolled down the screen. Nanette saw her stop at the comments section.

"If she needs one reason, I'd bet that 'not-an-emergency' is at the top of her list, you know. She could claim that medical cases have priority, and we don't have enough resources to do these kinds of publicity stunts," Nanette said.

"And that would be a mistake."

"You know Ilanda—"

"Look at all these thumbs-up," Octana said. "We can't beat Crazy at her own masterfully created game. She could unleash a tidal wave against us that would be more damaging than all of the previous fake news."

She clucked her tongue again and rapped her fingernails on the tabletop as if challenging Nanette's patience.

"So, money can buy anything? Do we want to, you know, sanction such a perception?"

"It's already ingrained in our DNA."

"We could be the exception," Nanette said, her back straightening in an unconscious defense measure.

"I really don't care if Ilanda accepts or not. I like my work on the crystals, and I don't want us to be shut down for putting ethical principles on display when it's not necessary."

"Don't you think that, you know, medical emergencies should prevail? If we bow to Crazy, we'll be flooded with similar requests." She quickly pressed on her arched eyebrows as to release some strain.

"Everyone is two-steps ahead of us because we don't think like potential users. We're scientists. We say yes to Crazy Velvet, but we announce rules that prevent the next movie star or billionaire from pressuring us."

"What kind of rules?" Nanette moved back to her side of the table, facing Octana.

"We'll alternate procedures at all locations, two medical cases and one for personal enhancements. The numbers for the former might increase if there's no demand for the latter."

"No exceptions?"

"For us, it's not about the money, so we go on a first-come-first-served basis. Exceptions should only be allowed for medical cases."

"I like that." Nanette leaned back in her chair. She stared at the barista behind the counter and let her mind drift.

Crazy Velvet was in the top echelon of the "wanna-be-connected-to-the-crystal-cloud" cohort. Nanette loathed the excitement of the players of virtual reality. Artificially created worlds and feelings had been the norm for the past four decades, and their limitations expanded with the increase of processing power. She'd grown up in a generation that wasn't identified by any particular letter—like the GenXers, GenZers, millennials, or boomers—but she didn't feel like being part of any of them. Not emotionally, anyway. Nanette had decided to step on a different path—that of the crystal research as a sound specialist. She wanted to deepen her recorded library of sounds created by Mother Nature as an extension of what she already had documented since her childhood.

The forest, its ground heaving with the bunions of ancient trees covered with a mélange of pine needles and branch debris in different states of decay, was her world, as was the chat between the leaves of an oak and a birch, ruffled by wind, or the scratching made by squirrels being chased by chipmunks. It was her world of sounds that soothed her soul and brought heartfelt memories of her tribe in Ontario—and later, in Victoria.

Nanette would never betray her Indigenous heritage by tainting her senses with crystal implants. Knowledge passed through the generations had made it to her as a verbal record. Her grandfather was the artisan of her transformational process from an innocent child into a time capsule of her people.

She watched Octana, still enraptured by Crazy Velvet's wizardry. Four million, seven hundred and forty-six thousand followers—it was a number she couldn't shake. There was an army watching Crazy's every move, virtual and real. They believed her statements, worshipped her look, and huddled around her like a thick, protective pelt of poison ivy. How could their team block such energy? What might become of this force if it were connected to the cloud? Still, it represented a fraction of the eight and a half billion humans roaming the Earth in different states of dissatisfaction.

"She submitted her application a couple of days ago," Octana said, reigning in the discussion about the YouTube starlet. "I'll openly take her side if Ilanda objects to the abrasive publicity."

"Becoming the rascal, aren't you!" Nanette said.

"She has to open up to such opportunities."

"Would you do the implants?" Nanette voiced the question that was really bothering her. She was afraid that in a society gone mad with consumerism, she would be one of only a handful resisting the change.

Octana raised her dark, penciled eyebrows at a dangerous angle until they seemed as if they might fall off her face. "I'd be an idiot not to." She had entered the word-tossing game so naturally, it was as if she had expected it. Up to that point, she had no one with whom to confess. "You wouldn't?"

"I like this world the way it is, you know, even if I sense that major changes are still to come. I refute the crystal enhancement for reasons other than medical."

"I believe in embracing the adjustments of the time we live in. Crystals are the creation of Mother Earth, and I honor her by allowing such assimilation." Octana flipped her tablet off and picked her croissant crumbs from the ceramic plate slowly.

"I believe in impermanence," Nanette said. "An organic, continuous change, fueled by our own way of life." There was an involuntary low level of sadness in her voice.

"How are we going to reach our mind's full potential without a boost? Synchronizing myself with the crystal's frequency could be one of the most rewarding experiences I'll ever have in my lifetime," Octana said, fueling the tussle.

"There are other ways, each of them, you know, requiring rigorous work and determination."

"Sorry, girl. I prefer the easy path."

"No hard feelings. I connect with Mother Earth through the practices of my ancestors. It's a duty that runs deep in our bloodline." Nanette sighed genuinely. None of her team members could comprehend the necessary wisdom for humanity's spiritual awakening was available for anyone to tap into.

"I recently read a *Bloomberg* article about how the twenty-eighty rule applies to the social media exposure as well—twenty percent of the most visible people on the net generate eighty percent of the traffic," Octana said.

"And how does that help us? We have no intention, you know, of hiring a social media guru." Nanette pushed her chair backward, ready to order another gluten-free apple pie.

"I was thinking about Crazy Velvet's followers and other public figures, like actors, politicians, or singers. Put together, they sway eighty percent of the online audience."

"Are you hinting that the pressure Crazy is exercising on us could be, you know, replicated by other crystal pretenders with world-wide influence?"

"That's exactly what's going to happen."

"That's when governments buckle and give in by forcing us to renounce, you know, the monopoly on our technology even if we haven't confirmed if it is completely safe," Nanette said as if finally awakening to the gravity of Octana's remark.

"I didn't get that far in my assumption, but that type of pressure would be real. Tens of millions of fans cheering for their idols' transformation. And a significant percentage of those people could get hooked on the 'cheap version' of the crystals."

"A generational fashion," Nanette mused. She was standing and holding the back of her plastic chair with both hands.

"They are the market DeBoers envisioned way ahead of us. Eyeglass stores will sell them without prescriptions," Octana said.

"That's the easy part. Where are they going to get the nanobots, you know, to mark the path to the pineal gland? Huh!"

"You underestimate the black market's appetite for making money and being creative. Mark built a darn solid software application for uploading the clients' characteristics into the crystal implants and onto the cloud without being hacked—"

"And it has to match the crystal's vibration. Yes, it's the process, you know, we all developed, and it's complex," Nanette said.

"If DeBoers makes the white version without locking in a certain frequency signature, then any punk could buy the nanobots and middleware from one of the clandestine labs, no registration required." Octana puckered her lips, pleased with the anarchistic message she'd delivered.

"Still, it won't be easy for anyone with an unregistered implant, you know, to connect to the crystal cloud. Not as long as Anonymous is the only one launching the crystal nodes in the cloud."

"Their monopoly will soon dissolve. Someone will come with a similar technology. As we expect to happen with ours."

"I agree these strongholds won't last, but we have the opportunity to suggest, you know, the future rules of the game, so users will be protected from the government watching," Nanette said, removing any doubt about her being a sympathizer. "I'm looking ahead at the time when people, you know, could get the implants from other suppliers. What would happen in case someone who was not our client gets a sensorial overdose through the implant?" she said, mimicking quotes with her fingers.

"In fact, a sensorial overdose could only have a temporary effect, so I won't worry too much. And not to be insensitive but why is that our responsibility?" Octana moved her head suddenly, and her fluffy golden hair took on a cartoonish halo look.

"It's not. I'm only saying hospitals will have to be ready and equipped to treat any crystal malfunctioning. As of now, they're clueless."

"So, what you're saying is that it's still our burden to train the trainers for such situations," Octana pushed forward, her voice gathering a tinge of anger.

"That's one option. At least at the beginning."

Without replying, Octana stood up and bagged her tablet. "I'm ready." She looked at Nanette, expecting her to pack her belongings as well.

"Let me grab some pies for the team," Nanette said.

As she stood in line, she thought about the new era that was upon humanity and the odds of turning people either into obedient AIs or enlightened beings and if there was even a chance of that happening.

Ilanda checked Crazy Velvet into the building at midnight on the day scheduled for her implants. The privacy of their location was a deal-breaker, and the law firm hired by Ilanda to represent the lab moving forward received specific instructions as to what was non-negotiable. In the end, the YouTube star reluctantly agreed that her fans should miss some of the steps in her transformational process.

A limo picked Crazy and a handful of her entourage up from the Billy Bishop Airport and delivered them under the cloak of darkness. There was no media and no live feeds—a total blackout had been imposed by the tight contractual clauses.

"Welcome to our abode," Ilanda said, spreading her arms out for a warm hug in an impulsive gesture that surprised even her. It felt like she was hugging a mannequin, stiff and docile before it sparked to life, flapping its arms frantically to escape the embrace.

"Yeah, yeah, great to be here, Doc," Crazy Velvet said. "My fans are watching old clips and cheesy advertising. I've never been offline for more than two hours at a time when I was awake." She waltzed around Ilanda making a pirouette, almost bumping into Octana and Nanette as they waited behind their boss.

"We can't rush the prep work. Your fans have to wait. We were quite clear when we negotiated the terms," Ilanda said curtly.

"Yeah, yeah, too much liability. I hear this crap all the time. Lead the way," Crazy swung her arms in all directions as if her body required it to maintain permanent balance. "My technical staff has to set-up."

"Follow me," Octana said, gesturing toward the steps. "The operation rooms are downstairs."

"Have you changed your mind regarding the full-body anesthetics?" Ilanda asked as she quickened her step to catch up with Crazy.

"I don't need it. I'm either aware through the whole experience, or I'll pull the plug."

"You won't be able to communicate during the procedure. Your face has to be immobile, so we'll do local anesthesia."

"My assistant will read the instructions you provided live. I expect a record audience to turn in. A thumbs-up from me while you work on me will mean a lot to them."

"The process is automated and hence, flawless," Ilanda said with confidence.

Octana leveled her head in front of the doors securing the lower floor for the retina scan, and they all hurried in.

"Your room is second on the left," Ilanda said, directing Crazy. "Change into the garment on the bed. It's in the color you ordered. We'll pick you up in fifteen minutes."

"Have you personally checked that the amethyst matches the shade I sent you?" Crazy Velvet asked.

"Your crystal implant is a perfect match for your hair color, fingernails, lipstick, and any other non-exposed body part painted purple," Ilanda said. She nudged the star gently toward the room before releasing more sarcastic words about the woman's single-color fixation.

"Nanette, show these gentlemen where they can set-up their equipment," she said before allowing a corrosive reply from Crazy Velvet.

The group split quickly like the crack of a whip.

"My brand is at stake if you're even slightly off-shade."

"Just tell your producers focus on your face, and you'll be fine."

Ilanda's fake pleasantries started to wear faster than she'd expected. In spite of all the pre-arranged requirements, Crazy's stringency for details kept everyone on edge.

The hallway cleared, leaving Ilanda alone. She walked into the antechamber leading to the operation room and leaned against the back of the door, palms over her heart as if trying to keep it from pushing through. She took several deep breaths and slowly calmed down. Ilanda ran her palm heels over her sweaty eyebrows and checked the timer on the wall. They were minutes away from the live broadcast.

Panes of smoked glass parted the room into smaller partitions, denoting the command center, observation room—where the techs were plugging their gear into the main video system, and the operation room, as they were readied for Crazy Velvet.

In the command center, Dr. Roppocone, the ophthalmologist who had worked on Kahuna Lapa'au, had finished uploading the patient's facial coordinates into the application that would instruct the robotic arm. He was now sitting quietly, waiting.

The preparations would take longer than the actual implementation. Ilanda mused that millions of Crazy Velvet's fans would be disappointed by the simplicity of the automation. Ilanda simply couldn't buy into any of the fluff supporting Crazy's brand of edginess and sharp language. A minimum risk in a safe environment was the least expected from her crowd, and the only request Ilanda compromised on was having a permanent online feed in the recovery room.

The undisclosed-to-the-public exorbitant fee Crazy had paid provided the revenue that would keep the lab financially afloat without reaching out to additional external sources. Ilanda had already shared bonuses with everyone as early Christmas gifts and threw a party at the Beer Bistro, the place where they'd had their first get together as a team.

Tangible results following Kahuna and Marinka's initial trials had boosted the morale, mellowed her attitude regarding the concept of franchising, and tempered any remaining shreds of tension.

Ilanda couldn't have dreamed of a more fortuitous personal relationship than the one she was having with Ojani. Their love was on a level of maturity that allowed for eccentricities never reached while married to Maahes. She had rediscovered her femininity through his hungry eyes, and the shape of his hand tracing her body countless times. Without voicing her thoughts so as not to disturb the settled energy in the room, she imagined Ojani as blind, reading the Braille embossed on her skin. The repetition of this gesture was a way for him to memorize the lines.

She had never been an "open book"—not completely open, anyway, not even with Maahes—but now, she had cracked her senses, her mind, and her body wide open for Ojani, a new chance for unconditional love.

The door from the hallway opened, and the medical crew rolled Crazy Velvet in. They glanced at her, she nodded back, and they pushed the patient through the next door and into the operation room. The star seemed composed while looking up at the ceiling as if immersed in a meditative state.

Ilanda joined Dr. Roppocone, and they both waited for Crazy's hands and head to be strapped to the angled chair.

Everyone stepped back—the lead nurse signed-off on the preparation checklist on her iPad. A green light pulsed on the translucent screen in the command center, confirming that the patient was ready for the implants.

"Here we go again," the ophthalmologist said, but he let Ilanda initiate the procedure.

The robotic arm moved as instructed, quickly and precisely. After the amethyst crystals were in place, several drops of structured water from Tenzin's Buddhist temple, the same one that had stirred Kahuna's and Marinka's implants, were placed on their surface as an activation agent.

Fixated on the YouTuber's stiffened body, the feed had to sustain the fans' interest for another five minutes before Crazy would be moved to the recovery room.

There was no glory, no script to follow, no voice crescendo swinging moods and increasing page views. There was only the motionless body of a girl that was supposed to emerge changed and whole, more potent and daring. The confidence of the crystals would put her over her normal threshold, raising her fan's energy several notches. Alternately, Crazy could also lose tens of thousands of her adorers if a shift in consciousness altered into a sophisticated, encrypted message if the notion of life's purpose, introspection, and awareness were put forward.

Dr. Roppocone's words, muffled by the haze floating around Ilanda, didn't make any sense, but she said, "Okay." It was the right answer, and he left the room.

The checkups in the months to come would provide Ilanda with the insight into what Crazy would become: a nuttier, eccentric, sense-driven, crowd-fanatic woman, or a self-aware, meditative, mature young person, ready to risk her star status to develop fully as a human being.

Ilanda was incapable of exercising her will over her tired, frozen muscles, and she let herself lean back in the chair in the dimly-lit command center. She scoffed when she realized that by accepting

Ojani's love, she had gone through a recent transformation herself, one in which she rose to a better self, molded by love and tenderness. A second metamorphosis awaited her in the fold: the implants. It wasn't like a removable tattoo, but she was convinced the rebellious act of implanting enhancements would trigger an evolutionary step for humanity. Or, at least, a significant leap. She wouldn't be around long enough to see it or to receive the Nobel. Or maybe she would if the crystals worked miracles to growing back her cells' telomeres, thus extending her life.

The respite would give her the time to find the language of water, bridging a much-needed communication gap that might help avoid another extinction in the billions of Earth's cycles. Maahes would be proud of her achievements and tease her lovingly. There were moments when she missed his caustic jokes and sarcasm, but then, Ojani's caring face morphed from Maahes's as he saved her from a dry and professionally-oriented life.

Nanette came in looking for her, and Ilanda yanked herself reluctantly out of her numbness.

"The crew is leaving, but Crazy's assistant had requested she stay. The boss's orders are that she's not to be left alone."

"Is the online feed still on?" Ilanda asked.

"Yes. It's on auto-pilot until morning when the techs are back."

Ilanda wanted to get a closer look at her patient, still subdued by the local anesthetic, without being identified by the online crowd.

"I'll be right back," she said, and she went to her office to put on the black wig.

"Daniela, isn't it?" she asked the young woman sitting on the leather armchair by the side of the bed punching something on her iPad.

"Dr. Mazandir? You look different."

"Long story. It's about valuing my privacy in these invasive times."

"Lucky you!" Daniela said.

"Is the sound on?" Ilanda asked, pointing toward the camera mounted opposite Crazy's bad.

"Video only. We very rarely enable the sound if Crazy isn't the one talking. Like earlier today, when I read the operation steps to the whole world," the assistant clarified.

Ilanda moved closer and checked the woman's vital signs on her tablet. Unexpectedly, she was asleep. "There's no sign of struggle in your boss's head. Everything's all chugging along as it should be."

"How fast could you remove the pads from her eyes?"

Daniela took her sneakers off and pulled her feet under her. Piercings ruled her ears, nostrils, and her right eyebrow, and Ilanda wondered what the rationale had been for not pairing that particular ring on the left side. Different shades of purple colored the complex contours of the flowers and geometrical shapes on her exposed arms—there was no doubt of her allegiance to Crazy Velvet.

"Tomorrow, if the vitals behave."

"And if they don't?"

"It'll be a bit longer. That's all I can say for now. If the crystals don't unlock, we might have to drop some more structured water on them."

Daniela glanced at Crazy, for once quiet and unresponsive, and touched her left arm as a reassurance that she was taking care of her.

"We should plug her batteries back in as soon as possible. People aren't used to seeing her like that. I voted against it, but the sponsors outnumbered me."

"What batteries are you talking about?" Ilanda asked.

"C'mon doctor. Don't take it verbatim. I meant to have her up and running."

Ilanda smiled at the figure of speech Daniela had used to show Crazy's vivacity. "She's a mover and a shaker, from what I was told, but I've never heard of her before," she said unapologetically.

"She's pretty niche on YouTube, but the broadband is slowly getting wider. The older brackets hear about us, check her out because of curiosity, and they're hooked before they know it. They rarely unsubscribe."

"Is it true that you have more than four million paid subscribers?" Ilanda asked, hoping to get, in a moment of full disclosure, the real number that probably wouldn't be as dizzying as the one articulated on social media.

"Things change fast in Crazy Velvet's world. We're edging five million, and we'll push through that quickly as the Chinese market —which has been sluggish until now—is waking up. We had to change the marketing message, some distribution channels, and . . . bang, the paralysis melted."

The color on her arms wavered in the dim light from the wall-mounted fixture.

"Do you think her fans will follow her example?" Ilanda knew she would never have the same quality time with Crazy, and Daniela was the best alternative to poke around for answers about the average person's perception of the crystal implants.

"Most will immediately, or, at least, as soon as the crystals are available for mass consumption. Those with limited financial means will have to save up for a year or two. They'll settle for used cars, shrink a two-week vacation to one, or skip it altogether. They'll be delayed but not stopped," the young woman said confidently as she described a market segment so familiar to her.

"And is this a good thing to have all of these people hooked virtually?" Ilanda said, pushing forward.

Daniela leaned her legs on the edge of the bed, delaying her answer.

"It's not meant to be a trick question," Ilanda said, sensing Daniela's hesitation. "I only want to know your honest opinion."

"Yeah . . . Crazy isn't only my boss but also my mentor. This crap has to stay between the two of us—understood?"

Ilanda crossed her heart solemnly.

"She's encouraging me to reach a certain level of dexterity to match the mathematical algorithms she uses on her AugReality compilations. The two of us work in Reality, record it, and then mix and compile it in AugReality."

"And that's unique?"

Had Ilanda uttered an abject profanity, it wouldn't have changed Daniela's features as fast as that question. "Are you nuts, doctor?" She could barely hide her indignation.

Ilanda rolled her eyes. "Watching YouTube isn't at the top of my daily activities list. Holding off government goons, combating fake news, and doing real work like what was done on your boss fills my day. Your stuff is important to you, and mine is important to me. It's pretty obvious."

"Right, right. Crazy never had a partner for her real-life recordings. She can't stand being touched during her sexual fantasies, hence all the additions through the algorithms. She feels different in my presence, and we'll give it a try."

"I wish you luck."

"We want to enhance our fans' experiences. The implants should produce an additional sensorial layer as if being in the room with us, feeling what we feel, seeing what we see. At least, this is what's being depicted by everyone in the know."

Ilanda wondered who, exactly, were those in the know—the butchers that had sliced through peoples' heads two years ago or the wanna-be franchisees?

"How might the crystals change her?" Daniela asked, staring at the immobile body lying in the bed.

"I can't tell you for sure. Everyone is aware of how helpful the procedure proved to be for Kahuna and the two medical cases we worked on last week."

"So, you're positive about Crazy's outcome as well?"

"Setting aside concerns about the body's reaction? Yes, I'm confident," Ilanda said, trying to chase her fear away. "She might experience sensible changes to her awareness, which could shift to a level that . . ." She paused, looking for the right word. ". . . We are not comfortable with yet."

"What does that mean?" Daniela straightened a bit in her armchair.

"When the crystal connects to the pineal gland, there's a certain alteration that's fired-up in the brain. More areas are animated, coming to life in a domino effect."

"More brainpower, more thinking power, added awareness, and we become more present. Did I get that right?" the young woman asked. She crossed her arms and moved her hands on her upper arms in a gesture that gave Ilanda the impression she was calming down the fever boiling through the decorative tattoos.

"You catch on fast," Ilanda acknowledged.

"Is Kahuna on a different level of awareness?"

"It is my understanding that Kahuna was already on a higher-level, even before the explosion, and the crystal and water combination helped bring him back by healing some of his broken internal connections."

Ilanda hadn't expected a lengthy conversation, and only now did she move to sit on the other armchair in the room.

What if Kahuna surpassed his initial threshold of awareness? What about Marinka? Where did she fall on that scale? Ilanda had asked herself these questions many times without the courage to face the pair as if afraid of her own success.

"And here's an epiphany that might give you the shivers: what if, in two months, Crazy Velvet goes through a cleansing process, revealing the triviality of her lifestyle?"

Before Daniela could reply with a motivated justification, Ilanda continued. "I'm not trying to minimize her art or offend her team, you included. I'm just saying."

"You mean like she could walk away from her fans?"

Ilanda noticed Daniela shiver in the warm room. She couldn't acknowledge a scenario so dramatic while Crazy was still on the ascendant curve of popularity.

"Or she might encourage them to *upgrade*, as you hinted earlier."

"And fill the gap," Daniela said.

"It is my hope that such a metamorphosis would help us evolve to a vantage point from which we are able to assess the destructive path we're on as a species."

"Do you think that's possible?"

"Definitely. I would be really disappointed if it wasn't. People want the implants, but for the wrong reason." Ilanda smiled to ease the gravity of her statement, and hopefully distract Daniela from fully comprehending its ramifications. She had said too much, and any misinformation leaked to the media might turn into another terrible nightmare she doubted the team would survive.

"I think that could be a sneaky trick to play on them," Daniela said.

"Really?"

"It's a transformation we all need but don't know that we need it. Or we don't have the time and patience for ourselves—there are abundant distractions around—and Crazy is one of them."

Ilanda was impressed with Daniela's acuity when connecting the dots and diagnosing the positives without judgment or unethical reasoning.

"Slowly introducing the most visible influencers in the world to the crystal implants would help change the perspective of their followers," Ilanda said, suddenly feeling on safer ground with Daniela. "Critical mass is required like for any worthy initiative."

From the young woman's body language—laid back and totally relaxed—Ilanda had the impression she had already accepted her future self as an evolved being.

"Create your own reality," Ilanda liked to remind herself, and now, time had brought humanity's Renaissance to an emergent reality. "I leave you to your duties now." She stood up and walked toward the door. "I assume the online crowd watching the feed is ecstatic seeing so much action." Her back was still facing the improvised webcam.

"You and I are invisible to them. Until Crazy puts the limelight on one of us, then everything changes," Daniela said.

"In other words, I should ask her not to thank me publicly or post photos of us together, am I correct?"

"Completely correct. And explain the reason to her if she doesn't get it right away."

"It's a deal. See you in the morning. I need my beauty sleep, too," Ilanda said as she closed the door gently behind her.

She was in the presence of a person with indomitable will and astonishing charisma, able to sway the meek toward an irreversible decision. Accepting Crazy's bold demand had demonstrated a lesson she had to learn by taming her ego in a callous world which wasn't aware yet of the imminent debasement of its social values and structure. Create something the influencers craved, an intellectual trap, and they'll implant the crystals, trampling personal principles and societal rules. Ilanda thought it a pragmatic method for reaching the critical mass Daniela had mentioned.

A shaft of light pounded her mind. The word "*influencers*" palpitated in a strident red. Below the letters, she saw her face coming through the light fog. The message was clear—she was an influencer, too, even though she had never counted her followers, on or offline. She never considered assessing the impact of her speeches and published papers, but now might be the proper time. It might embolden other doctors and practitioners to leave their trivial life behind, the shallowness of a job that had turned into a burden and lapse into the transformational unknown. Suddenly, she felt the desire to take on such responsibility and give up fighting the people who keep pressuring her to be complicit.

Standing in the lobby outside Crazy's room, Ilanda recoiled from the fear that her blunder of honesty in front of Daniela might generate another crisis. The idea of a spokesperson came to her mind but was quickly dismissed.

A message on her phone reminded her that Ojani had cooked a vegetable dish seasoned with Indian spices the way she liked it. "*And more surprises*," he added, leaving her to wonder if they were food-related or some sort of sensual game meant for the intimacy of his bedroom.

"*OMG*," she replied, and she picked up her purse and hailed an Uber at the lab's address. She was famished—for food, for him, for the extension of the existence she experienced, for what it promised to be after the implants: even more sensorial.

CHAPTER 22

Ilanda had bad memories from previous live TV interviews, but today, she'd accepted the challenge from the man of faith on the Toronto's Evening News Show on the condition that it will be done via remote connection from her office. The church had designated Father Onofreio to carry the message of prudence and humility for those willing to alter their bodies with the crystal implants. As usual, the religious institution didn't mince words on its position, and the secular history of its mistakes was immediately disregarded as irrelevant. She was ready to face the onslaught of words.

Lately, she felt more confident and emotionally balanced since she openly let Ojani step into her life. He filled her soul with yearning for love and her mind with images of his dark hand mapping her naked body. During the days in the lab while recording notes on how the informational signature of the nanobots should be improved or what additional tests should be pursued on the quartz implants , Ilana entertained thoughts of Ojani in her mind's eye as a mental respite. He was not a destructive disturbance from her scientific work. Somehow, talk of crystals and water always came up during the breaks between their romantic encounters, percolating ideas and meanings in her mind that needed a particular infusion of love and self-confidence to come up.

Cherry was right—it was a good idea to share the news of her relationship with the team. No one cheered or congratulated them. They all nodded and said thank you for considering them trustworthy. Hiding her feelings from her family, her schoolmates, and sometimes even from Maahes was in the past now. The warmth of Ojani's Jamaican roots melted that fear of being emotionally exposed in front of those that cared for her. Ilanda confessed to Ojani how her parents' distant attitude slowly built the shell surrounding her heart. They toughened her up by ignoring her most of the time, unless a milestone such as high-school graduation could have shed on them some parental pride.

But Ojani was a survival of a life harder than hers, and she felt ashamed to complain or compare anymore. At her age, no safety net was necessary for love or for a relationship that would give her sentimental stability years before Maahes's death.

Ilanda pushed her shoulders backwards, ran her fingers through her hair so no locks were caught behind her ears, and checked one more time that no unwanted items from her office would show up in the AugReality broadcast. She looked at her phone. It was five minutes before the interview would start, so she dialed in for the visual and sound checks.

An assistant adjusted the brightness of the image and increased the volume. "I'll patch you in right after the commercial," she said.

"Good evening, everyone. We start another edition of 'Debates That Could Alter Our Lives' bringing forward not only two personalities that were very much present in the public eye recently, but also a subject that has incited worldwide turmoil and disrupted certain religious and spiritual beliefs. I am your host, Marrilou Lam, and my guests tonight are Dr. Ilanda Mazandir, the neurosurgeon who developed the crystal implants technology, and Father Onofreio of the Roman Catholic Archdiocese of Toronto."

"Good evening, Father, Marrilou," Ilanda said. She had prepared for the interview this time with a professional team that listened to Father Onofreio's previous TV and radio interventions revealing the church's perception of what the crystal implants were trying to achieve.

"Are we self-sufficient as we've been created by God or do we need artificial alterations for increased mind and physical potential?" Marrilou Lam asked, bringing context to her audience. "Are we upsetting our Creator by bringing these changes to ourselves or are we just exercise our free will as we see it fit? These are some of the questions we hope to answer during tonight's debate. But I'll start with a piece of news that came in yesterday. Dr. Mazandir, you just opened twenty-six crystal implant franchisees, most of them in North and South America, with a handful in Europe. Why not more than that?"

"The reason is very simple: they owned their buildings, so they didn't need special approval from the landlords. They trained their personnel on the premises and assimilated our processes faster. A similar number will be announced in a couple of days throughout Europe and China."

"Has the online registration form gone down yet?" Marrilou Lam asked.

"If you're implying everyone has been expecting a demand beyond any means of being fulfilled sooner than four weeks, then yes, the response has been impressive. There are potentially higher delays for those selecting the entertainment option. As we've mentioned in our official declaration, medical cases take priority."

"I understand that even if the crystal implants are popular these days, there are medical doctors and some neurosurgeons that are putting a negative spin on this fairytale," Lam stated. "What would you say to that?"

Ilanda had no patience for naysayers, but she learned to keep a polite tone so as not to attract any more enemies or envy from her fellow colleagues, some of them who already reached out offering their services.

She quickly glanced at Father Onofreio. There was no smile in his eyes. She was not convinced he was even listening to her. Instead, he was waiting for the proper breach into her defense to deliver the same script the church put in his hands. There wasn't enough makeup on his shiny head, and perspiration was coming down his white sideburns, vanishing into his perfectly trimmed beard, that, for a moment, Ilanda had the impression was glued to his face to enhance the authority of his tiny shoulders and a narrow upper body that made him look like an aged child.

"History has often shown how revolutionizing ideas or technologies are not welcome or understood when the markets are young and unprepared to receive them," Ilanda said. "Just think about how long it took for the governments and forces in control of the society to accept the crypto currencies and electric cars. Both technologies have improved our lives. The crystal implants represent a shift in how we should perceive human evolution and I understand some peoples' reticence in accepting this shift."

"An assisted evolution, that is." Marrilou Lam's peppery tone made Ilanda and Father Onofreio smile but each probably for a different reason. It was one of those questions the lab's public relations team had prepared her for.

"Yes, indeed. Sometimes, we need to help ourselves—"

"And not ask for God's help, Doctor?" Father Onofreio interjected. "Aren't we going against God's will by artificially enhancing our bodies using the same decadent logic that destroyed the society in the first place through drugs and alcohol?" Father Onofreio asked. "What if—"

"With all due respect, Father," Ilanda jumped back on her own script, "how do you know the crystal implants' positive effects aren't God's answer to my in-depth research on the subject?" Away from the studio lights and not being in close proximity to the religious figure, Ilanda felt no pressure to align her voice inflection with his, which was a bit menacing.

"It can't be. God wouldn't allow it—"

"Father, I'll answer by referring to the book of scripture so familiar to you, the Bible. God didn't accept the chosen people to remain slaves in Egypt. He acted on the pharaoh's denial to free the Israelites by unleashing various plagues and the sacrifice of the innocents, so don't you think God will also show us specific signs or actions if this enhancement, as you call it, is not in line with His will?" Ilanda had the itch to stand and walk around her office, but she only pushed her body forward instead as if to stop Father Onofreio from interjecting. "We started the discussion mentioning that medical cases are our priority. We want to save lives, first and foremost." Ilanda remained as composed as possible. She feared it was a futile argument with a man of faith whose purpose in life was to reform others to his rigid beliefs. She was one of the few doctors who believed in a candid and protective God, one who was ready to help when asked. She didn't regard science as the ultimate healing solution when she knew perfectly well the medical prescriptions of the chemically-based drugs would only temporarily alleviate the pain and the symptoms.

"Doctor Mazandir, there is always an altruistic reason on the facade of Satan's plan. One has to go deeper to figure out what that plan is." He smirked back at her.

"We've heard public figures approving of the implants and even admitting their willingness to get them," Marrilou Lam said during the awkward pause that ensued, probably because silence wasn't good for the ratings. "Are they all wrong?"

"They're gullible," Father Onofreio said, "attracted by a novelty, which, like any other drug, will bring them misery and disillusion." He projected a sadness that seemed to indicate his inability to change the situation.

"Nevertheless, are they all wrong?" Marrilou insisted.

"No, they are not," Ilanda interjected. "I'll admit for some, the reasons are selfish. They seek enhanced pleasurable experiences. The expectation is that the crystal implants could help one's mind with the creation of additional virtual worlds that go beyond the ones generated by the video games. But there is no certainty that this is going to happen. If it does, it's possible, for some to remain there, undisturbed, as conscious energy."

"That's even—"

"Father, I used my wildest imagination for that last statement. Don't take it literally, please," Ilanda winced. She shouldn't have mentioned the concept of inner virtual worlds. She only read about it on the net a couple of days back, but it stuck out as a radical application to her benevolent technology.

"You just mentioned enhanced pleasure, which is not in line with the Church's teachings. The godliness in people is being removed and mocked, and your technology is giving it a harder push."

Ilanda stood up as if she couldn't bear the insult, but then sat back, remembering she's on a live show. "The lotus is a beautiful flower, revered all over the globe, but especially in India, where it has significant spiritual implications."

She sensed that Father Onofreio was itching to cut her off again, so she raised her hand to put him back in his place. "It grows out of smelly mud. It's not pretty down there, but it's a fertile soil needed to create the elegance and grace of the lotus."

"I don't see the correlation," the man said, his face reddened, his voice wavering.

"The Church thinks that implanting the crystals will exacerbate sin—what if the outcome exceeds all expectations? What if a reformed person is the equivalent of the lotus flower? Would the Church still raise concerns?"

Ilanda had willingly cracked the confessional's door. If he would hold off on his condemnation for a while, he might see how they can activate the finer side of the patients' human character, even if they were originally implanted for entertainment. That would be proof enough for Father Onofreio and the Catholic Church to delay their judgment until God divulged His real intentions.

"If I understand your encrypted statement, you have huge expectations for the way the crystals interact with the human brain. Positively, I mean. Correct?" the man asked.

"Yes. I would like for us to put aside the duality that runs our lives—good, bad, inappropriate, well-behaved, and so on and so forth."

"Easier said than done."

"We all make concessions, Father. We do our best to forgive, and in turn, we ask for forgiveness. Isn't this teaching one of the fundamental foundations of the Catholic Church?"

Father Onofreio nodded. His hands were in his lap as if he were listening respectfully to a respected clergyman.

"People want to transform themselves for various reasons. Let's not take that away from them by pointing fingers and judging," Ilanda said. She was leaning forward.

"What if you're wrong?" Father Onofreio asked.

Ilanda observed his hunched shoulders and coy grin, a humble posture she was not sure to be calculated or sincere.

"Great question, Father," Marrilou said, confirming she was still the moderator. "A significant number of our viewers are interested in the answer."

"Look around at where we're heading right now as a society," Ilanda said. "Ecologically, we've made blunders on Earth". She pointed to the vertical scroll on the TV screen behind Marrilou. "Before the fall of 2055 we witnessed the daily worldwide occurrences of hurricanes in the United States' Midwest region, tornadoes in Southern China, earthquakes in Chile and Guatemala, and mudslides in Brazil that each have buried at least three hundred people. And those were only the ones that were newsworthy. After the awakening of water, these incidents not only had increased in number but in intensity as well," Ilanda said.

"Not all environmental reports agree on the main cause of these climatic events," the anchorwoman said, playing devil's advocate. "Way before water had that strange behavior, the debate was about the effects humanity's industrial revolution had on climate change. We all linked the melting of the ice caps, the increased carbon dioxide levels, and the depletion of the aquifers, to climate change, now you are—"

"True, but there is no denying that these occurrences are not normal. We all know that money and power feed such reports, and I'll leave it at that."

"Are there other reports?" Lam asked.

"The ones U.N. Water posts on its website. There is a graphical comparison of the atmospheric events, before and after the awakening of water in the regions I mentioned a minute ago, along with many others that are known as tornadoes and hurricane corridors.

The graph also refers to new areas that were outside the path of any significant weather phenomenon," Ilanda leaned back on the chair. "What better time to improve ourselves than now!"

No political interests or Church official could derail the trend of crystal implants, but they were trying anyway. During her preparation for the interview, Ilanda watched a three-minute video clip in which the clergyman answered the question 'why should people avoid the implants?' He misspoke by saying '... they could see more clearly,' but corrected himself immediately.

Suddenly, Ilanda recognized the real meaning of Father Onofreio's statement, and his presence in the studio as the desperate act of an institution that, throughout the centuries, had tried to prevent the masses from being educated, cognitive, and inquisitive about their purposes in life.

That thought took the air from Ilanda's lungs, and she paused. She couldn't focus on Marrilou's words. Father Onofreio's eyes fixated on her, hungry and cold, stirring shivers on her back. The Church knew the implants would tighten people's awareness, diminishing the ranks of the parishioners and implicitly weakening the influence of secular institutions. They would embrace spirituality instead of religious dogma. They would find God everywhere they looked, not only in a secular institution. She had only her intuition as proof.

Ilanda felt empowered by her realization. "As the only sentient species on Earth, our disdain, greed, and lack of compassion have increased proportionally to our scientific discoveries. We are proud of these achievements, yet these very achievements undermine our survival through unchecked pollution, GM-ed foods, and drugs that cause a palm-long list of side effects."

She saw the screen behind Marrilou change to the social media channels, overloaded by comments and questions. They couldn't stop her now. Not anymore. The genie was completely out of the bottle, and no charm would trick him back in.

"Going back to your question, Father Onofreio, this personal transformation the church is against can't make things worse than they are now, but I'm hopeful for a positive change." She was done. There was no more beating around the bush.

"I understand your enthusiasm, but it is the church's conviction that you're playing God with peoples' lives." The man's voice was harsh, sounding as if he were being choked by invisible hands. "How will you justify the loss of lives if things go wrong? Would you say that it was God's will for these people to perish? Or, filled with grieve and remorse, you'll ask God for repentance?"

Ilanda took in the vortex of his words, but she had no intention of backing down.

"Science, religion, and spirituality are closer than they've ever been. There is acceptance of what until recently were considered intangible concepts, such as self-healing, in scientific circles that slowly are being replicated in labs all around the globe. Even at public gatherings, people are taught how breathing and focusing inwardly can unlock energies that repair damaged cells. To me, it's like God is leading us to an understanding that's escaped us until now."

"And this could be the theme for another debate," Marrilou Lam said. "There are still a number of unanswered questions that our social media team will send to Dr. Mazandir. Do you think your team could post the answers under the FAQs section of your website?" she addressed Ilanda directly.

"I promise only pertinent questions will be answered. We are busy ourselves with so many projects on the go," she said. "Thank you for the invitation, Marrilou. Nice talking to you, Father Onofreio." She disconnected as soon as the host finished her closing script.

THREE DAYS AFTER HER RELEASE, Crazy Velvet was back in her professional studio, recording new material. Ilanda assigned Octana to monitor the YouTuber's online activity and report on images or posts that weren't characteristic for the star.

They were in the lab's kitchen, refilling their mugs with coffee for the second time that day. It was a luxury afforded after they'd changed the classification of the building from "research facility" to "medical unit with a unique designation," a vague enough legal term that was potent at the same time.

"Look for before and after type of behavior," Ilanda suggested." Have the posts change their cadence? Their content? Are they now more profound or borderline silly when compared to before the implants? Anything out of the ordinary is important."

"You really expect her to stop cracking jokes and become more profound in such a short amount of time?"

"I don't know what to expect. She might feel different, but she's afraid to expose her newfound depth. Adjusting to the new sensation of awareness can be traumatic for some."

"Why?" Octana asked.

"Because they realize they've been asleep for most of their lives."

"But Crazy is fearless. She won't hide behind feelings or put on masks for society."

"It could be traumatic, even for her, as she has to untangle herself from her previous personality, now that it's served its purpose." Ilanda sat down, facing Octana. "It might be easier for me because I can anticipate the kinds of changes to look for. My transition will be short and sweet. And I don't have the kind of public exposure Crazy has."

"Should we reach out to her?" Octana sounded like a mother concerned for her daughter, who hadn't worn a hat on a cold winter's day.

"We checked on her yesterday, and we'll do it again tomorrow. Anyway, her vitals can't tell us much about her emotional state."

"What if we ask her directly?"

"We can, but before we do that, let me talk to Daniela—she knows her boss intimately. Don't drop the monitoring yet."

Ilanda left the kitchen, letting Octana clean the rings of coffee off the table.

Daniela answered minutes after Ilanda had sent her a text message.

"Hey, Ilanda. Thank you for keeping an eye on us."

"That's my job for the next little while. We all agreed on that from the beginning," Ilanda said.

"I assume Crazy's vitals are humming in sync. There's no emergency, so how can I help?"

Ilanda admired her direct approach, assuming it had somehow rubbed off on her from Crazy Velvet.

"The night the two of us had that lengthy chat, I indicated a certain type of behavior that might occur as a consequence of the implants—"

"Like not being so jumpy at every single stupid thing or saying thank you a hundred times a day, even when asking for a smoke, or sobbing uncontrollably when seeing a cat chased by hungry dogs—that type of change?"

Ilanda froze on the couch in her office, aware that she had just been given evidence of Crazy's adjustment to the implants but not knowing how to react. "Is it that obvious?"

"Only for those close to her, for now. The team had a working session yesterday at which Crazy presented new concepts for her show."

"And?"

"First off, she's never asked for feedback before. Never. We just did what we were told."

"That's a very good sign," Ilanda said, not sure if she'd meant it as a statement or a question that needed Daniela's confirmation.

"Yes, indeed."

"What did she propose?"

"Mellow scenes, more profound, focused on love and a bond that transcends the trivial sex scenes we've peddled so much in other versions," Daniela admitted to what Ilanda had hoped would happen.

"Are you happy for her?"

The young woman shuffled herself in the chair as if riffling words in her mind.

"I think she finally sees me for who I am: smart, beautiful, and reliable. Thank you, Ilanda." Tears spilled down her cheeks, dropping fast off the edge of her chin. The apprentice's inner-beauty transpired through the AugReality transmission; she was appreciative of regaining her confidence and pride. "This procedure will change many lives."

Ilanda's gaze fogged under the tears that had welled in her eyes, and her throat produced a peculiar rumbling, barely forming the words. "It's the crystals and the structured water. I just put them together."

"It's a divine combination, a gift disguised as a source of decadent pleasure and unlimited entertainment."

"The multiverse uses intelligent ways of disseminating messages to us. And again, like in so many previous instances, we are prone to missing their meaning."

Daniela's tattoos were subdued in the room's scant light, and Ilanda sensed throbs of energy pulsing around the young woman, like a cleansing process, long overdue.

"Is she aware of her transformation?" Ilanda asked. Details were important for the knowledge database the team had started to build.

"Probably. She's more inquisitive about our puzzled looks and reticence to provide feedback. We weren't sure if it was a trap, and she might explode in one of her random breakdowns. The discussion we had that night helped me understand what's going on."

"Did you talk to Crazy? Make her aware of her new . . . state of being?"

"Yes. I also told the team to ease off."

"And Crazy?"

"She only smiled at me like I was a childhood friend she hadn't seen since first grade. I can still feel her hug. She showered me with love and gratitude and said, 'Let's make the world a better place.'"

"That's beautiful," Ilanda muttered, an effulgence of energy fluttering through her body like sap in a tree. She felt whole and motherly, even though she had never given birth.

"She'll make a public announcement next week, after the release of the latest video," Daniela said. "The fans will notice the change immediately. They're very perceptive."

"Some might be bitter, with no desire to accept such a personal revolution."

"Crazy expects that to happen. She'll stay the course and make this world a better place," Daniela repeated.

"Are you willing to stay by her side?"

"More than ever. Before the crystals, I stayed for the fame, but now, I have a purpose."

In her youth, Ilanda realized that 'purpose' was a word loaded with meaning. To her, purpose meant drive, direction, and success. But only a fraction of humanity really understood the concept, actively contributing to the achievements of modern society.

"Let me know how I can help," Ilanda said with an open heart.

Daniela smirked at her as if she'd expected the offer.

"What do you have in mind, Daniela?" Innately, Ilanda knew she wanted the implants, but she waited for confirmation.

"A pair of shiny crystals. I can pay for it—I only need my name on the list. I'll submit the form today. I'd have told you anyway. I'm glad you called."

"We'll get you a fine grade of crystal. Is there any particular color? Purple?"

Daniela giggled loudly. "Anything but, purple. Let's be original."

"Did you tell her about your intention?"

"Not yet. I'll do it today. Before I apply."

"I'll see your friend tomorrow for the check-up," Ilanda said, nodding at Daniela before disconnecting.

Her mind had already acknowledged that the connection between the two women transcended barriers of any kind. Calling them friends was natural.

"How did it go with Tenzin?" Ilanda asked Ojani, who was sagging on the couch in her apartment.

They'd decided to split the working days in the week fairly, spending time at one another's places, living together for a while to see how many compromises they had to make to keep their relationship healthy. She was barely able to wrangle an answer out of him. It was as if his throat had clogged with immensely painful words and couldn't manifest sounds. "Was it that bad?"

His gaze met hers. "He's not capable of judging me. He's always loved me like a brother, but I could feel the shrieking inside of him, even if his face never flinched."

"Does he blame me for your decision to do the implants?"

"He knows it's entirely my judgement, and the reasons aren't important, eh."

Ilanda heard the words come out of Ojani's mouth as a hissing sound paired with a wide grimace. "It's the end of a story in which I played coyly with the idea that someday I'll become a monk and wrap myself in those soft robes. Tenzin bought the lies, but it wounded him deep inside, a permanent wound that will never heal."

"But you'll still see each other, won't you?" Ilanda asked.

Ojani snorted, and tears tumbled from his cheeks in straight lines like dry ruts in the mud. He never let his guard down in front of her, and Ilanda drew closer to him. She had infringed her will on the relationship that would break Ojani's last connection to what represented his family. It was selfishness on her part, as she should have guessed Tenzin's reaction.

"You can still change your mind," she said, and she'd meant it. "At least you can postpone the intervention for a while. He's so dear to you."

Pain racked his body; hers took in the tremors. "I've made up my mind, not because I promised you, but because I need to experience the technology I've always dreamed of as safe and reliable."

"Did he say you're not welcome at the temple?" she asked.

"Not out loud, but I'm familiar with their customs. They will suffer seeing me *altered*." He blew his nose into a tissue.

"But the abbot and the monks could find refuge at the farm you're planning to buy if need be," she said, trying to sound positive to bring his mood up a little. Her words sprouted a glimmer in his eyes, and his orange skin took on a brighter hue.

"That's another deed I'll have to fulfill, eh."

"It's going to be okay. You, me, the team, our patients, and our customers—they're all in good hands," she said as further encouragement. "We'll keep an eye on the temple and send help through a third party if they're too stubborn to accept it from you."

Ojani nodded and cuddled deeper into her embrace. It wasn't a motherly embrace, but that of a lover.

"Speaking about help, Cherry asked us for donations for Water for All, whatever we can afford. No amount was specified. It's up to us. Their clean-up and pollution prevention projects are still active and need funding."

She felt his short nods on her chest, and she kissed his sturdy hair.

"Can I start making preparations for the implants next week?" Ilanda asked, not sure if she was pecking away too much at his emotional endurance.

"Do you expect me to go public, too?" Ojani's gaze took on a dull sheen as if overtaken by sudden worry.

"No, there's no point to drag you along with me in the public eye—unless you think otherwise."

"I'm good."

Their bodies seemed to meld into each other like moss on trees as they mourned the broken tie that would leave Ojani floating by himself on troubled waters with Ilanda as his only lifeline.

"We've received the first shungite crystal shipment from Anonymous, as they promised last week. I'm relieved they've agreed with Cherry's business agreement."

"I've always wanted black eyes, eh," Ojani said, pain still ringing in his voice.

"Your eyes are already black, silly, and starry-beautiful. I can vouch for that." She kissed the cut above his right eyebrow. Ojani's determination in keeping his promise to her added value to what she considered a string of qualities that even Maahes couldn't match entirely.

"Feeling ready for it?" she asked, still holding him tightly. It was as if the two of them were a piece of corundrum crystal, intermingled with layers of love and brilliance.

He let out a meek and muffled yes, and she pushed back again.

"You can do better than that," she said as if challenging a toddler to try to tie his shoes one more time.

"Yes." The word has come out sluggish, but forceful.

"I'll do it first, draw the media's attention, and let them watch my transformation. What better example to give than the reputable neurosurgeon getting hooked."

"You'll put on a great show, eh."

Ilanda sensed a raise in his energy in opposition to the apathy that had engulfed his mind since he'd returned from the temple. "I hope so. We've received rating estimates from a company specializing in surveys. They expect fifty million viewers during the intervention and approximately half of that number in-and-out during the night."

"That's a healthy audience." Ojani released himself from her gentle hold and lifted his feet onto the couch. The cut above his eyebrow seemed lighter against his dark skin.

"Three advertising companies called the PR guys, asking for live broadcasting rights, and providing a quote. They have clients salivating for this type of crowd. Crazy Velvet drew in thirty million, all of them thrumming with enthusiasm and hankering for eccentric AugReality videos of her transformation."

"Are you getting more numbers than her, eh? My own YouTube star." Ojani puffed manly pride.

She burrowed her fingers under his ribs and tickled him.

He let her play piano notes on his side with little reaction, but he wore a grin that was large enough to whittle away the grimace of abandonment he'd had moments ago.

"Yes, I'm your star. Yours only. In private and not on slimy

AugReality. I hope that physicality still means something to you," she said, overly morose, knowing he wouldn't take it seriously.

"I appreciate physicality more than you know, eh," he shot back. "You are perfect for the job of taunting an unseen audience while the shungite dust activates in the presence of water."

"I like the compliments," she said, and she got up on top of him, tightening her legs around him as a jockey would do to her noble partner.

He stroked her hair and cupped her head in his strong palms.

Ilanda didn't feel as if she were in control anymore. When the kiss followed, waves lapped at her lips, and rivers of melted emeralds coursed through her aged body. She felt the liquid life of the rocks returning to her heart, cleansing it and calibrating its out-of-sync rhythm. She perceived the instant elation, like a cherry on a sundae, and she was ready for any move on his part, to surrender to desire, love, and any other cravings a woman of her age might have.

"I love you," he said, and he kissed her again and again, repeating a mantra that ascended their senses to a level of detachment. "I'm ready for the implants, eh," Ojani muttered, caressing her face.

"I'll be waiting for you on the other side," she replied, and she let herself roll onto the couch so he could get into a position of domination. She caught a glimpse of them, asleep in a prism of amethyst, and Crazy Velvet looking at them through a magnifying glass.

Ilanda was one week away from enhancing her brain and potentially reaching a higher level of consciousness. She didn't expect to become one hundred percent smarter; just a bit more would do it. She and Ojani would connect in a different realm where even the structured water of their own bodies might communicate with them.

She paused when the thought struck her. The intensity of working on high profile clients had distracted her from asking the team about the results of the resumed research on water. The compelling behavior of the liquid in various states of excitation would have caused a commotion, and everyone would have gathered around her to interpret the outcome. Instead, they kept silent, heads down due to their hectic schedule, each a carbon copy of the next.

"You know," Ilanda said, "Cherry wants the implants, too. She told me the other day. Shungite, as well."

"If the shungite is so darn adaptable, Kahuna might sue us for not giving it to him in the first place, eh."

She didn't laugh or reply, but affected a morose mask to remind him how much she respected the Hawaiian leader.

"Sorry. Bad joke. Didn't mean it."

She smiled. "The quantity Anonymous can supply us with is limited. We'll have to be selective.".

"Friends and family, eh?"

"Perhaps. Plus, dignitaries, politicians, CEOs, and public figures that want to set an example."

"Isn't that what we aimed for, eh?"

"Indeed. Attract the masses through influencers." She agreed, but she didn't feel comfortable with the indirect manipulation they were exercising.

"What's bothering you, eh?" He pulled away to look her in the eyes.

"Do you think the quality of the crystal implants will change in any way the social structure?"

"What do you mean, eh?"

"We and those with financial means will get the shungite. The next well-off level can afford the quartz, the amethyst or a similar, high-grade quality. And the rest will have to settle for the artificial whites. There will be a handful in between, and nothing else."

"It might be an obvious stratification, but the market is an unpredictable animal."

"What's your take on it?" Ilanda asked.

"I've heard through the grapevine how certain companies would like to pre-pay for crystals in bulk and offer them as an incentive to employees, eh."

"Really?"

"Even those who can't afford a higher grade will get it for their smarts, blending into the social strata you just mentioned." Ojani thrummed with enthusiasm.

"That's fine, as long as they don't circumvent the process." She sounded alarmed, not for loss of profit, but for the potentially ruined lives at the hands of butchers.

"A legal contract is already being drafted for such requests. The company is responsible for registering employees with one of our franchisees. No one will fall through the cracks, eh."

"I like delegating," she said, re-energized by one less worry that could have been added to her list.

"Will we go away for a week after the implants are in, eh?" Ojani changed the subject, hope rounding his eyes.

"Not right after. We'll still need medical supervision, and we'll have to give our fans a cooling-off period before we can travel."

"Your fans, not mine. I'm incognito."

"Not if you're on my arm, dear. I can't go through customs wearing a wig, even if the chip will prove my identity." she winked at him.

A getaway with Ojani sounded romantic and in line with her early daydreaming. In their later years of their marriage, Maahes rarely suggested a vacation without being tied to a business meeting with a potential local partner in a South American country or a supervision trip to a water treatment plant half way built. He just couldn't let go of business, disconnect, and enjoy her presence fully. With Ojani, she didn't feel anyone's second choice.

"When is the launch of the next batch of franchisees?" It was her turn to lean on his chest and feel the rhythm of his heart like waves lapping on the beach of their destination.

"In three days, then, twenty more in three weeks, eh. Mark is doing the last check-ups before enabling the franchisees to download the software routines and the clients' list."

"Yes, Sarafian is pretty thorough at his stuff."

"Costa Rica, Uruguay, Kolkata, and New Delphi are coming online in that batch. There's a huge demand."

"Is it the middle class or only the one percent?"

"Predominantly middle class, eh. We've cross-referenced their applications with their social security chips. They're in the upper bracket. "Then we can leave afterward. There are three-week intervals between launches, and work is done well ahead of time. Should I make the bookings?"

Without leaving the warmth of his body, Ilanda muttered the confirmation for which he yearned. "It will be my last trip of the year. No more international romantic getaways for a while."

"Island or mainland, eh?".

"Thirty years ago, I would have said Key West, but now I don't feel comfortable vacationing on that leftover sliver of land. I need to see more landscape around me."

Ojani squeezed his lips, weighing other options, and she let him struggle with the decision. "The beaches are gone, no matter where we go. Costa Rica is safer, and we could do a safari in the jungle and mingle with the wildlife and the locals." He raised the tip of his nose in the air like an important person that had just given an ultimatum. Only his was friendly, making a mockery of it.

"I'll accept if you promise that no one will find us that week," she conceded. Then, she turned around and kissed him on his lips.

"We'll have a fantastic time, eh."

It was all she needed as assurance.

"We look absolutely amazin', eh!" Ojani exclaimed when he saw himself in the mirror in one of the lab's recovery rooms the day after his own intervention.

"Yeah! Like zombies in the *Night of the Dark Souls*," Ilanda grinned mirthlessly.

"I see darker shades of grey. It's a bleak world, for now. Do you see the same, eh?"

"Yes, and it's going to be like that for a while until the brain readjusts itself. Marinka, Kahuna, and even Crazy Velvet reported the same effect."

Ojani shrugged at the confirmation and continued to move from side to side in front of the mirror, admiring his shungite implants.

"Should we wear shades or let people stare at us, eh?" He wasn't sure of Ilanda's approach to this massive change in their life.

"Broadcasting the intervention has its purposes, but I'm not going to expose myself publicly just to show off the crystals. Not until more people do it."

"You received two-dozen interview requests from major TV stations. What are you going to do about it, eh?" Ojani asked. He looked at her. It was a marked contrast between the combination of her blonde hair and light skin and the grim black of the shungite implants.

"I'll let the PR department select a few on the condition that I won't step into their studio. It's AugReality or nothing."

"Sounds reasonable. Is the team pumped-up? Who is next, eh?" He turned to face her.

"Other than Nanette, they're all in. They've tried convincing her, but they pretty much understand her reasons."

"Ancestors garbage, eh?" The insulting words came out unchecked, and Ilanda saw his body convulse for a moment as if an assertive spike of shame had hit him, like an eel discharging its electric defense. "Sorry, I know it's a sensitive subject," he said.

"I suggested that the team spread the crystal implant interventions out over a period of six months. In case of unexpected developments, we'll have time to recover," Ilanda explained.

"What type of developments, eh?"

"Like clarity of mind, awareness, identification with oneness, you know . . . trivial things."

He frowned at her sarcasm and sat on the bed, thinking of the probability of that happening. "Could the perception of what we're doing change so drastically, eh? It's still important work that's barely started." His eyes bored into hers as if he were seeing her for the first time as an equal life and business partner. He loved her, but something burnt into his subconscious—he perceived his eviction from Tenzin's life to be a high price to pay to be with her and to potentially evolve to a more aware human being.

"Should we start training replacements for ourselves, too?" he asked. He lurched toward her and grabbed her hands gently. "We'll enjoy a permanent vacation. That would be terrific, eh."

Ilanda pushed him back to the bed. "The business is almost on autopilot. The franchisees will take care of it in every corner of the world. All we need is trusted people at the helm so no scammer can squeeze in, no matter the reason."

"So, I was right when I said we need replacements, eh."

She grinned blearily. "Ethics and integrity—qualities required for my blessings."

"The eye-assessment is done from this location remotely and sent to DeBoers for customization. The final crystal, cut to the client's specifications, is shipped out to the franchisee with whom the customer has registered. As a final step, we upload the software routine that will be run by local personnel on the cutover day. Where is the weakest point, eh?"

Ilanda sat on the bed beside him. "I don't know. DeBoers doesn't get the client information—only a record number that matches on our end. The routine sent to the franchise is an unhackable file, and they don't have the expertise to even think of breaking in. It could only happen before the whole process starts," she concluded.

"Like the deaths linked to the stolen identities reported so often lately, eh?"

"Yes." Her shoulders seemed to age, and Ojani leaned toward her to offer support. "There are also voluntary exchanges of identity for money. Poor areas in India, China, and South America are prone to such practices. Then, they go off the grid. They were living a simple life before giving up their name, anyway," she said.

Ojani released a nervous laugh over an uncomfortable situation. He patted Ilanda's hand but suddenly felt devoid of any comforting energy that might put her at ease.

"Let's focus on our vacation. We talked about our window of opportunity, and that's coming in two weeks," she said, reinvigorating the link between them.

"I'm glad you're not backing out."

She snorted at his worry and kissed his lips, nudging them as if she was sucking on a candy.

"Should we leave for your apartment now, eh?" he said.

"Strenuous movement is out of the question. Doctor's orders." Her voice was forceful, but a smile percolated on her face.

Ojani pulled her closer for another kiss, but she masterfully worked her way free and sauntered toward the door.

"One more night. It's not too much to ask of you. I'll keep an eye on your vitals from home. Rest now."

Left alone, he went back to bed, raised its angle to a comfortable position, and snuggled in. Ilanda was right. Lying down did calm the restlessness in his stomach, and the darkness behind his closed eyes seem natural.

Aware that he wasn't dreaming, Ojani floated, caught between slices of time and the memory of his grandmother's storytelling about how she and her brothers used to race in the spaces between the freshly washed bed sheets hanging on the tight strings in the backyard. They could only escape the long, white corridor at the end of the rope or by bending underneath the fringe of the fabric, which almost touched the ground. They were dear memories like the ones he wanted to build with Ilanda.

Still in the dream, he found that he couldn't move in any direction, and he imagined kicking backward like a mule hitting an invisible abusive owner. There was no movement, no sensation of breezy air cruising across his prickled ears.

Weightlessness.

An imponderable feather.

Where was he?

Had the transformation started already?

He couldn't tell if the starry panoply of pulsating lights was near or far, or only decorative fixtures on the universe that kept him confined. Claustrophobia had never plagued him; nevertheless, the inability to appreciate distance and depth unsettled him now. Ribbons of silver and gold light flickered from nowhere, intertwining and connecting the dots pulsating in the blackness surrounding him like the extinct, bewildered monarch butterflies that found themselves in a different location than the one they'd entered in their internal GPS. There were countless patterns that lasted long enough for his awareness to acknowledge them, and he looked for a key to decipher the last hold on the labyrinth of his mind.

"It's beautiful in here, eh" he said internally, but no other stimuli overtook his senses.

He brought his attention back to the white parallel walls he identified as a wedge in the time-space dimension of his mind. *What sedative had they used on him?* He mentally scolded Ilanda. The vibration of the incoherent words spoken by an unidentified voice was imperceptible as it wobbled with the smoothness of the vertical walls waiting for his scrutiny.

Who was talking?

The words approached him from all directions, clear and not threatening. His skin prickled, and he felt his body's vibration synchronize with the one closest to him.

"We are one," the sound hissed. "We are all water. Everything is water in permanent shift and evolution."

He dared a question. "*Are you part of the awakening?*"

Ojani thought he heard a chuckle. "Yes, we are the awakening. The awakening within and without."

His analytical mind couldn't fully latch onto the to-and-fro with the intangible entity.

He felt a gentle touch on his shoulder, and then someone whispered, "Dinner is here."

CHAPTER 23

Cherry touched the volcanic rock she had brought back from Hawaii, a gift from the island itself. Its usual coldness made the hair on her arms stand on end, giving her a brief respite from the furnace of another summer day.

The twisted branches of the backyard cherry tree, deeply attached to her childhood memories, was slowly coming back to life. Timid leaves stippled the lower branches while the bark had come out thicker, prodding intense shades of brown. Fruit was still two, maybe three years away.

Along the left side of the fence, the greens of parsley, celery, and lovage had no shame exposing their bushy shapes. The grass was way past its shyness, rising two inches tall. It tickled her bare feet, and she loved it.

This growing frenzy had taken place in spite of the city-wide water restrictions preventing Cherry from contributing to the energy boost released by the lava rock. Since she'd returned from Hawaii, she'd thanked Pelé, the spirit of the island, many times, and each time, the reach of an echo perked up her senses like an invitation to return to a sacred place that would be propitious for her spiritual development.

Kahuna's and Marinka's presence would be a blessing. Some days, the draw to the island had a tangible force on her as if she had been the one chosen for a certain task that wouldn't be revealed except in person, deepening her desire to go back.

She envisioned multiple scenarios in which she moved to Hawaii. Her education as a limnologist, along with her U of T credentials, would make her a desirable asset.

The thought of travel reminded her of Romana Pilb. They hadn't spoken in more than two months. At the U.N. level, country and corporate compensation agreements had been signed, and strict implementation guidelines had been drafted. Under the new terms, geopolitical domination had shifted so smaller countries had a better chance of being heard when resolutions were negotiated.

Cherry went back into the house and dialed Romana. "What corner of the world are you saving these days?" she asked when the president of Water for All and U.N. Water answered.

"Hello, my dear. I'm still in Varanasi, roaming the east coast. Been dismantling the tanneries to convert them into small manufacturing facilities for flexible solar panels, home scale wind turbines, and atmospheric water generators."

"Not wasting any time?"

"We need more volunteers for the array of projects we can finance. Educating people on how to stop dumping garbage in the water streams is one of them," Romana said. Her upper lip scar tinged with sweat and her black eyes gave Cherry the impression she was wearing shungite implants.

"Not liking New York anymore?"

"If I come back," Romana said, "certain forces will draw me into the politics of the place. Here, I can choose my battles. I garner more respect with these simple people than with those sophisticated diplomats. I make my own schedule and the lifestyle suits me."

"Are you going to celebrate your fifty-second birthday in India?" Cherry asked.

Romana nodded, her face brightening for few seconds as if already imagining the gifts and the cake.

The AugReality image showed a small room equipped with an

aged table and metal filling cabinets. Romana leaned on a chair and closed the window. The car horns, the chatter of the crowd, and the call of street vendors diminished. "They all come to life at dusk." She stood up to turn on the light in the room.

"I like your sari," Cherry said. The core material, dyed in red at its fringes, contrasted pleasantly with her charcoal hair and light chestnut skin.

"I have some beautiful ones, custom made. I fell in love with the craft, and Srinitham introduced me to one of his aunties who is an amazing designer and seamstress."

"How is he doing as the head of the Varanasi office?"

"He's grown professionally. He's more confident, and he's gained the respect of the village elders involved in our projects."

Cherry sensed a pride in Romana's statement as if she were claiming the man's achievements as her own. The blue of her eyes had gleamed when she mentioned Srinitham's name. Cherry recognized the same nuance in Ilanda when she spoke of Ojani.

What was the likelihood both of her friends would find love with younger men? She resigned herself to the fact that a May/December romance wasn't in the cards for her.

"He's emphatic, and he knows how to handle them. He helped me identify the government sponsors for a law prohibiting imports of plastic and electronic garbage. We might have enough support to see it pass next month."

"Has the river dumping diminished?" Cherry asked.

"The dumping in the Ganges is minimal and is coming mainly from smaller effluents. The Central Pollution Control Board reported that there are still active tanneries and manufacturing businesses that haven't complied with the new stipulated rules."

Romana re-arranged the folds of her sari on her shoulders, and took a sip of water from the mug on her desk. "The EcoCity Program related to better urban planning for reaching a zero-carbon footprint has been expanded to cities with five to ten millions people. Recycling programs are enforced throughout the province, and for the first time in this school year, the education board has introduced in grade 9 subjects such as climate change, environmental protection, and renewable technologies," Romana said.

Cherry had the impression that Romana indirectly assigned these accomplishments to her protégé.

"That's fantastic. Did this behavior translate to a mellowing of weather activity?"

"Are you referring to the fact that water understands and accepts our initiatives and measures as a sign of backing off?"

"Yes."

"Not everyone is convinced of the correlation between implementing climate change prevention measures and a diminished number of atmospheric events. Mother Nature has her way, and I am not sure we can so easily make her believe of the honesty of our intentions."

"It takes time," Cherry said.

"Definitely. At least the Indian business community that negotiated financial compensation for the loss of profit, also accepted the harsh reality that they still have to pay for the extensive pollution they caused."

Cherry chuckled and shuffled her feet on the couch. "At the end of that financial exercise, did they get any money?"

"Yes, but not as much as they expected," Romana said. "Only now they understood the high cost of clean-up. And that cost was deducted from the amount they negotiated."

"I have no doubt they'll build better businesses even with the new restrictions in place," Cherry said, and she meant it. She read about India becoming the hot spot for renewable technologies under a specially funded department inside IIT[1]. U.S. hedge funds and investment banks opening office in Bangalore, Hyderabad, Pune, and Mumbai. Young minds churning ideas to better a world that was dissolving in front of their eyes.

"Government agencies," Romana said, "such as Central Pollution Control Board and National Biodiversity Authority were enforcing the U.N. resolutions, and for once, all the other political forces, left, right, and even the communist party, played the same tune. I also befriended the prime minister's liaison, a forty-one-year-old guy, totally sold on the reality of climate change and with sparkling integrity. So I have his ear when necessary," Romana said.

"Have the water restrictions tighten over there beyond the daily ration of ten liters of potable water? In Canada they shrink by ten percent every three months like clockwork."

"I've heard that you are the spoiled ones. Forty liters of grey water per day per household. Is that true?"

"Yes, but it won't be long before the numbers even up all across the world. No more favoritism," Cherry said. "Aren't you missing the U.N. sterile office environment?"

"Not at all. India is a good place to work. At least for me. It doesn't have the air conditioning, the clean toilets attended daily by the janitor, or the pristine cafeteria, and to be honest, the camp in Mongolia where we stood up to Mosamoni and Narankama when they discovered the source of primary water was much worse."

"Yes, you mentioned it."

"We lived in tents," Romana said, "at minus five-degree Celsius for most of the time, food barely made it to us, mainly dehydrated fruits and vegetables, and oatmeal that we only mixed with water. Six long months of a tug-of-war with the Mongolian army and the private army forces hired by the U.S. water bottling companies operating in that region."

"I'm still pampered here in Toronto," Cherry said. She grabbed her cell and walked into her windowless office. The AugReality, showing Romana sitting, followed. She switched on the light. "I want to show you a rendering of me with crystal implants."

"What the hell is that?"

"Romana, what do you mean—"

"Why is Hayyin's mask in your office?" Romana Pilb was standing, her finger pointing at the wooden mask on the filing cabinet, leaning against the wall.

She stammered. "It only represents Hayyin, but it's just a reproduction." Cherry was so excited to share her decision about the implants with her friend that she completely forgot about her hidden identity. It represented a slip in judgment that would require patching up where her dear friend was concerned.

"Cherry!" Romana set her fists on the table. Her lips pulled into a thin line as if she'd swallowed them in a moment of rage. "Who are you covering for?"

"Romana . . . it's complicated," Cherry whispered. All the fight she had in her for defending the water and building the momentum supporting environmental protection initiatives had vanished, leaving her feeling empty, timid, and exposed to Romana's challenging gaze. Knots in her stomach twisted mercilessly. A scale on her well-built armor had lifted, and it threatened to come completely off if Romana wouldn't let go.

"Are you in any danger? I can ask to have a security detail assigned to you."

"That won't be necessary, my friend. I'm tired of carrying this burden . . . I'm Hayyin."

Confessing the way Hayyin had entered her life, how it had grown into the empowering entity that manipulated significant crowds of people, and how it had become an egregore[2] sustained by the thoughts and actions of its followers had shifted its burden to Romana.

It was a truth that couldn't be shared any further. Hayyin had fulfilled its purpose and given Cherry's existence the meaning for which she yearned. She was grateful and wished never again to tie the strings of that mask behind her head.

Over the years she had identified her personal struggle to find her own voice and purpose, with the toil of the mask that travelled to a new continent in search of a master that would make a difference in the world from behind the battered and emotionally charged identity.

The chronological details she provided only increased the rate of Romana's breathing, giving away the internal struggle Cherry knew she would think a betrayal for not sharing it willingly.

Announcing her decision to do the crystal implants no longer seemed like a badge of honor but a trivial gesture made by an immature person who was only willing to appease the energetic entity that controlled her.

Romana had loudly declared her lack of interest for the implants, though she understood Cherry's and Ilanda's reasons for getting the brain enhancement. "It might not provide the sanity you expect in a world gone berserk," Romana explained, "a world whose roots come off as brittle dirt."

"You need to stay grounded for us," Cherry said, more to appease Romana than anything else.

"I'll resign if they make the implants mandatory for the U.N. officials." Romana's voice sounded resolute. "And I'll never return to the U.S.—India has everything I need at my age."

Including love, Cherry thought. She smiled back as a way to ease the shame of her admission. "You know, there is more to the crystal implants than what's been advertised," she continued. "More depth —bordering inner-awakening."

"Soul redemption?" Romana asked.

"The interpretations are many. The end goal is the same. What Ilanda stumbled upon might have a significant impact on all of us."

"It's tempting, but no, thanks. I'll keep my wits, damaged or not."

The flashes of rage subsided, and her neck jerked awkwardly as if she were hanging from an invisible collar.

"I aim for Hawaii when the time is ripe," Cherry said when Romana extended her silence.

"I assume Marinka and Kahuna will be glad to have you. Their fight isn't over yet."

"They won the legal one. With the U.N.'s help, the chemical companies are out of the islands and they can start reintegrating the farmland that is back in their possession."

Her cheerleader tone surprised even her, raising Romana's eyebrows.

"That outcome was to be expected, given the new circumstances. Rising water levels have been affecting the life on the islands for a while now. I got the latest reports one week ago."

"How bad is it?" Cherry asked. "The beaches are gone. I saw that when I visited them a couple of months ago."

"Ten inches higher in the last three months. The chemicals accumulated in the plots used for years by Monsanto, BASF, Agrigentics and DuPont are washing into the ocean due to heavy rains. The marine life along the shore line will take a long time to adapt and recover to safe human consumption levels."

"How will people survive?"

"Supplies will be brought in as a temporary measure. You might be safer in Toronto, short and long term, as well."

Cherry kept to herself. She had spoiled the delight of reconnecting with Romana, and mistrust and pressure had seeped into their friendship.

"I won't divulge your secret to hierarchical ranks within the U.N. or Water for All," Romana said. "I truly believed that Hayyin's involvement has geared the water movement toward the light. There wasn't a single selfish decision on your part that I can recollect."

The confirmation put Cherry at ease. "Next time we talk, I'll be a different person," she said, thinking again how much the crystal implant will change her.

Romana leaned forward in her chair and whispered back, "I assume I won't see you on the other side." She grinned widely, pondering her words.

Cherry felt an earthbound heaviness at the thought that somehow, like Nanette, Romana would be left out from experiencing a jolt in their consciousness of their own volition. At least, this was what she had expected, as Marinka had attested.

"Coherence," Ilanda had told her a while back, "is the quality that takes place between the heart and mind as soon as the water decoded by the crystals kicks in. It will balance you emotionally."

Cherry had no reason not to believe her, and that was why her name was high on the priority list for the shungite implants.

"Romana, if you return to the U.S. anytime soon, let me know, and I'll fly to see you in person. Like last time, we'll enjoy a chocolate cupcake at Sanjay's bakery by the U.N. building."

Romana smiled. "That's a sweet they don't make here." She looked over her shoulder as if checking on the street swarming. "Probably I won't return any time soon. I'm pulling any possible excuse to extend my stay here. And when I do return, I feel it'll only be so I can hand my baton over to my replacement."

"That will be a sad day for the water movement. You've done so much for us." Cherry stood up as if she wanted to salute her older comrade. "But I'll still come to see you in New York when you're back."

"Thank you, my friend," Romana said, and she disconnected, but not before Cherry saw her unrestrained tears.

CHAPTER 24

Between several glasses of red Chardonnays, a meal of steamed vegetables with tofu, and the discussion about the latest book published by Michio Kaku, *Humanity's Future in a World Controlled by IAs*, the flight to San Jose, Costa Rica, was just a blip on a radar for Ilanda and Ojani.

They'd worn dark shades in the airport to conceal their identities while waiting for their flight. Only during the security checks did people whisper behind their backs as if they'd seen them naked, and their appearances weren't up to par. Several youths gave them the thumbs-up. One of them said, "We're saving for that piece of technology you're wearing," loud enough for everyone to hear.

"That's encouraging," Ilanda said to Ojani, and she put the shades back on as soon as they'd cleared customs.

Once she agreed to go on vacation, she let herself be surprised by his choice of resort, though she reigned-in her expectations. The notion of taking the unforeseen break swelled her chest, transitioning her psyche into aloofness. It would also give them the opportunity to check if the crystal implants were activated by playing mind games with each other and using telepathy the same way Marinka and Kahuna did.

"We should have told you earlier about our mental achievements," Marinka had explained during the first AugReality checkup session after Ilanda had her implants done, "but you had no way of indulging in a similar experience. Now you can."

"It will entail some fine-tuning on everyone's side," Kahuna had added in his electric tone, further piquing Ilanda's curiosity. "Shungite's frequency, and in my case, amber, have to find a common vibratory scale, and then we can connect."

"Mentally?" she asked, beaming with energy at the unlimited potential opening ahead of them.

Kahuna nodded, his shaved, tattooed head, made him look like a lizard that swallowed a grasshopper.

"How did you figure that out?" Ilanda asked.

"We could only assume that once the nanobots had connected the pineal gland with the implants, it triggered a dormant area in the pineal gland's own crystal, increasing the depth and vibration of the broadcasting of our thoughts," Marinka said, disclosing her theory.

"Is there a shungite cloud hovering above Hawaii?" Ilanda pushed with her questions. She hadn't keep track of the worldwide deployments Anonymous had promised.

"Yes. They made the announcement weeks ago. It's a small tenterabyte cloud that can be expanded on an as-needed basis. Anonymous specifically said that they did it for Kahuna for his bravery when facing the multi-nationals," Marinka said.

"Have you tapped into the cloud yet?"

Ilanda was as famished for details as if this were the first she'd ever heard of the technology and its implications.

Marinka turned toward her father, and their smiles obliterated any doubts they might have had about their achievement that they hadn't shared before.

"We've matched the vibration of our implants," Marinka said, "with that of the pineal gland, creating a powerful frequency amplifier. Our brains can now, when we focus intensely, find and 'hook' with the cloud's vibration. Anonymous has only uploaded minimal information—an operating system that accepts everyone like us.

When we connected, we couldn't feel anyone else's mind prodding at the time."

"And more clouds are being launched every week," Kahuna said.

"You mean other shungite clouds?" Ilanda asked.

"Yes. Much, much bigger above Europe, the US, Canada, and parts of Asia. There is also a schedule to launch many more of the same."

Ilanda grinned mischievously at the father-daughter pair as if she had her own secret that was about to share with them. "I told you a while back about Ojani joining the team?"

"Yes."

"He's done it, too. We both have the implants, and we could start practicing the same way you two did."

"It's great that you have someone you can trust," Marinka said. "And after you acquaint yourself with the tuning-in process, we should all try to connect and hop from one cloud to another."

Ilanda remembered giggling at the prospect of such a feast but said nothing more.

Now, Costa Rica and its tranquil space could become their mindfulness playground.

While Ojani did the check-in at the front desk, Ilanda kept her mind occupied with studying the wooden nervures of the ceiling, sustaining the weight of red ceramic tiles and the textile hanging on the walls depicting parakeet and macaw parrots in red, yellow, and green nuances. She sauntered down a winding path toward their room. The warmth coming down through the palm tree leaves, the moist of her skin, and the hand of the man she definitely knew she loved, blended in a balm that soothed her soul. The tugging at her heart felt like a sewing machine stitching together shredded tissue, healing the wounds Maahes had left behind.

"Does it meet your standards, eh?" Ojani asked as soon as the bags were in the room, and the tipped bellboy had gone.

She looked at the king bed, its immaculate sheets pegged beneath the mattress, the shiny ceramic floors that matched the furniture with mahogany insertions, and the local landscape, immortalized in three oil paintings hanging on the walls. It was modern, clean, and completely theirs.

"It's ours for a week, and this is what matters. Believe it or not, we'll spend more time outside on the beach than in here," she said, and she saw disappointment flicker in his eyes. Maybe it was just an impression on her part.

Ojani jutted out his chin as if he were about to make a serious announcement. "I'm sure I'll get my share of you, eh." He gave a few short spurts of laughter.

They jumped on the bed simultaneously, like synchronized gymnasts. Their clothes twisted on their bodies, revealing skin caressed by hungry hands. They settled for a long kiss into which Ilanda put fire, passion, and a longing to live life fully. Her body signaled that she was ferociously and unconditionally his.

"Let's get some fresh air, eh," Ojani said in the middle of their entanglement, and she liked it.

They changed into shorts and slippers and went outside.

"The beach used to be over there." Ojani pointed to their left where water sloshed against an improvised cement levee seventy feet away. Seagulls hopped on top of the barrier, avoiding the splash and seaweed on its edges, left behind by the waves.

"If the water level advances, this will be the line for the second levee, eh." He indicated where they were standing. "Beyond that, there is no future for this resort."

"Where's the real beach? You promised me a beach." She lamented like a spoiled child. Ilanda felt guilty for having brushed off the visible signs of climate change that mattered to her.

"They made one with the sand saved from the original beach, straight ahead. It's tiny, but it has the right vibe, eh."

They walked toward it hand-in-hand, and the scent of flowers she didn't recognize filled her senses. She breathed in short jolts of it as if adjusting to the air on a different planet. At the end of the alley, the aromas of grilled meat and pastries from the nearby restaurant enticed her. The afternoon was breezeless. Tourists lay immobile on wicker chairs with blue cushions. Only a few seats were occupied.

"Hungry, eh?" he asked.

"Not really. Maybe a snack," she said, and she let him take the lead on suggesting the right dish.

"I was told that the street vendors make a delicious cheese pie, eh."

She nodded, but she didn't move when he nudged her. The smooth skin of the palm tree edging the path seemed to talk to her. She took off her slippers and stepped on the grass, hugging the palm tree with both arms.

Ojani smiled at her, but he didn't join. He looked out at the restless waves as they slapped the artificial border.

After a while, Ilanda released her embrace. "I'm ready for that snack," she said, clutching Ojani's arm.

"Let's follow the exit signs, eh," Ojani said. "The market is just outside. When we get back to Toronto, I'm going to drive to Sudbury," Ojani said.

"What's in Sudbury?"

"An idyllic piece of property, eh."

"Oh?"

"I've already done an AugReality tour of it, and I'm waiting for the inspection report, eh."

"Is this the farm you've been obsessing over?"

"It's not exactly a farm. It has a patch of forest, a miniature lake, and a cleared area that can sustain crops of any kind. The legal designation of the land allows for additions to the existing house, eh," he declared proudly.

"So, you can tick the farm off your bucket list."

They smiled at each other and continued sauntering through the resort. The security guard greeted them at the gate, and Ojani exchanged words with him. The man pointed to the left and said, "*Ninos*."

"We're in the right place," he told her.

Ilanda followed Ojani toward the kids in the street as if in a trance. Ahead of them, a man in shorts and a floral shirt was paying a vendor for his pies. The man looked like an altered version of

Maahes, physically improved, somehow, sporting a fresh haircut and a thick, groomed beard.

The man laughed with the seller. When he turned around, Ilanda locked his gaze for a moment. She thought she could recognize Maahes's eyes in a crowd, but these weren't them. They were implants. She gasped and tugged at Ojani's hand.

The man's face turned white as a ghost and he glanced erratically left and right. He quickly saddled an electric golf cart and vanished along the side of the road hidden by the lush vegetation.

"What's wrong, eh?"

"Implants in Costa Rica! So fast!" She turned to him inquisitively.

"It's been a month since we opened the local franchise, and it's already logged two months' worth of requests within forty-eight hours, eh."

"Do we charge less in Costa Rica?" she asked, unsure of the price policies upon which they'd agreed.

"Nope. Blanket prices, eh."

"So how . . .?"

"Ex-pats. The requests came mainly from ex-pats who moved here years ago, as well as a handful of locals, eh," Ojani said, justifying the surge in demand.

"That guy that took off in a golf cart . . ." She paused as she wasn't sure how to explain the eerie feeling stirred in her by the man's resemblance to Maahes. "I don't remember working on his profile."

"Could have been Nanette. The more we do, the less we'll remember. In time, with all due respect for our work, these people will become clusters on the crystal cloud map, eh. We'll give them a new life and meaning—don't fret about such a detail."

Ojani offered her a cheese pie wrapped in paper, and he bit into his. "Marvelous, eh," he said while chewing.

Ilanda kept her eyes on the road in the direction in which the man had disappeared. She reasoned that there were many lookalikes in the world—why shouldn't there be one of Maahes, too. Still, the sauntering walk, the laugh that had always induced a sense of calmness in her, and the overall attitude, troubled her. She would definitely look him up in the database, and maybe on the cloud. Maahes would surely approve of her new-found happiness.

She finally tried the cheese pie and nodded complimentarily to Ojani who was waiting for her reaction. “I could eat these all day long.”

They walked back into the resort, ready for a dip if the water buoys floating close to the shore showed it was safe.

CHAPTER 25

"I can feel your thoughts," Cherry said to Marinka, who was sitting in front of her on the lawn between her house and her father's. "Something about going to the farmers' market tomorrow, am I right?"

"You got it. It only took you three days to do that because we already knew how to go about it."

Cherry's face was exposed to the sun, and the shungite implants worked like a set of shades. She embraced the direct heat and sunlight unabashed. It was as if she could breathe the energy in, process it through an efficient internal mechanism, and send it as a wave to every cell in her body.

"In one week, you'll be able to connect to the shungite cloud to chat with Ilanda and her team. You'll be able to visualize each other in your minds and 'talk' in silence," Marinka said.

"Exquisite! I'm happy that I got over my fear and moved to the island with you."

Without letting her gaze slip the rustle of the ocean, the Hawaiian asked, "Is there nothing left to go back to?"

Cherry pondered the question, dreading the answer. "There's nothing or no one to go back for. Selling the house was the most painful thing I've done in my life—my childhood, my parents' memories, all of it is in strange hands that will rip it apart to modernize it in the renovation." She teared involuntarily, leaving a wet mark on her cheeks to attest to her pain.

"At least, you've brought back the lava rock."

"It didn't belong there without me. The miracle I witnessed in my backyard . . . it helped sell the house." Cherry laughed, imagining the puzzled faces of the new owners when the dryness whitened the grass, parsley, and especially the cherry tree, whose happiness to be alive again showed on its bark and in the multitude of leaves.

"Have you listened to Crazy Velvet's confessions? She came clean about the effects of the implants, and so did that actor, Doug Suariano," Marinka said.

"Not entirely, but it's positive, isn't it?"

"That depends on what one's expectations are. They've experienced what we now know is normal: inner-peace, increased awareness, the downloading of information they are not familiar with—"

"Did they say downloading?" Cherry asked incredulously.

"Not exactly, but they were specific about the alien nature of it."

"Alien?"

"Not extraterrestrial, just knowledge they hadn't accumulated in their formative years or since," Marinka explained.

"We should ask Ilanda if applications have surged as a result of the revelations from these influencers." Cherry hoped such actions wouldn't deter the power players and other influencers of the world from getting their own implants.

"It doesn't matter anymore," Marinka said. "People always react emotionally to external stimuli, and the first few steps have already been taken. Slow or fast, it's an enhancement that, in my opinion, will only go upward."

"I agree. I only want to see the onslaught of weather come to a stop and water go back to its dormant stage," Cherry said, acknowledging her worries.

Marinka didn't reply.

Cherry noticed her smiling at the seagulls, their feathers ruffling as they flew in the breezeless day.

"Water will stay vigilant for a long time," Marinka said, confirming her beliefs.

"I've been working with Ilanda's team for the last eighteen months on what we thought could be a scientifically-based pattern for a language for water," Cherry added. "We tweaked previous cymatics[1] experiments with no visible changes in the molecular structure. Dr. Masaro's results of exposing water to music and feelings proved to be a threshold we couldn't improve on." She crossed her arms and continued. "When frozen, the water molecule displays messages of love, gratitude, or fear, hate, so on and so forth. The challenge comes when we try embedding a whole sentence in the same format. The same frozen molecule won't display a different message on each side of its hexagonal form. What else can we do?"

"But you all agreed on the concept that water has memory?" Marinka asked.

"That concept is indisputable." Cherry waved her hands in the air to emphasize her conviction. "Making the water reveal what she knows is the hard part. We see it as a limited display mechanism. We don't know yet how or what triggers a 3D visualization of the information water assimilates."

"Are you saying there is a limited alphabet for water and we don't know how to create full sentences that she would display back to us?" Marinka asked.

"Yes. The display will prove her interpretation is correct."

"Father and I talked about it. We even asked for advice from the spirit of our ancestors."

"And?"

"Our actions, like the ones implemented through the U.N. resolution, are the best language for water's awareness—it's all connected. Indirectly, water forced us to get the crystal implants, and now our consciousness is shifting to the next level. From the height of our new-found understanding, we recognize the deep scars and the still festering wounds we've inflicted." Marinka paused, breathing deeply. "We'll grieve, but we'll stop the madness.

That is when water will smile at us, the seasons will return, the crops will flourish, and we'll all express our inner-beauty on the crystal cloud."

She smiled, and Cherry had the impression that Marinka's dark skin had become lighter, as if she'd morphed into a different person.

"Do you miss the sparkle of your green eyes?" The words had jumped from Cherry's lips without warning.

Marinka's smile grew larger and warmer until it encompassed her, the lawn, the houses, and the immediate landscape. "The benefits are many, and we are transitory anyway. Who gets attached to a pair of eyes?"

Marinka chuckled, and Cherry joined her, amused by the easiness her friend showed while talking about her transformative process. "Water is a part of the shungite cloud from now on. She will read our minds and feel what we feel. There is no place to hide, but there are no reasons to do it either."

"She's on our side," Cherry added.

Coming to Hawaii felt like the end of a journey she had been guided on a long time ago. It was a journey that followed the water in an attempt to understanding her own growth as a person, and decoding her own life's purpose through the thick of challenges, noise, and fears, that intertwined with her two identities. It could also be the end of Hayyin's journey. She had decided to leave the mask wrapped in a plastic bag in a storage unit in Toronto. She had said her goodbye and, once again after selling her house, she had practiced the non-attachment attitude to material belongings. The moment she locked the metal door behind the items she kept, her body had come alive with an energy that tripped her every single cell. Her first thought was that she could light-up the Christmas trees in a whole neighborhood even if the winter festive celebration was months away. The elation of a new beginning had poured out of her in an interrupted stream of tears that lasted until she reached home, fifteen minutes later.

"Water was always on our side—we were the ones who strayed," Marinka said. "It's time to understand who we really are and behave accordingly."

"Energy beings?" Cherry asked as if she knew the answer.

Marinka nodded, "Water and energy," and she turned her face toward the sun. Cherry felt a gentle thought touch her mind like the kiss of a trustworthy lover she had never met. She replied in kind before extending her reach to anyone who might be hovering in the ether to exchange their love and gratitude.

NOTES

CHAPTER 10

1. Palmaria Palmata is a red alga that grows on the northern coasts of the Atlantic and Pacific Oceans.

CHAPTER 20

1. 1 Apatite – type of gemstone
2. 1 PATH - downtown Toronto's enclosed pedestrian walkway linking 29 kilometers of shopping, services and entertainment

CHAPTER 23

1. IIT – Indian Institute of Technology
2. Egregore - is an occult concept representing a "thoughtform" or "collective group mind", an utonomous psychic entity made up of, and influencing, the thoughts of a group of people.

CHAPTER 25

1. Cymatics - the study of visible sound and vibration, can demonstrate the power and beauty of vibration's influence on water.

ACKNOWLEDGMENTS

Crystal Cloud came out of me like an unexpected snow fall on a sunny day. I had no intention of writing a sequel to *Water Entanglement*, but after re-reading it, I realized how much potential the plot has and it would have been a shame not to explore it further.

Most of the time, the creation process takes me away from family and friends, transporting me into the infinite space of my mind, where I mould my characters, while being moulded by them in return. Therefore, a new book is a fresh opportunity to thank them profoundly for their understanding and support.

Special thanks to Yvette Kendall for her valuable input to the crystal technology ideas I used in the book.

Thank you to all who took the time out of their busy schedules to read the book and provide testimonials: Jonas Saul, Yvette Kendall, Rainey Marie Highley, Nanette O'Neal, Christopher Douglas, and Fredric Lehrman.

BIBLIOGRAPHY

Dispenza, Joe. 2012. *Breaking the Habit of Being Yourself.* Hay House.

Highley, Rainey Marie. 2012. *Water Code.* Divine Macroverse LLC.

Masaru, Emoto. 2004. *The Hidden Messages in Water.* Beyond Worlds Publishing.

Munteanu, Nina. 2016. *Water Is ... The Meaning of Water.* Pixl Press, Vancouver, B.C.

Nuday, Carly. 2014. *The Water Codes.* Water Ink California.

Wetzel, Robert. 2001. *Limnology: Lake and River Ecosystems*, 3rd ed. New York Academic Press

ABOUT THE AUTHOR

Claudiu Murgan is an engineer with a deep yearning for writing with a meaningful message. Originally from Romania, he started writing Sci-Fi at 11-years old and was involved in the Romanian fandom until 1997 when he decided to immigrate to Canada.

Inspiration resurfaced within Claudiu after nineteen years of a creative drought. The result of that blessing from God was *The Decadence of Our Souls*, a Fantasy novel touching on spirituality. The journey that culminated with the book mentioned above taught Claudiu that Love, Gratitude and Compassion are necessary life companions that should open one's sensibilities to the Divine Creator.

Writing *Water Entanglement* was a blissful joy that transported Claudiu into the fascinating world of water and crystals. *Crystal Cloud* is the sequel to *Water Entanglement.* The novels are works of Eco-Fiction bringing to the forefront water's ability to heal us when treated with reverence and hurt us when treated with ignorance and disrespect so prevalent in our society.

Claudiu's experience in various industries such as IT, renewable energies, real estate and finance, helped him create complex, realistic characters that bring forward meaningful messages.

Connect at ClaudiuMurgan.com. Please leave your testimonials at Amazon.com and Goodreads.com

Patreon.com/ClaudiuMurgan

Instagram.com/claudiumurgan
facebook.com/ClaudiuMurganAuthor
www.ageofwater.ca

www.ingramcontent.com/pod-product-compliance
Lightning Source LLC
LaVergne TN
LVHW021656060526
838200LV00050B/2380
* 9 7 8 1 6 4 7 4 6 4 1 5 8 *